Amazon in Darkness

Amazons of Themyscira Book Two

Elizabeth Salo

EBOOK ISBN: 978-1-962460-02-6

PRINT ISBN: 978-1-962460-03-3

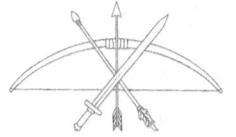

Chapter One

THIS MIGHT HAVE BEEN a terrible mistake.

The coastline of Türkiye was far rockier than Colin had realized, and his tiny boat wasn't exactly the most seaworthy vessel in the Black Sea. He watched impotently as the choppy waves crashed over the side of his ancient fishing boat. He was surprised the engine hadn't yet given up the ghost with all the luck he was having on this trip. First, he'd nearly lost track of the person he was following, then he'd been forced to detour to acquire his current means of transport, and now he was on the verge of having to bail water out of his boat with a bucket.

His plan to approach the target area after dark had made total sense when his only concern was being spotted, but now that he was trying to navigate the rocks without wrecking himself on them, he wished he'd given his plan more thought.

Too late to turn back now.

He fished his flashlight out of his bag and checked his notes again. He was certain he was in the right spot. He had to be. Clicking off the flashlight, he scanned the coastline. He saw nothing but hills, rocks, and scrubby trees. The area was probably gorgeous during the day, but it was almost one in the morning. Nothing ever looked welcoming in the middle of the night.

Straightening his back, he squared his shoulders. He'd never been wrong before. It was no time to start doubting himself. He steered the beat-up fishing boat toward the only stretch of the coast that wasn't a sheer cliff. He gritted his teeth and braced for impact in case the waves slammed the boat into the nearby boulders. Instead, the boat beached itself gently, the rubber bumper on the side nestling up to one of the jagged rocks. Colin let out a sigh of relief as he cut the engine and dropped the anchor.

The boat had better be there when he got back. Having an escape route was just good practice.

He grabbed his trusty canvas bag from the back of the boat and headed for the side closest to shore. He was going to get wet, but it wouldn't be the first time. At least he'd been smart enough to wear his old shoes. The drop from the deck wasn't far, and he landed with a soft plop in the shallow water. He hitched his bag more firmly over his shoulder.

"That's far enough."

Colin froze, his left hand still adjusting the straps of his bag. Slowly, he lifted his head, coming up short when he saw the arrow pointing at his face.

Half a dozen heavily armed women were standing in front of him, blocking him from going any farther. The swords and bows they held might not have been the most modern of weapons, but the razor-sharp edges glinted like diamonds in the moonlight.

Colin scanned the line of women. Each of them was at least as tall as he was, which put them in the neighborhood of six feet. They were wearing armor made of finely tooled leather and shiny bronze, and their expressions ranged from distrust to outright hatred.

What had he gotten himself into?

Moving slowly, he raised his hands like he'd seen in the movies. "I come in peace?" His quip landed like a lead balloon. These women clearly weren't the joking type.

The one in front took a step toward him, her sword flashing inches from his neck. "Why have you come here?"

Focusing on the immediate threat of the muscular brunette with dark skin and glaring brown eyes, Colin took a deep breath. There was no way to truthfully answer that question without making the situation worse. He tried tact. "I mean you no harm."

She sneered. "That much is obvious." Her gaze flicked quickly over his meager possessions.

Colin took offense to that. He wasn't a total dud in the fighting department. "I think this is all just a misunderstanding. With your permission, I'll be going now." He tried for a harmless expression and gave a tiny shrug.

The point of her sword twitched closer to his carotid artery. "But you do not have my permission."

Not the answer he'd been hoping for. Colin frantically searched for some way to safely extract himself. Sadly, nothing was coming to mind. "Um," he finally started but was cut off.

"What's the meaning of this?" A new voice cut through the tense standoff, making the brunette flinch and her blade twitch closer to Colin's throat.

"We caught this man landing on our beach," the brunette explained without turning around to address the newcomer.

A woman with curly red hair now stood on top of a nearby boulder, staring down at Colin, daggers shooting from her piercing green eyes. Unlike her friends, she was wearing jeans, a green tank top, and leather boots that went almost up to her knee.

"Is that so?" she asked. Before he could breathe, she flung herself off the rock, performed a jaw dropping acrobatic flip, and landed mere inches in front of him.

"Selene," the brunette said, her voice pitched with a hint of warning.

So the feisty redhead's name was Selene. It fit. She looked like a goddess of the moon, her skin so pale it appeared alabaster in the moonlight. Unfortunately, her stunning face was only a hairbreadth from his own. He swallowed, meeting her stare without a blink.

"Don't worry, Frona. This one isn't going to try anything, now is he?" Selene didn't ask it like a question.

Colin considered his options. Even if he'd been thinking of trying his odds at escaping, the Beretta he could see attached to Selene's belt was enough to make him reconsider. "Look, ladies, I'm sure we can work something out." Colin pasted on his most charming grin.

He'd successfully found his way into more than one pair of panties with that smile.

Selene didn't even blink.

He tried again. "This is a mistake. If you'll just lower your weapons, I'll be on my merry way, and you'll never have to look at me again." He tried to put his hands out in a calming gesture, but since Selene was standing right in front of him, he accidentally brushed up against her arm.

Several of his captors drew in quick breaths, and he heard the stretch of a bowstring being pulled tighter.

Selene took an immediate step back. Her right hand grabbed the gun she had strapped to her hip, and her left pulled a lethal-looking knife out of a thigh holster.

"Whoa, take it easy," he said, trying to make his voice as soothing as possible. "I didn't mean to touch you. It was an accident."

"Touching an Amazon without her permission is punishable by death," Frona said.

Colin felt like he was drowning, frantically treading water to stop his head from going under. Had the scary brunette just threatened to kill him and claimed to be part of an extinct race of warriors all in one breath?

When Colin had set out for Themyscira—the supposed homeland of the race of Amazon warriors that most people believed to be entirely mythological—he'd expected to find at best a ruin of an ancient city and at worst nothing but rocks and blowing sand. He had not been prepared to find actual Amazons. At least he knew he was in the right place, not that it was much of a comfort at the moment.

"I'll keep that in mind," he said. "I think we got off on the wrong foot. I'm Colin Wolfe. I'm in the antiquities business." He offered a hand to Selene, who just stared at it, her fingers flexing around her weapons. With a shrug, he dropped his hands to his sides.

Selene slowly lowered her dagger, tucking it quickly into its sheath. "We should take him to the prison. I'll go brief the queen on the situation."

Murmurs of agreement spread through the crowd of women. Selene turned and walked away, Frona stepping in to take her place, her sword once again pointing at his throat. "Psyche, bind him," Frona called to a blonde woman with skin like honey. The Amazon took his bag, then tied his hands behind his back.

Crap. It was time to play his nuclear option. "You don't happen to know Dr. Samuel Treadwell, do you?"

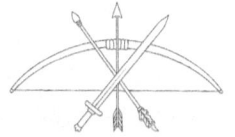

Chapter Two

SELENE COULDN'T BELIEVE HER ears. The intruder on the beach had just dropped Sam's name. Her face an impassive mask, she led the small band of warriors and their captive through town. Her feet itched to march this Colin Wolfe character straight to the prison, but it wasn't the right move. If he knew Sam, then there was more to him than just a simple lost boater, and she needed to figure out what.

It seemed impossible that he could have found their city on his own. Up until two days prior, Themyscira had been hidden by a divine veil, blocking the knowledge of its existence from all outsiders. Hermes, the Greek god of travel and boundaries, had hidden the city twenty-five hundred years prior at the request of Kalli, the queen of the Amazons. Two days ago—after they had defeated a paramilitary group that invaded their homeland and tried to annihilate them—had Kalli removed the veil. There was no way this man could have managed to locate the city in the short time since the veil had disappeared. No one was that good, and Selene didn't believe in coincidence.

Selene skirted her small group around several disabled Humvees, leftovers from the battle that had raged the day before. The crunch of gravel under Colin's shoes was the only noise as they made their way through the town, his heavy tread drowning out all other sounds. They approached the Royal Hall, where earlier in the evening they'd had a celebration of life to honor their fallen sisters and rejoice in their victory over the invaders. However, it was late enough that the sounds of the revelry had vanished—no music, no sound of chattering voices.

The Royal Hall, despite its fancy title, was not a particularly impressive building. It was the largest one in the city, though it was only one story and relatively low to the ground. It was built out of the same native stone and mortar as the rest of the buildings in town, with the main indicator that the building was important being its location at the edge of the city square.

She walked up the short set of stairs that led to the front door and shoved it open, grabbing it before it banged into the wall. The crowds had dispersed, leaving just three people gathered at the far end of the room. Selene crossed the stone floor and dropped into a kneeling bow. "My queen," she said, gazing somewhere around her friend's feet.

"Selene," Kalli said. "Rise and report."

Selene stood as she heard the rest of her small group enter the room behind her. "A boat just landed on our beach. There was only one occupant, a man."

Kalli nodded. "Was he armed?"

"It doesn't appear that way, though we haven't thoroughly searched his belongings yet. We were going to bring him to the prison and deal with him in the morning, but I thought it might be more prudent to bring him straight here."

"Oh?"

"He mentioned Sam." Selene nodded toward the blond man standing behind Kalli.

The band of Amazons came to a halt a respectful distance away from the queen, with Psyche and Frona flanking the prisoner, each with a steely grip on one of his arms.

"Wolfe?" Sam said incredulously, taking an unconscious step forward. He squinted through his glasses at the man like he was seeing a ghost.

The prisoner looked sheepish, if that description could ever be applied to a man as confident as he was. "Hello, Sam."

Kalli turned to her fiancé, the silver circlet that signified her position winking in the flickering firelight. "You know him?" Her eyebrows went up.

Sam looked at Kalli and nodded. "Yes, or at least I used to. His name is Colin Wolfe. He used to be one of my anthropology PhD students at Georgetown, but I haven't seen him in at least four years." He turned to Colin. "What are you doing here? How did you find this place?" Sam demanded, his gaze pinning Wolfe in place just as firmly as the Amazons holding him.

The other man shrugged as much as he could with his hands tied behind his back. "The same way you did, I imagine."

Selene doubted that very much. "Answer the man's questions," she said, giving the intruder a scathing look, her fingers twitching near the hilt of her knife.

Colin noticed the slight movement of her fingers and bobbed his head. "I did research, looked at old maps, read old diaries. I visited your exhibit at the Smithsonian," he said, glancing at Sam. "Everything I saw was pointing me in the same direction. Here."

"He had this on him when we found him," Psyche said, dropping the canvas bag at the queen's feet.

Kalli and Sam exchanged meaningful glances. "Why now? Of all the days to explore, why did you pick today?" Kalli asked, her skepticism obvious.

Selene wondered whether her friend was thinking along the same lines as she was.

"It seemed like as good a time as any," Wolfe responded, trying his charming grin again. It had no more effect on Kalli than it had on Selene, who hid a smirk.

Kalli frowned but quickly masked it. "Anything else you have to say for yourself?"

Wolfe shifted from one foot to the other but didn't try to shrug off his guards. He glanced around the hall, his eyes tracing the shields, swords, and spears that decorated the walls. He noticed the long table that was pushed up against the wall and held the remains of the party that had ended a few hours prior. Finally, his gaze settled on Kalli, inspecting her circlet and the matching ring. "This place is pretty lively for a long-dead civilization."

"Take him to the prison," Kalli ordered. The troop of Amazons spun to leave, tugging Wolfe along in their midst.

Selene watched them go. A slightly panicked look crossed Wolfe's face right before he was shoved out the door. She turned back to the others and said, "This cannot be a coincidence."

"Agreed," Zoe chimed in, weighing in for the first time from her position leaning against the wall. "This man shows up mere hours after we defeated an armed invasion staged by one of our former sisters and her band of mercenaries? It has to be related."

Sam shifted, tucking his thumbs into the pockets of his jeans. "I don't buy it. I know Wolfe. He may not be the most upstanding citizen in the world, but I can't believe he would've been part of Eris's plot against the Amazons. He used to be an anthropologist like me. There's no way he would stoop to destroying an entire civilization. Plus, he seemed genuinely surprised to find you guys alive."

Kalli sighed, reaching out to take Sam's hand in hers. "Tell us what you know about him."

"Not much to tell. He used to be a grad student of mine. One of my colleagues, a friend I trust, saw him steal a priceless ancient Greek artifact from my office at the university. He was kicked out of the program four years ago—which he blames me for—and I haven't seen him since. We never recovered the artifact." He squeezed Kalli's hand.

"He stole from you?" Selene asked, dropping her gaze to the olive-green canvas bag on the floor. "He said that he looked at maps, did research, and came to the same conclusions you did on how to find this place. Is it possible he's following you? Maybe even stealing your research?" She gently kicked the bag with her toe.

"The same thought crossed my mind," Kalli said, eyeing the bag. "When we left Washington, DC, to chase after Eris, we left in a hurry. Sam grabbed a lot of his books and papers, but maybe we missed some?" She glanced at Sam.

"It's possible." He shrugged. "I was only able to grab the papers from my house. There was probably more research in my office."

"He broke into your office?" Zoe asked. She shoved away from the wall and came to stand next to them.

"It wouldn't have been the first time," Sam said.

It was certainly possible. Colin Wolfe seemed morally questionable enough to pull off something like that.

"Let's not jump to any conclusions quite yet," Kalli said. "It's late, we're all tired, and we may not be thinking clearly. Perhaps tomorrow morning we'll be able to look at this situation with clearer eyes and see something we missed."

Selene grabbed Wolfe's bag off the floor. "I'll look through this. See what he might have been up to." With a nod to her friends, Selene turned and left the hall. Her steps sped up with a renewed sense of energy. Finding out what bad guys were up to was sort of her thing, and she loved it. She was going to dig into Colin Wolfe and see what dirty secrets he may be hiding. Depending on what she found, Mr. Wolfe might be in for a really bad morning.

She walked down the quiet street, mentally counting the small houses until she found her own. She paused at the door, her hand tracing the battered wood, sliding to the stone doorway. She remembered building this house thousands of years ago. At the time it had felt like the biggest accomplishment of her life. She'd been in countless battles, defeated thousands of enemies, and yet this small house had felt monumental.

Things had changed. Selene was now a nomad, not staying in any one place for very long. Part of that was practical. Your enemies—and the authorities—had a harder time finding you if you moved around a lot. Part of it was also personal. For reasons she'd never wanted to examine too closely, she now shunned the sense of permanence that came with owning her own home.

Selene pushed open the door, her eyes taking in the entire interior in one glance. The one-room house had a slim leather cot in the front, the straw mattress long since disintegrated. The back of the room held a small table with a candle on it and a chair. There was one small window high in the back wall. Along the pane there were several small trinkets that she'd collected throughout the years: a bent arrowhead, a small smooth stone, and a tiny carving that looked like a cat.

The entirety of this house would have fit inside the living room of her London apartment. It was astonishing how much things had changed over the years. It was a stark reminder that this was where she had lived for hundreds of years. This small, simple life used to be the one she lived and breathed.

It was nothing like the comparatively opulent life she currently lived. Her penthouse was enormous, the furniture soft and comfortable. The miracle that was electricity powered everything from her Sub-Zero refrigerator to the hot tub on her balcony. She could have food delivered to her door with a quick call or a few clicks on the internet. All these advancements would have been indistinguishable from magic had she been exposed to them thousands of years ago. Instead, most people, including Selene, now took them for granted.

The life that she'd grown up living had been harsh, but they hadn't known any different. They'd trained, they'd fought, and they'd done what they needed to support their people by hunting and growing food. Their lifestyle had made them tough, but they'd needed to be tough to live the life of warriors.

Would she and her sisters have grown into the women they were if they hadn't lived the spartan lives they'd always known? Something told her that it would be far more difficult to get out of her current lush feather bed in the morning to go outside and get the crap kicked out of her during fight training than it had been to wake from the cot that was barely better than sleeping on the floor.

With a sigh, she pushed the past from her thoughts. Her stay in Themyscira was only temporary. Soon enough she'd be back to her normal life, and her days would once again revolve around Blackburn Industries. For now, however, she needed to focus on the task at hand, and that was to figure out what Colin Wolfe was up to.

Selene crossed the dirt floor to the small table. She pulled a lighter out of her pocket and lit the candle, which cast a weak glow that barely reached the edge of the table. Longing for electricity, Selene sat on the rickety wooden chair and plopped the bag down on the table. Time to see what Wolfe was hiding.

She opened the drawstring, and the first thing she saw was a flashlight, which almost made her shout with joy. She flicked it on and used it to continue digging through the bag. He'd been traveling light. There was a small stack of notebooks and papers, which she set aside to go through more thoroughly. Apart from that, he had a lockpick set, a jeweler's loupe, a small folding shovel, and a box of granola bars. No weapons anywhere.

She turned her attention to the small hardbound notebook. She opened it but couldn't make heads or tails of what she saw inside. It didn't look like any language she was familiar with, which was saying something since she'd been alive for more than four thousand years. She huffed, closing the notebook with a snap. She picked up a few of the other pages, which appeared to be photocopies of the originals. These, at least, were in English and looked vaguely familiar. She thought they might be related to Themyscira and the Amazons, but she wasn't certain. She'd have to have Sam check them out tomorrow.

She sighed, then stood up and stretched. She should probably try to get some sleep, considering that the sun would be up in a few hours. She crossed to the uncomfortable cot, but before she got there, her phone vibrated in her pocket. Glancing at the screen, she saw Ambrose's name and smiled.

"We've found him," Ambrose Moretti said as soon as she answered.

Satisfaction swelled inside Selene. This, at least, she could be happy about. Taking scum off the street was always a joyous occasion. "Where is he?"

"Paris," her lieutenant answered. "Should we wait for you to meet us there before we approach him?"

She desperately wanted to tell Ambrose yes. Phillip Brauer had been on her radar for months. The spoiled son of the Earl of Nottingham, the prick was forever committing mild infractions, and his rich and influential family simply made them disappear. That was until two months ago, when he raped and beat his girlfriend. Now Phillip was in hiding while his family tried their hardest to make the charges go away. They'd tried to buy his girlfriend's silence, but Anna Rayner hadn't taken them up on it. She'd gone to the police and reported it, but ever since, she'd been dealing with harassment from Phillip's family.

That was where Selene and her Special Operations arm of Blackburn stepped in. She'd heard about Anna's situation through her network and was determined that this time, son of an earl or not, Phillip Brauer would pay for what he'd done. Anna Rayner would get the justice she deserved, one way or another.

Regrettably, as much as she wanted to go after Brauer herself, it wasn't practical. She was still in Themyscira, and it was kind of an awkward time to bail.

"No," she finally said with a sigh. "Don't wait for me."

"Right," Ambrose said, though she could hear the hesitation in his voice even through the phone.

"I'll be fine, darling. I have total faith that you'll get the bastard, even if I'm not there to see his face when it happens."

"You're the boss."

She smirked even though Ambrose couldn't see her. She was that and so much more. "As always, please ensure there won't be any undue interest in this matter from the authorities."

"Not from our end," he assured her.

She nodded in satisfaction. "Good. Well done." She paused, then plowed ahead. "I have another name I need you to look into for me."

"Simple stuff or full workup?" Ambrose's voice was clipped. He was in full business mode. Personal stuff could wait.

"Give me everything. His name is Colin Wolfe."

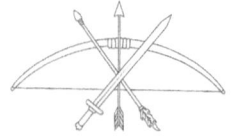

Chapter Three

THE MURMUR OF QUIET voices woke Colin from his fitful sleep. It took a moment to remember where he was and why his back was killing him. Prisons in general weren't known for their comfort, but the straw pallet he was sleeping on definitely did not come highly recommended.

Opening his eyes just a slit, he tried to pinpoint where the sound was coming from. The jail wasn't particularly large. The building was a giant rectangle with a hallway running from front to back down one long wall and a row of four cells separated by nothing but bars taking up the rest of the space. He could see the entire interior of the building at a glance, which wasn't super great for privacy, but at least he'd been given his own cell. The two cells closest to him were occupied by groups of hulking men in black military garb. It wasn't often that Colin felt small, but in this group he would have been at the bottom of the food chain.

Only one person in the jail wasn't behind bars. Colin tried not to move as he assessed the situation. The newcomer was crouched in the hallway near the door to the cell next to his. She had ghostly pale skin and a huge mass of black hair piled on top of her head. Her outfit consisted of strips of black leather that could loosely be dubbed a skirt and a skintight bodice that did almost nothing to protect the ample breasts that spilled out over the top.

The black-haired woman glanced around surreptitiously. Her eyes darted from the exterior door at the end of the hallway to the window in the wall behind her, then skimmed each cell. He closed his eyes, not wanting her to know he was awake. The pale light he'd seen through the window told him it was probably just before dawn, and her twitchy behavior made it obvious she didn't want anyone to know she was there.

The woman appeared to be having a rapid conversation with one of the commandos in the next cell. The conversation was low, and he couldn't hear much. The few snatches he caught didn't make a lot of sense. It sounded like she said the word *belt* and then maybe asked about a boat. He really hoped she wasn't planning to steal his boat. It wasn't exactly his in the first place, but he'd had every intention of giving it back to its rightful owners. Eventually.

It was the last word he overheard that got his attention. *Heracles*.

His eyes opened just wide enough to watch the black-haired woman pull out a large metal key and slide it into the lock with a slight clang. Still crouching low to the ground, she opened the door just wide enough for the soldier to slip out, then quickly closed it again, leaving his compatriots inside. He mirrored her crouch, and the pair crept down the short hallway and slipped out the front door.

It was obvious to Colin that the woman was one of the Amazons, but her behavior screamed stealthy. If Colin had to guess, she wasn't authorized to be doing what she'd been doing. It raised the question as to why she was sneaking around the jail and breaking out one of the prisoners.

The really interesting question, however, was why she was talking about Heracles, especially to a guy who, at a guess, wasn't exactly the scholarly type. The myths about Heracles, more commonly referred to as Hercules, didn't normally come up in everyday conversation. Why on earth would she be asking about it now?

Colin racked his brain, and the answer finally jumped out to him. There were many different myths around Heracles's adventures, but only one of them was tied to the Amazons. It was said that Heracles and his men had sailed to Themyscira and stolen a priceless artifact from their queen, Hippolyta. The item he had stolen was a girdle—a belt that was part of her armor and was supposedly what she'd used to carry her weapons.

But Heracles was a myth, right? There was no way that the impossibly strong and brave man described in the old stories could possibly have truly lived.

Colin glanced around at the building he was trapped in. This prison wasn't a myth. The Amazons clearly weren't a made-up story. He'd seen with his own eyes that not only had they existed thousands of years ago, but they existed to this day. If they were real, why not

Heracles? And if both Heracles and the Amazons were real, then it was quite possible the belt was too.

Colin lay back on his pile of straw and stared at the ceiling, his mind buzzing. If the Amazon was going after the belt, it meant that she believed it still existed. And if it still existed, there was no telling what a four-thousand-year-old artifact would fetch on the underground markets. In fact, he probably wouldn't even need to advertise widely. He could reach out to a few of his prior clientele, and he was sure one of them would be frothing at the mouth to acquire it.

All Colin had to do was figure out how to beat her to it.

Several hours later, Colin was pacing his small cell, wondering how he'd gotten himself into this mess. He'd been in his current line of work for four years, and he'd never once landed himself in jail for his trouble, much less at the hands of a race of women who by all accounts shouldn't be alive. His hopes had spiked when he'd seen Sam standing among them, clearly a bit more than just friendly with their queen. Those hopes had been dashed when he'd been hauled off to his cell for the night.

It was too bad they'd taken his canvas bag and his lockpicks, though the lock on the door was so ancient he wasn't even sure his picks would work. Maybe he should start carrying a pocketknife. He examined the hinges, looking for weak spots or signs of poor construction.

The door to the jail opened, admitting a beam of sunlight and Selene. One of the men in the cell next to his let out a catcall, moving closer to the bars to get a better look at her excellent body, which today was attired in tiny khaki shorts and a navy-blue tank top that hugged her curves. She had his bag carelessly dangling by a strap over her shoulder.

Selene walked down the hallway, her green eyes assessing each cell and the prisoners inside. As she passed in front of the cell next to his, her arm flashed out—snaking through the bars before he could blink—and grabbed the man who'd catcalled her by the front of his shirt. She gave a careless tug, and his face met the inside of the bars of his cell. His nose crunched loudly and spewed blood down his front.

She took a quick step back—escaping the spray—and continued on her way, stopping directly in front of Colin's cell. "Nice moves," he commented.

"The queen would like to see you," she said, pulling out the same iron key he'd seen the black-haired woman use earlier. He held out his hands in front of him, wrists together. "I think we can skip that this time."

Colin glanced at the man in the next cell, whose eyes were already starting to swell shut. "I'm good if you are." He wasn't in the mood for a black eye.

The town appeared to be arranged in the shape of a cross, with a long street running from the Royal Hall toward the Black Sea. Both sides of the street were flanked by what appeared to be small houses. The shorter street that crossed it led from the jail on one end to a long low building at the other, which was nestled at the foot of the surrounding hills. Right at the intersection of the two streets was a large, grassy square that held grazing goats. Selene led him through the herd of goats and to the same large building as the night before.

Someone had cleaned up the mess, the long table now empty and sporting a series of low benches on either side. The back of the room held the same ornate chair as before, not quite fancy enough to be dubbed a throne, but still much nicer than any other seat in the place.

The woman sitting on it intrigued him. She had medium-length brown hair decorated with a thin silver circlet that contained a sapphire so large it made him want to weep. He could only guess at the price that one piece of jewelry would fetch on the underground market.

Something about her didn't seem to make sense. She, like Selene, was an anachronism, something out of time that didn't quite fit the world around her. Despite her obvious role as the queen, she was perched on the chair in jeans and a polo shirt. He didn't know exactly what to make of it or of her.

A movement to the right of the chair drew his eye to yet another puzzle, a woman with long, flowing blonde hair who was wearing jeans and a body-hugging T-shirt. She'd been there the night before but hadn't said anything, so he hadn't been able to figure out what her role was in this strangely assorted group.

Colin's eyes lit on Sam, who was once again standing behind the queen. The good doctor Treadwell was sporting quite a few bruises Colin hadn't noticed before and appeared to be favoring his ribs. What on earth happened to him?

Selene stopped in front of the trio and bobbed a quick bow. "My queen."

Colin wasn't sure if he should bow and settled for a quick bend and a nod.

With a flick of her wrist, the queen gestured in Selene's direction. Colin watched as Selene dug into his bag and pulled out the papers. Without a word, she handed them to Sam, who took them and began flipping through the pages.

Colin had hoped it wouldn't come to this, but he was stuck now. The evidence was right in front of the only person who would understand what he'd done. Sam muttered under his breath as he opened the red notebook and flipped through it quickly. He snapped the notebook closed and moved on to the stack of loose papers, his growling getting louder as he made his way through the pile.

"Son of a bitch," Sam cursed, rapidly flipping through them. "These are mine." His fist clenched around the papers, wrinkling them as he shook them in Colin's direction.

"Technically, they're copies of yours. The originals are still in your office," Colin said. Selene rolled her eyes at him, and he shut up. He probably wasn't helping his case.

"Is this how you found this place?" Sam demanded.

"In part," Colin agreed. "But as you well know, the exact location wasn't in those papers. I did my own research." *Take that, Professor.*

"The location wasn't in there because no one knew the location of Themyscira until two days ago," Selene said, her eyes narrowed. "How did you figure it out?"

He had no idea what she was talking about. How was it possible that no one could have known where it was? It was not like the city was hiding or anything. And the four people in front of him had clearly gotten here somehow.

Colin glanced from face to face, each one staring at him with varying degrees of suspicion or accusation. Only Sam seemed mildly concerned. "I'm afraid I'm lost," Colin said. Two days ago? What were they talking about? His brain started whirling, trying to make the puzzle pieces fit.

He thought back to the commandos in the cells and the damaged Humvees scattered throughout town. It was clear that something serious had gone down, and recently too, if he had to guess based on how much of the damage still hadn't been cleaned up. Had the town been attacked? It would make sense, given the military-looking dudes holed up in the prison. What did that have to do with him?

Everything fell into place.

He shot both hands out in front of him. "Wait, wait, wait. Do you think I had something to do with whatever went down here?" He searched each person's expression in turn. It was Selene's terrible poker face that clued him in. "You do. No wonder. I can promise you, unequivocally, that I have nothing to do with the rest of those guys. In fact, two nights ago, I was in Samsun acquiring a boat. You know, the town about an hour from here?"

"Do you mean stealing a boat?" the blonde asked, pulling out a cell phone from her back pocket.

"Borrowing might be a better term." He had intended to give it back, honestly.

The queen nodded at the blonde woman, who stepped away from the group and placed a call. He didn't have time to wonder who she was calling.

"Would you also say that you 'borrowed' my research?" Sam asked. He crumpled the documents into a little ball.

Colin shrugged. "More or less." Sam scowled at him, but he was unmoved. They hadn't exactly parted on the best of terms. Colin still hadn't forgiven him for getting him kicked out of school. Colin hadn't done what he'd been accused of, so anything he could do to pester and annoy his former mentor was fine by him.

The blasting ring of a cell phone drew everyone's attention to Selene. She fumbled in the pocket of her short shorts and pulled out a smartphone. She glanced at the screen, then answered it and walked out of earshot. The blonde woman returned, sliding her phone back into her pocket.

"Well, he was telling the truth about being in Samsun. A boat matching the description of the one on the beach was reported stolen two days ago."

It was Colin's turn to be suspicious. There was no way she could have been able to verify his story that quickly unless she was some sort of cop. She didn't look like much of a cop, but after watching Selene bloody a guy's face for catcalling her, he was willing to withhold judgment.

"Thanks, Zoe," the queen said. She looked at Colin, considering. "It appears we may have misjudged you. Slightly."

Maybe he was going to get out of this after all.

"Not so fast," Selene said as she flipped her long riot of curls behind her shoulder and tucked away her phone. "He may not have been helping Eris and her men, but he isn't exactly innocent either."

"What do you mean?" Sam asked, resting his hand on the back of the queen's chair.

"Turns out Colin Wolfe has quite the rap sheet for grand theft," Selene said with a sneer.

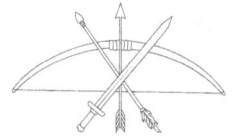

Chapter Four

COLIN CROSSED HIS ARMS over his chest and cocked his hip, meeting Selene's eyes without blinking. "I prefer to think of it as being a purveyor of antiquities. You're only a thief if you get convicted," he said.

Selene scoffed. "Now you're just splitting hairs." Ambrose had just given her an earful about Colin Wolfe's shady past. Typical, she supposed. She couldn't manage to go more than a few days without running into some sort of criminal or another.

She turned to Kalli, Zoe, and Sam. "The police suspect, but have been unable to prove, that Wolfe has been dealing in contraband antiquities for years. No one knows where he gets his merchandise, but once he has it, he sells it to the highest bidder."

"When you say it that way, it sounds bad, doesn't it?" he asked, and she rolled her eyes. She knew his type. He thought his charm and devastating good looks could get him out of any situation. Not this time. Clearly he had no idea who he was dealing with.

"Did you honestly think it was a wise decision to try to steal from a race of immortal warriors?" Zoe asked, her head cocking sideways and her eyes narrowing.

"Not exactly. I didn't know about the whole immortality bit. I assumed you were nothing but dust by now." Colin cringed.

"So, if you weren't planning on stealing from us, then what were you after?" Kalli asked, her fingers tapping out a rhythm on the arm of her chair.

"Me." Sam stepped out from behind Kalli. "You've been stealing from my dig sites. That's where you've been getting your merchandise." Anger laced his tone, and his hands clenched and unclenched repeatedly as if he was stopping himself from hitting something. "Artifacts have been going missing for years, but I always just assumed it was a local guide who was skimming a bit off the top. I never would have guessed it was you."

Colin's chin came up and his shoulders went back. He stared Sam down. Selene had to admire his guts. "I became the type of person you always believed me to be."

Selene crossed her arms. "That's what this is about? A little tit for tat?" She stared into his hazel eyes and did her best to ignore his gorgeous mouth.

His eyes narrowed, his arms crossing to mirror hers. He took a half step closer to her but seemed to think better of it. "Can you blame me? Dr. Samuel Treadwell"—he sneered as he said his name—"ruined my life. I was never going to be taken seriously as an academic after he accused me of stealing from him and got me kicked out of school. I chose to put my skills to use in another way. If I also used them to get back at the man who screwed up my life, that was a bit of a bonus."

Kalli stood, immediately drawing their attention. "Enough," she said roughly. "It's clear that Mr. Wolfe wasn't part of the plot to attack Themyscira. His actions may have been questionable, but they're hardly worthy of him being drawn and quartered."

Colin's gaze whipped around to meet Kalli's, disbelief evident on his face. "Seriously? You guys do that?"

Selene wanted to smirk but kept it to herself. "For the right person," she said sweetly.

She wasn't sure exactly what it was about Colin Wolfe that got under her skin. He was sickeningly handsome, but that wasn't it. He had questionable morals, but hadn't she also done some things she'd rather not admit to? What made her so different from him?

Selene's mirth died. She'd been standing here playing holier-than-thou with a man who wasn't all that different from her. If she ever confessed the truth of her own actions, she was certain Kalli would have no choice but to lock her away and lose the key. Doing the wrong thing for the right reason was still against the unwritten Amazon code.

"What do you want to do with him?" Zoe finally asked, taking a step closer to Kalli and Colin. She'd stayed mostly quiet during the exchange. Selene couldn't imagine what her little Interpol agent heart was doing at the thought of capturing an international thief.

Kalli examined Colin from the top of his brown hair to the spot where his boots met the stone floor. Then she turned to Sam. "What do you think we should do?"

Sam took a half step back, staring at his fiancée with uncertainty. "You're the queen."

Kalli's smile softened. She crossed the floor and planted a soft kiss on Sam's lips. "And you're my future husband. You're also the person he's been stealing from. I think you should get a say in his future." Kalli pulled back, but her hand remained on Sam's arm.

Colin shifted from one foot to the other, his eyes darting from Kalli to Sam—then, for some reason, landing on Selene. She tried not to think about why. "Look, I know I'm not exactly in a position to bargain here, but seriously, I meant no harm. The things I re-home . . ."

Selene coughed out the word *steal*, but he ignored her.

"The things I re-home are well taken care of. Most of them wind up in the hands of private collectors who can pay ten times what a museum could. My clientele are very careful with their collections and often have higher security than most high-end gem dealers."

Selene rolled her eyes. He was just trying to save his own arse. She would do the same if their positions were reversed. It was obvious he was saying whatever he needed to to get out of this unscathed. She wasn't going to let it work.

"I think you should detain him, at least for now," Sam said. Pity filled his eyes.

"What?!" Colin's voice lashed out. "I guess I should have expected as much from you." His hazel eyes narrowed, and his biceps bulged slightly as he clenched his fists.

A look of sorrow crossed Sam's face. "He knows how to find this place, and he knows that the Amazons are not only real but are, in fact, still alive. We aren't ready for that information to go public."

Colin laughed bitterly. "Sure, use that as your excuse if you'd like. You're doing this because you still believe Dr. Aldridge's word over mine. Here we are, four years later, and you still don't trust me." He thrust his chin at Sam threateningly as heat poured into his cheeks.

Sam's face was a stone mask. He took a deep breath before he continued. "Whatever I do now, I do for Queen Kalliope and her people. Whatever you think is between us pales in comparison to the need to keep them safe."

Colin rolled his eyes. "Oh, yeah. How could I forget? Your fiancée." He sneered. "What sort of Amazon falls in love and gets married?"

Selene reacted on instinct, thrusting her knife to Colin's throat before he'd finished asking the question. "You forget yourself, prisoner." She pushed on the tip of the razor-sharp blade just enough to draw a single drop of red from his neck. Blood was racing through her veins, throbbing in her ears. How dare he say something like that to Kalli, to a queen? She should bloody his face for the mere thought that Kalli was doing something improper.

Colin slowly relaxed his hands, holding them cautiously in front of his torso. He swallowed, bringing his throat even closer to her knife. "I'm so sorry," he said, his voice dropping to a low murmur. "That was so out of line that I can't even begin to make it right."

"Selene!" Zoe called her name sharply.

She glanced around the room. Sam was slack jawed, Kalli looked mildly concerned, and Zoe's hand was hovering over her gun. Selene looked back at Colin and saw an instantaneous flash of fear in his hazel eyes before he masked it. Normally, she didn't mind putting a fear into people—it was part of her job at Blackburn. This, however, was out of line.

She lifted the knife away from his neck, sliding it smoothly back into its sheath. She took a deep breath and rolled her shoulders, trying to settle her racing pulse. "It seems we both need to apologize." She bobbed her head quickly but refused to drop her gaze.

Colin took a half step away from her, his hand instinctively rubbing the spot where she'd nicked his throat. "I'd say we're square. I insult your queen, you try to kill me. Seems like a fair trade."

Selene had to fight down a laugh. How was it that she'd gone from boiling over with rage to amusement in the span of a few seconds? His charm had nothing to do with it, she reassured herself. Or the ever-so-sexy grin playing at the edges of his mouth.

Colin turned and faced Kalli, bowing deeply from the waist. "I apologize for the slight against you. I was angry, and I took it out on you, and that isn't fair."

Kalli regally lifted her head as she returned to her seat. "I thank you for your kind words. Be that as it may, I have to agree with Sam. I think, for now at least, you'll have to remain in custody. Guards!" The doors of the hall flew open, and two Amazons wearing full armor strode in. They marched across the floor, stopped in front of Kalli, and gave her a quick bow. She waved them toward Colin. "Please escort Mr. Wolfe back to his cell."

Selene's heart twinged slightly when she saw the panic on Colin's face. Clearly she'd gone soft over the last few hundred years. He was a thief and he'd invaded their land. End of story. If he were any one of the people on her organization's most wanted list, she wouldn't have had any trouble locking him away. There was no reason for her to feel any different now. Still, she watched him until the guards had dragged him out of sight, then reluctantly turned back to face her friends.

"How long can we keep him that way?" Zoe asked, one eyebrow going up as she crossed her arms and leaned back against the wall.

Kalli sighed. "Not long. It isn't fair to keep him locked up just for landing a boat on our shores, but we need time to think." She sagged in her chair, her crown slipping slightly.

Selene felt sorry for her friend but was secretly glad that their positions weren't reversed. The burden of ruling had always seemed unfair. The queen had to make thankless decisions that did nothing for herself but hopefully bettered her people in the long run. Selene operated differently. Sure, she wasn't the victim of the crimes she avenged, but she got to use her skills and abilities in a way she greatly enjoyed. Plus, every time she and her people rid the world of yet another scumbag, everyone benefited from it, including her.

"It will get out, you know," Zoe said, tapping her foot. "People will figure out that this place exists sooner or later. We must be prepared for that. Who knows what danger that might open us up to?"

Kalli pushed a lock of brown hair behind her shoulder and straightened her royal circlet. "I know. We'll have to come up with some sort of response for when people figure out that a city just appeared out of thin air, but I'm at a loss. Any ideas?" she asked, glancing at her friends.

Sam shook his head, but Zoe asked, "Can we at least bring in a generator and a few port-a-potties? I'm dying here."

"That can be arranged," Selene said. As usual her friends didn't ask how or why, which was for the best. Some of her contacts weren't as on the up-and-up as Zoe might hope.

"One of our first orders of business will need to be to acquaint our people with the wonders of modern technology. They have twenty-five hundred years to catch up on, so it'll take a while, but better we teach them than they find out the hard way," Kalli added. "Plus, we can't all just drop our old lives and not look back. We need a way to communicate with the outside world."

"We should probably start weapons training too," Zoe added, gesturing to her holster. "If we get attacked now, it won't be with swords and bows."

"On the list," Selene said, but her mind was elsewhere. Instead of being focused on the planning conversation she was in the middle of, her thoughts wandered to the prison and to one particular prisoner. She had no reason to think of him—and she chided herself for doing so—but she was worried about Wolfe. She'd seen the conditions in the prison, and while not exactly torture chambers, they weren't the Ritz either. He wouldn't be used to living in those conditions.

Stop it. She shook her head. Colin Wolfe's well-being was none of her concern. He was a prisoner, nothing more. Just like all the other creeps they had in lockup. The fact that she could still picture his smile had nothing to do with anything.

"Isn't that right, Selene?"

Selene yanked herself back to the conversation, lost. "I'm sorry, what?" she asked.

Zoe rolled her eyes. "I said we should be able to outfit our fighters soon, get them practicing on targets, that sort of thing."

Selene nodded. "Sure, sounds like a plan. I should be able to get some supplies here in the next few days. We'll have to make plans to meet my men outside the city, unless you don't mind them seeing all this." She made a large circle with her hand.

Kalli's lips pursed. "It's probably best if we meet them, at least for now. It'll keep down the number of people asking questions on both sides."

"Understood." Selene pulled her phone from her pocket and placed a call. Organizing the delivery of supplies was at least a distraction to keep her mind off a certain cocky jerk with a great smile.

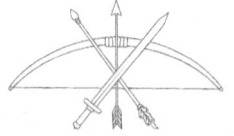

Chapter Five

C OLIN WAS SUDDENLY A lot less excited about being in Themyscira. The old stone buildings no longer seemed quaint
and interesting since one of them, and probably the least comfortable one, was going to be his home for the foreseeable future. He
couldn't believe what he'd gotten himself into.

His guards escorted him back to his cell, the barred door closing
behind him with a loud clang. The Amazons walked away without
a word, but the commandos in the next cell over weren't as pleasant.
Several of them crossed the floor and stood at the bars that separated
the two cells.

"Couldn't talk your way out of your cell?" a big blond man
taunted.

"Talking isn't exactly what I want to do to that redhead," another
man said, smacking his buddy on the arm.

"Where's your friend? Blond guy, kind of jacked, arms covered in
tattoos?" Colin asked innocently. "Did he leave you in there to rot

without him?" The big guy smacked his hand into one of the bars with a dull thud and growled.

It probably wasn't smart to taunt a bunch of guys who could break him in half without even trying, but Colin couldn't bring himself to care. For the moment, a wall of bars separated them. He'd care later, assuming he ever got out.

He turned his back on his less-than-friendly neighbors and stared at the low stone ceiling. He needed to figure out how to get himself out of this jail before he rotted in it. Plus, the siren song of Hippolyta's belt was calling his name.

He systematically inspected the mortared stones of the exterior wall of his cell. He cautiously ran his hands over it, looking for any loose blocks he could remove or cracks that he could exploit, but the wall stood firm. Not surprising. The jail had stood this long, and it wasn't going to topple over just because he pushed on it.

He glanced at the door at the front of the building. The door was guarded at all times, making him wonder how the woman from that morning had sneaked in and out undetected. Even more surprising, as far as he knew, no one had reported the prisoner missing.

The long wall of the hallway contained the sole window. It didn't have glass in it, so if he could escape from his cell, he might have an option to go out that way. The opening was narrow, which made him glad he wasn't nearly as ripped as the guys in the next cell. They would never have fit.

He was about to inspect the bars in his cell door for weaknesses when the outside door opened and Selene strode in, her hair flashing in the sun and a pair of sunglasses perched on top of her light-red curls.

She walked up to his cell and held his red notebook in front of her, pointing it at him accusingly. "We can't read this."

Colin slowly spun to face her, staring at her through the bars. "I know." Maybe he had a ticket out of here after all.

She rolled her neck, then tapped the book on the door to his cell. "Sam says it's in some sort of shorthand code."

He took a small step toward her, just barely holding back a laugh. He nodded solemnly instead. "He's right."

"Translate it for us," she demanded, her eyes narrowing accusingly. Her fingers began tapping out a staccato rhythm on the notebook.

He finally cracked a smile. "Now, why would I do that?" He crossed his arms over his chest and enjoyed watching her eyes flash. He'd always been a sucker for a fiery temper.

"We need to know how much you know about this place, about the Amazons." Her voice lowered as she glanced sideways at the men in the next cell.

Colin's eyes swept from the top of her head to the toes of her combat boots, enjoying every glorious inch of her, including her furious gaze. "Not nearly as much as I'd like to," he said with a smirk.

She let out a huff, crossing her arms to mirror his position. He couldn't tell if she was annoyed or amused.

She glared at him before glancing around the jail. "I . . . ," she started, but she trailed off, looking more closely at the cell next to his. She took a few steps to the right, and he saw her eyes zoom around the cell. He could practically see her counting the number of prisoners in the adjacent cell and coming up short. "Guards!" she yelled, dropping her arms and reaching for the gun at her waist. She pulled it from its holster, holding it loosely but competently at her side.

The two guards came running into the building, their swords drawn and eyes immediately searching the entire prison. They came to an abrupt stop next to Selene. "What is it?" the one in front asked.

Selene turned to them, eyes blazing green fire. "Have you two been on watch all day?" she asked.

The women snapped to attention. "Yes," the same guard answered.

Selene stalked closer. "Then perhaps you can tell me why one of our prisoners is missing!" She was shouting by the end. She stared them down, inches from their faces. The guards took a step back, their leather armor creaking. Selene wore nothing more protective than shorts and a tank top but didn't look the least bit concerned. He admired her daring.

She simply radiated power.

"Well, Tanis? Nothing to say for yourself?" she asked the woman who'd spoken. The woman rolled her shoulders and looked Selene in the eye but said nothing. "You, Alekto?" Selene rounded on the other woman. Alekto glanced at Tanis, but her partner didn't look back. Alekto turned her gaze back to Selene with a grimace. She dropped her eyes to Selene's torso and said nothing.

"Fine," Selene continued harshly. She pulled out her cell phone, tapped it once, and then said, "Zoe, I need you in the prison ASAP." She shoved her phone back in her tiny pocket. "Now we wait."

Colin watched the scene play out in front of him like a reality television show, only with considerably more weaponry. He had a sudden craving for popcorn.

The other prisoners were enjoying the show every bit as much as he was. The men in the next cell had come to the bars to watch, several of them taking side bets on who would win. One poor schmuck even made condescending kissy noises at Selene and Tanis. Without bothering to turn and look at them, Selene aimed her gun through the bars of the cell and pointed it directly between the eyes of the closest commando. "Who wants to push me right now?" She pulled back the hammer with a quiet click.

God he loved her fierce determination. The commandos beat a quick retreat from the bars, the one who had the gun pointed at his head putting his hands up in defeat. Those guys deserved everything she dished out to them.

Colin watched, fascinated, as Selene took in a deep breath and visibly relaxed her entire body, every muscle slackening. Whatever she was doing, he needed to learn how to do it. It would probably come in handy in his line of work.

Zoe burst through the door to the jail. She glanced around, instantly taking in the situation. "What's happened?"

"One of our prisoners escaped, and our guards here," Selene said, gesturing to Tanis and Alekto, "didn't feel the need to tell anyone."

Zoe immediately grabbed Tanis's wrists behind her back and marched her over to the only remaining empty cell. "We're going to run out of space in the jail at this rate," Zoe muttered. She ushered Alekto in with her partner. "You stay here and deal with that"—she gestured at the book in Selene's hands—"and I'll go inform Queen Kalliope. She'll want to question the guards and possibly form a search party."

"You'll also want to tell her to look for one of your own," Colin offered as Zoe turned to go.

Selene's fierce green eyes snapped to his. "What are you talking about?" she asked, coming to stand in front of his cell.

He shrugged nonchalantly, but his mind was whirling. He may have a bargaining chip after all. "Black hair, big boobs, likes skimpy black leather."

Selene gave Zoe a significant glance before turning back to him. "Why would we look for her?" Her skepticism was obvious.

"Well, she's the one that busted G.I. Joe out of jail this morning. I figured that might be important."

Zoe took a step closer to him, her blue eyes pinning him. "What did you see?"

He crossed his arms over his chest. "What's it worth to you?"

Selene rolled her eyes and let out a huff. Bull's-eye. He'd hit his mark.

"Why shouldn't I just beat it out of one of these guys?" Selene asked, waving her hand vaguely in the direction of the cell next to his. Several of the occupants muttered under their breaths.

"You could try, but you wouldn't get very far. Everyone else was asleep."

Selene's fingers wrapped around the bars of his cell, squeezing so tightly her knuckles turned white. "Now that we know who took him, what do we need you for?" She dropped her hands to her side, again deliberately relaxing her tense muscles.

Colin walked slowly toward the front of his cell, stopping a few feet away from where Selene stood on the other side. "Because I know where they're going." This was his ticket out of there. He just hoped he'd played his cards right with Selene. He'd been trying to irritate her just enough that he could surprise her with his information, but not enough that she left him there to rot out of spite.

She rolled her eyes. "Let me guess, you'll tell us once I let you out of your cell?"

He smiled smugly. "Nope. I'll tell you once I'm on a boat in the middle of the Black Sea."

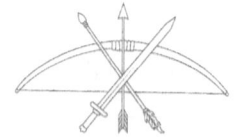

Chapter Six

S ELENE STALKED BACK AND forth in front of the queen's throne like a caged animal. "You can't possibly be considering this," she said, rolling her neck to loosen the muscles. "He's our prisoner."

Kalli gave her a bland look. "And he may know the whereabouts of a traitor. If Nyx really did let the soldier out of his cell, she's betrayed us. Again. Not only that, but if Wolfe is right, they have almost half a day's head start on us." She looked at Sam, who was uncomfortably shifting back and forth. "Can he be trusted?"

Sam grimaced. "I honestly don't know. If you'd asked me a week ago, I would have said no. After listening to him this morning, I would still say no."

"He's a thief and a criminal," Selene spat out. "He can't be trusted." She tamped down on the feeling that she was being hypocritical. Now wasn't the time.

"Zoe, what do you think?" Kalli asked, turning to her friend.

Zoe glanced from Selene to Sam, then shrugged. "We can always track Nyx the regular way. I can get Interpol on the horn and see if they've picked up any chatter."

It wouldn't be enough. Despite her better judgment, Selene said, "That won't work. Whatever it is that Nyx wants, she doesn't know the first thing about the modern world. She has no money and would have no clue how to drive a car or get on a plane. That's where Eris's goon comes in. He can show her around, help her get whatever she's after. He'd be smart enough not to draw the attention of the authorities. She's not likely to blend in."

Kalli nodded. "I agree. As much as I'd like to think the best of all our people, there is no logical reason Nyx would have left Themyscira unless she was up to something."

"She can't be happy you're back," Sam commented. "She ruled for the last twenty-five hundred years. She isn't going to give that up without a fight."

Kalli absentmindedly touched the silver circlet she wore. "No, she wouldn't." Nyx had worn the crown just days ago, and she hadn't been happy to surrender it.

"Can't you ask the gods for some assistance?" Selene asked. As the only Amazon with a direct connection to the Greek pantheon, Kalli was uniquely qualified.

Kalli shook her head. "It's not a good idea to bother the gods for something so trivial. Besides, since when are the Amazons unable to handle their own business?"

Frustration ripped through Selene. Logically, she knew they needed to go after Nyx and stop whatever she was trying to do, but letting Wolfe go just rubbed her the wrong way.

Why was he trying to bargain now? Why hadn't he said something earlier? Of course Wolfe wanted to get out of jail, but Selene's gut was telling her that there was more to it than that. Given enough time, he'd figure out how to escape Themyscira himself, or perhaps Kalli would just let him go, deciding it was unfair to hold him hostage any longer.

If what he'd said was true, Nyx had broken the commando dude out of jail before they'd talked to Wolfe the first time. The fact that he hadn't tried to use what he knew as a negotiation tactic was odd. If all he wanted was to get out of jail, he could have mentioned the information earlier and shortened his stay. He'd clearly been concealing the information on purpose and hadn't wanted to draw their attention to the situation. That implied there was something else he knew that he wasn't sharing. Something he wanted to keep for himself.

Like Zeus's lightning bolt, it hit her. She stopped pacing and stared at Kalli. "He wants it."

Kalli sent a confused glance at Sam, then Zoe, and they both shrugged. "Wants what?" she asked.

Selene continued pacing while she worked it all out. "Here's what I think happened. Nyx came to the jail this morning looking for help with something she felt she couldn't do herself. Wolfe probably overheard them talking about whatever it is that Nyx is up to. So why wouldn't he have just told us and used the information to save his own ass? But he didn't. Which means the topic of conversation was probably near and dear to Wolfe's own heart, arts and antiquities. Clearly Nyx is going after something, and he wants it for himself." It made total sense. He was a thief that specialized in ancient relics. The only objects Nyx even knew about would fall under the category of ancient, assuming they still existed. "Think about it. It makes total sense. He's going to try to take it for himself, then sell it to the highest bidder." She smacked her hand against her thigh, barely feeling the slight sting.

"It does match his style," Sam added with a nod. "But what do you think they're going after?"

"No idea," Selene said.

"But Wolfe would know," Zoe added.

"Yes, he's keeping that from us." A sense of calm spread through Selene. If Kalli was going to go along with Wolfe's proposal to get the information she needed to find and retrieve Nyx, then Selene could at least comfort herself with the fact that Wolfe was no different from anyone else she went after. She could think of him as one of her prey and lure him into her trap. Then she could pounce and recapture him before he was even aware of what she was doing. "I'll go with him," she said.

Zoe started forward, but stopped short, a deep vee forming between her eyes. "What? Why?"

Selene wanted to dance with excitement. She had been missing her real-life hunting down bad guys and this seemed like a great way to jump back in. She'd do what she did better than anyone, and she'd make sure Colin Wolfe didn't spill the secret of the existence of the

Amazons in the process. It was perfect. "He won't tell us what he knows until he's away from here. I don't want to let him out of my sight. Win-win."

"Selene," Kalli said, exasperated. "That isn't necessary. He's not hurting anyone."

"Tell that to your fiancé and his research team." It was a low blow, which made her stomach twist slightly, but she wasn't wrong.

Kalli glanced at Sam's stony face. He cocked his head, and his eyes narrowed, telling Selene everything she needed to know. She was right to go. Colin Wolfe may be gorgeous and charming, but he was still a thief, and he'd wronged one of the only men she'd ever really cared about. Sam might be Kalli's fiancé, but he also meant a lot to Selene. He was living proof that there were good men in the world, men who weren't emasculated by strong women, men who could let women be themselves.

Most importantly, Sam had reenforced a lesson that Ambrose had originally taught her. Not all men deserved her wrath.

As she waited for Kalli's answer, she bit her tongue, fighting the sensation of blatant hypocrisy. Here she was offering to play prison guard to a man who stole stuff for a living. It wasn't like he'd raped or killed anyone, and yet she was treating him like vermin. Who was she to judge when others bent or broke the law? She wasn't exactly an angel, or even much of an Amazon. She squashed that thought when Kalli spoke.

"Are you truly set on doing this?" Kalli fixed Selene with an appraising gaze.

Selene nodded firmly. "Yes."

"Then you have my permission. Figure out what Nyx is up to and why she left Themyscira. She doesn't know anything about the outside world and wouldn't have left here without a reason. Do what you need to, use Colin Wolfe in any way that you need to. Just get the information we need."

Zoe's eyebrows waggled, her blue eyes sparkling. "I wouldn't mind using Wolfe in a few interesting ways myself."

Selene rolled her eyes at her friend. "Mind out of the gutter, please. This is a mission, nothing else." Not that she hadn't had similar thoughts herself.

Zoe unsuccessfully tried to wipe the smile from her face. "Of course not. Riding off into the sunset with an uber hot guy. No possible way that could turn sexy. Work comes first." She added an exaggerated nod and a quick salute.

Selene crossed her arms, her right foot tapping on the stone floor. "We won't be riding off into the sunset. This mission is important. Don't you agree we should find out what Nyx is up to?" Sometimes it was easier being around mostly men. They didn't gossip like schoolgirls.

Zoe took a small step closer to Kalli. "Notice how she didn't deny he was hot?" she stage-whispered loud enough for everyone in the room to hear.

"Are we done now, children?" Kalli asked, amusement simmering beneath her stern words.

Selene reeled in her irritation at Zoe. She made it sound like there was something dirty about what Selene was doing, and that simply wasn't the case. Colin Wolfe may be hot as sin, but he was a means to an end and nothing more than that. She took a deep breath, using it to soothe her senses and relax her entire body. It wasn't worth getting worked up about. She was doing her job.

"I'm done. I'll be ready to leave in fifteen minutes, my queen," Selene said, dropping into a small bow out of respect for her friend's position.

"Come back alive, Amazon," Kalli said, echoing words from long ago.

"Don't plan your wedding without me," Selene responded, wagging a finger between Kalli and Sam, making them both smile and bringing rosy spots to Kalli's cheeks. Selene still couldn't get over that their once man-hating queen was engaged to be married. It just proved that after four thousand years, she could still be surprised.

"Same goes for you, Selene," Zoe chimed in with a cheeky grin.

With a quick nod to Sam and an eye roll for Zoe, Selene spun on her heel and left the Royal Hall.

Her first stop was to her own quarters to grab the meager possessions she had with her. When she'd left London to chase down the tip she'd gotten about her former Amazon sister Eris—who had been trafficking weapons, among other things—she hadn't known how long she'd be gone or where she'd wind up. She definitely hadn't expected to wind up back home. At the time, she'd decided to travel light to make it easier, just a handful of outfits and some tech so she could keep in touch with Ambrose and Blackburn. She grabbed her gear from its small pile on the table and shoved it into a bag before slinging the strap carelessly over her shoulder.

She wasn't sure what felt stranger, coming back to Themyscira after twenty-five hundred years or leaving it again after less than a week. Of course, she had missed her sisters while she had been exiled and unable to return. It was amazing to see them again and catch up on everything that had happened while she was gone. But having been gone for as long as she had and having experienced the modern world in all its splendor, it was like she no longer fit in quite the same way. It was like she was trying to shove a shotgun shell into a handgun. It wasn't going to work. Maybe it was a good idea she was leaving.

After grabbing her stuff, her second stop was the jail. A new pair of guards had come on duty, and Selene was pleased to see who was standing watch. Melina and Frona had always been loyal to Kalli and wouldn't let any of the prisoners waltz out of jail.

"I've come for Colin Wolfe," Selene said as she approached the door.

Frona nodded. "Queen Kalliope sent word you would be escorting him on a mission." She handed Selene the large iron key that opened the jail cell doors. "Come back alive," she said with a nod. Selene returned the nod quickly and headed inside.

Her target was lying on his pallet, arms behind his head, staring at the ceiling. He glanced in her direction when she came in, then went back to studying the coarsely cut stones above him. She knew he was ignoring her on purpose, which just made it more irritating.

"On your feet, Wolfe." She stopped outside his cell and crossed her arms, the key dangling quite obviously from her fingertips.

"Oh, you're here for me?" he said, feigning surprise. He swung his long legs over the side of the bed and stood. He stretched, putting all his glorious muscles on display through his thin cotton T-shirt. She tried not to notice and failed miserably.

"The queen has agreed to your terms," she said. "If you tell us what you know about where Nyx and the missing prisoner have gone, you're free to go."

His eyes narrowed suspiciously. "Just like that?" His arms crossed over his chest, making his pecs bulge, and his eyes narrowed. "What's the catch?"

Wicked delight rushed through her. She cocked her hip and her head to look at him sweetly. "I'm coming with you."

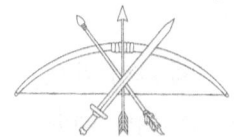

Chapter Seven

H E WASN'T GOING TO make the clean getaway he'd been hoping for, but looking at the fiery redhead in front of him, Colin couldn't complain. It wasn't like he'd expected them to just let him go.

He was sure he could handle her, even if she was an Amazon. Selene might be a fighter, but she was still a woman. He hadn't met a woman he couldn't charm. Eventually, at least.

"Done," he said, shrugging. "When do we leave?"

A smile spread across her beautiful face, highlighting her dimples. "Now."

She opened his cell door and gestured for him to leave. He glanced behind him at the commandos still cooped up and glaring venomously in his direction. He gave them a cheeky grin. "Sorry, boys, I guess this one's all mine." The blond man in front growled and slammed his hand into the bars, making them rattle ominously.

Selene glanced at the prisoners, then back to Colin. "Do you have a death wish?" she asked.

He strolled out of his cell, enjoying the satisfying clank of it closing shut behind him. "Not particularly. I'll need my notebook, by the way."

Her eyes narrowed, and she glared at him. "Why?"

He began walking toward the jail door. "I suppose we could leave it behind, unless you actually want to find the thing that Nyx and her jailbird are after." He tucked his hands into his back pockets and watched her, immensely enjoying how easy it was to push her buttons.

She yanked her hand through her hair, then pushed the curly mass over her shoulders. "Fine."

Smiling brilliantly, he swept his arm in front of his body, gesturing for her to lead the way. "After you."

Selene marched out of the jail, head held high and eyes glaring. She handed the key back to the guards at the door and headed toward the center of town.

The sun was just setting when Colin set foot outside, and he paused to enjoy the feeling of freedom. He wasn't out of danger yet, but knowing that they were heading to his boat and away from this place was enough for the moment.

The burning reds and purples of the sky were striking, casting a warm glow over the ancient city. Colin felt a pang in his heart that he would never fully explore the wonders of this place. Spending another day in captivity wasn't exactly high on his list of things he wanted to try again, but, despite being a thief by trade, he was an academic at heart. He'd had hours to contemplate it, and yet he still couldn't wrap his mind around the fact that this place and these people still existed. As both he and Sam had believed, the Amazons weren't mythological.

Oh yeah, and apparently, they were immortal. Go figure.

Of course, he still had questions. He had no idea how his old rival had wound up here engaged to their queen or how that queen and her friends appeared to be far more modern than they should have any right to be. Queen Kalliope, the blonde named Zoe, and the fiery Selene were all a mystery to him, but as he watched Selene's perfect rear as she walked in front of him, he couldn't wait to figure out the puzzle.

They walked through town, retracing the same path they'd taken the night of his capture. Curious Amazons appeared from inside buildings and crouched upon rooftops, but no one said anything as Selene escorted him past the edge of the city and toward the sea. They came around a slight curve and stopped dead.

His boat was gone.

Selene seemed to realize the problem at the same time he did. She sighed. "Nyx and her soldier must have taken your boat."

"That's too bad. I was hoping to return that to its rightful owner."

She cocked her head in his direction and gave him a dubious look out of the corner of her eye.

"I was, honest." Colin raised his hand with three fingers up, his thumb grabbing his pinkie.

She rolled her eyes. "I sincerely doubt you were a Boy Scout." She pulled a phone out of the tiny pocket in her shorts and pressed a button. "Yeah, I need a boat."

The conversation took less than ten seconds. Colin had no idea who she'd called, but they must have had some resources, because Selene said, "A boat should be here in forty-five minutes."

Colin leaned up against a boulder, eyeing his companion. She paced rapidly, making circles and figure eights in the dirt. Her long, shapely legs ate up the ground, her arms shaking like she was getting ready to take on a punching bag or an unfortunate sparring partner. The energy practically vibrated off her, making him tired just looking at her.

"So what's your story?" he asked, cocking his head sideways and squinting in her direction.

Selene stopped pacing and glared at him, shoving her long curly hair over her shoulder. "I don't have a story." She crossed her arms, making her breasts plump nicely.

"Everyone has a story. Especially a woman who is thousands of years old and yet looks like she just stepped out of *Guns & Ammo* magazine." He eyed her top-of-the-line pistol and the deadly tactical knife strapped to her left thigh.

She huffed, and turned away from him, planting her foot on a large rock. Without even trying, she jumped off the rock and landed on a boulder ten feet away, her back still to him.

"See what I mean?" He raised his voice in her direction. "There's always a story. Normal people can't do that."

She turned back around and looked at him. "You're well aware that I'm not normal." She glanced in the direction of Themyscira but quickly looked away, her eyes clouding.

He crossed his arms over his chest and studied her. "Being an Amazon is some of it, obviously." He gestured to the distance she'd just jumped without thinking. "But there's something else not quite right with you, Zoe, and your queen. You may be from here, but you're not really at home here. At least not anymore."

A line appeared between her eyebrows as she scowled at him. She launched herself off the boulder with a flip, landing within a few feet of where he was standing. "Show-off," he teased.

Selene closed the distance between them. When she was mere inches from his face, she stopped, her eyes blazing green fire. "Kalliope is the true queen of the Amazons. She belongs here and I should throw you back in your cell for saying otherwise."

He held up his hands in surrender. "I didn't mean to offend. I've read stories of Queen Kalliope, so I'm not going to doubt your word. But the three of you have a vibe that you don't get from spending the last four thousand years in isolation. Plus, if Beretta is now exporting to Themyscira, I'll eat my duffel bag."

Selene's hand twitched over her gun, but she took a few steps away from him. She rolled her neck, shrugging a few times. With one deep breath, she did that total-body-relaxation thing that fascinated him so much.

"The three of us . . ." She paused, then started over. "The three of us have spent more than half of our lives away from here." There was a faint wistfulness in her tone that she quickly covered.

"I don't suppose you'd care to elaborate on that," he said.

"I don't suppose I do," she responded curtly. "What's your story, anyway? You came all this way—traveling halfway across the globe—just to make Sam look bad? Isn't that just the tiniest bit childish?"

Colin shrugged. "You know my story. I steal stuff for money. Quite a bit of money at that. Getting back at Sam is just a side benefit." The words rolled off his tongue with practiced ease. He almost didn't notice the slight pang that he'd worked so hard to contain.

"Care to elaborate on that?" she repeated his question back at him.

"You wanna go tit for tat?" He raised one eyebrow suggestively, looking her up and down.

She rolled her eyes, but a small smile appeared on her face. "My tits are worth way more than your tat."

He scoffed in mock offense. "I'll have you know that my tat is quite impressive. Some might even say legendary."

She waved her hand dismissively. "I'll believe that when I see it."

He stood, taking a half step closer to her. "Anytime," he said and meant it. Selene might have a temper on her, but he could only imagine what all that energy could be used for in the bedroom. Plus, she was sexy as hell. Her soft red hair was long enough to make him drool, and her lithe body was fully capable of kicking his ass, yet looked soft in all the right places.

Selene was saved from having to respond by the sound of a motor. Spinning away from him, she grabbed her bags and walked to meet the incoming boat.

Colin watched from a distance as Selene spoke a few words to the man who was driving the boat. With a quick nod, she climbed aboard. She turned around, noticing him still standing where she'd left him. "Are you coming or not?" she asked, exasperated.

He had no idea what it was about him that riled her up so, but damn she looked cute when she was annoyed at him. He walked to the water and jumped in the boat. He didn't manage it quite as smoothly as she had—his left shoe was now drenched—but he made it. She gestured quickly to the pilot, who backed the small speedboat away from the shore and took off.

The sun had set while they were waiting for the boat, but Selene didn't seem to mind. She sat at the back, eyes closed and arms spread wide, relaxing. Her hair was whipping madly around her face, but she didn't seem to notice.

Colin sat across from her, contemplating the puzzle she present-ed. She was drop-dead gorgeous, obviously. She was also clearly a fearless fighter, even though he hadn't gotten a chance to see her in action. She moved in a way that was far too calculating to be anything other than honed perfection. But however he'd pictured the Amazons, she definitely wasn't it.

She'd admitted, reluctantly, that she'd spent much of her life away from her homeland. That, at least, explained the guns and the fancy cell phone that she'd used to call for their ride.

Glancing at the placid face of the man driving the boat, Colin wondered how she'd managed to get him there so quickly. From what he'd seen, it didn't look like they knew each other, and yet here he was, picking them up at night in a shiny boat that looked like it had hardly been used. He'd give anything to know who was on the other end of that phone call she'd made.

He was surprised that she didn't immediately start grilling him for information. He knew she wasn't happy about the deal he'd offered, so he'd expected rubber hoses and bright lights as soon as they'd shoved off. Instead, she seemed perfectly content to sit back and wait, her feet propped up on the edge of the boat, just barely catching the spray from the water.

After about half an hour, the pilot cut the engine and guided the small craft toward a rickety-looking dock that stuck out into the sea. Selene's eyes popped open, instantly alert. She watched him pull up next to the pier and stop, reaching out to grab one of the pilings. With a quick nod, he hopped out of the boat and rapidly strode away from them, not even bothering to tie up.

Colin briefly considered making a run for it, but he knew she would catch him before he made it ten steps. "Are we getting out?" he asked, confused. He hadn't told her where they were going yet, so he had no idea why they were stopped.

She stood and stretched like a cat, which did all sorts of interesting things to her lean muscles, and she thrust her breasts out like they were on display. She caught him looking but just rolled her eyes. At least she didn't punch him. "We're not getting out. He was."

She got behind the wheel and turned the boat, expertly guiding them away from the pier. Instead of sitting in the seat and hiding behind the windshield, she sat on the back of it, her long limbs more than capable of reaching the controls. She shook her hair so it fell over her shoulders and turned her face into the wind.

After another thirty minutes, when he could no longer see the shore in any direction, she cut the engine. The boat rocked a few times as the waves of their wake caught up to them, but Selene didn't seem to mind. She stood rock steady, arms crossed in front of her, and pinned him with her gaze. "Now, talk."

The moonlight was bright, for which he was thankful. There wasn't a city light as far as he could see. He and the forever-irritated Amazon were well and truly alone.

To be honest, he'd spent so much of his last twenty-four hours planning and plotting his escape that he wasn't quite sure where to start. If he just blurted out what he knew, there was nothing stopping her from dumping him at the first opportunity or sending him back to jail in Themyscira. He wasn't going to be cut out of this hunt, not if Nyx and her soldier were after what he thought they were after. One score like that and he could retire.

He chose his words carefully. "I believe they're going to the Mediterranean."

She cocked her head to the side. "The Mediterranean is a big place, a whole sea, in fact. Please tell me you have more to go on than that."

"I might," he hedged.

"Oh for God's sake, this is useless." She marched back over to the pilot's seat and reached for the key.

"No, wait." He held his hands out in her direction, sweat beading on his forehead despite the cool air. "Can I just see my notebook? Please?"

She cut him a look out of the corner of her eye.

"I promise I'm not making this up." At least he didn't think he was.

With an exaggerated roll of her head, she grabbed her bag and dug inside, producing his red hardcover notebook. He caught it with ease and pulled off the elastic band, rapidly flipping through the pages.

Selene came up behind him and peered over his shoulder. "How can you read that? It isn't any language that I've ever seen, and I pretty much know them all."

He waved his hand dismissively, his mind focused on what he was doing. "It's a shorthand I developed. Academia can seem boring from the outside, but I can assure you that it's pretty cutthroat. There's a whole publish-or-perish mentality that can lead people to do desperate things." He licked his finger and kept flipping pages.

"You mean like stealing priceless historical artifacts?" she asked innocently.

He glared at her, then turned back to his notebook. "This isn't about my history with Sam."

Her gaze narrowed, but she eventually backed up and tapped her toe rapidly as she waited. Finally, about halfway through his notes, he found what he was looking for. "We need to go to Mycenae."

There was a pregnant pause before Selene said, "You mean the one in Greece?"

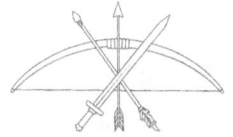

Chapter Eight

"DO YOU KNOW ANOTHER Mycenae?" Colin asked.

Selene was skeptical. "As in the town that hasn't been occupied since the thirteenth century?" He had to be joking. It made no sense that Nyx would break someone out of jail just to go to a long-destroyed city.

"Yep." He snapped his annoying red notebook shut and tucked it into his pocket. He sat down, stretching his legs as far as they could go on the small boat. As if he didn't have a care in the world, he lifted his arms behind his head and leaned back, closing his eyes.

She walked over and kicked him, shoving his legs off the seat he'd propped them on. His eyes popped open. "Hey! I was using that," he said as she sat down on the seat his feet had recently occupied.

Starting at the top of his head, she scanned his entire body. The way he was leaning, with his arms behind his head, was doing delicious things to his pecs and biceps. She found herself staring just a little too long, and when she glanced back at his face, she saw his knowing grin.

Refusing to be cowed, she scooted to the edge of her seat, invading his personal space. "Explain." She stared at him like she would a dog on the verge of biting, cautious yet confident.

"No," he said, a huge smile splitting his far-too-attractive mouth. He closed his eyes again like he planned to take a nap.

Fed up, she grabbed him by the shoulders and threw him to the floor of the boat, narrowly missing the seats on either side. In an instant, she sat astride him, glaring down into his face.

His shock turned sexy as his hands rested on her thighs where they bracketed his hips. "Well, if you wanted to take me up on my offer from earlier, all you had to do was ask." He waggled his eyebrows suggestively and smirked. His eyes moved from her face down to her breasts before glancing at where her thighs rested on his stomach. "I've always liked women who know what they want."

He was the most infuriating man she'd ever met. She'd just practically physically assaulted him and all he could do was proposition her. What was wrong with him? "Then you're going to love me," she purred, leaning down farther into his body, pressing her breasts into his chest. His eyes widened and his breath quickened. "I always know exactly what I want. And right now . . ." She trailed off, drawing one finger suggestively down his face from his temple to his lips.

"Yes?" he asked, his voice husky.

She could feel his cock hardening underneath her, and she fought to keep herself focused on her objective. She sat up, her finger under his chin, shoving his head hard into the floor and holding it there. "I want to know why we need to go to Mycenae."

He laughed, but it turned into a groan. "Red, you sure know how to push a man's buttons."

"Red?" she said warningly. No one called her that. At least not more than once.

"Glare at me all you want, Red. I'm not telling you what you want to know." He stared her in the eye as he used the nickname again. Arrogant prick. Did he think she wouldn't retaliate?

Her fingers itched to inch sideways to locate the pressure point where his neck met his shoulder. It was her business to know how to get uncooperative men to do what she wanted them to do. She had no doubt, with the proper application of force, she could get Wolfe to spill his deepest secrets.

She found herself hesitating and didn't understand why. Her mission was to track Nyx and the escaped soldier. Wolfe had information that would help her on that mission, and she knew exactly what it would take to get him to tell her that information.

She couldn't quite bring herself to do it.

Unwilling to look too closely at her own motives, Selene pushed herself up, towering over where he was still sprawled on the floor. "Don't think this conversation is over," she said. Sliding back behind the wheel, she turned the key with a flick of her wrist, and the boat roared to life. She diligently ignored him for the rest of the trip.

The boat ride took longer than she expected. Selene was grateful that her Amazon genes made her senses sharper than the average person's, because being in a boat in the middle of the sea at night would have been disorienting otherwise, even with high-end navigation equipment. All around her was an unrelenting inky blackness. The breeze washed over her face, and the darkness soothed her soul, calmness flowing through her.

Her anger always seemed to simmer just below the surface, but the last few days of being back together with her sisters had pushed buttons she wasn't aware she'd had. Being close to Colin Wolfe was only making it worse.

It had been a long time since she'd had to think about her life all those centuries before. She'd settled into her new life—into her new career—with ease, using her skills and abilities to right wrongs in the only way she knew how—by force.

The Amazons had been the fiercest warriors of their day. Armies had quivered when they'd approached, knowing they were fated for death and destruction. But even through all of that, the Amazons had always operated by a code. They always knew right from wrong, and there were certain lines they didn't cross. They didn't kill for pleasure and didn't torture people. If they did deal a killing blow, it was always swift and sure.

The passing centuries had changed her and not for the better. She'd seen firsthand, over and over again, exactly how much damage people could do to one another. She also watched them escape repercussions for their actions, especially men of power and wealth.

Their victims often weren't able to stand up for themselves, so she'd appointed herself their guardian. She could do what others couldn't, and she did it with relish. The stain on her soul was worth it for the justice she brought to others.

Just as the sun was starting to rise, glinting sharply across the water, a strip of land appeared in the distance. She pulled the boat up to an abandoned pier, tying it off so it wouldn't float away. She'd call to have someone pick it up later. No use wasting a good boat.

Grabbing her duffel from where she'd stuffed it near the front of the boat, she hopped off, waiting impatiently while Colin climbed out after her. They weren't far from Istanbul, where they'd be able to procure more supplies. Unfortunately, they were far enough away that walking wasn't going to be an option.

There was a small village near where she'd dropped the boat, and she headed in that direction, watching her squirrelly companion closely. She had no idea what game he was playing, so it wouldn't hurt to keep an extra eye on him in case he tried something.

It was still early enough that even the fishers weren't yet out and about. She saw a rusty old truck left next to a particularly dilapidated cottage. Hoping that the engine wasn't in as rough a shape as the body, she headed straight for it, throwing her bag in the back.

Colin lifted one eyebrow as he watched her. "And you gave me crap for borrowing my boat." He slung his bag in back alongside hers. Just as she hoped, the owner hadn't felt the need to lock the doors, and she opened the door with a quick tug. A loud creak split the calm morning air, and she cursed under her breath.

They jumped into the truck. Selene rapidly searched the console for a set of keys, but there was nothing obvious. She grabbed the sun visor, tilted it down, and was rewarded with the clink of a set of well-worn keys falling into her lap. She shoved them in the ignition and twisted, making the engine rumble reluctantly to life.

She stomped on the gas just as the door to the cabin opened, an angry-looking man in a bathrobe running after them. Despite the decrepit nature of the truck, it was still faster than he was, and they left him behind, fist still shaking in the air and screaming obscenities.

They rode in silence. Occasionally she could feel his gaze burning into her, but she didn't look at him. She still hadn't figured out exactly what it was about him that threw her so much, and until she did, she didn't trust herself to relax around him. It wasn't just his ridiculous good looks, though those were certainly nothing to scoff at. It also wasn't because he was a thief. She wasn't exactly a model citizen herself, so she couldn't judge him too harshly for his choice of profession. At least his line of work didn't leave a trail of dead or damaged bodies in his wake.

The road started out as dirt ruts and gravel, but the closer they got to Istanbul, the nicer the roads became. On the outskirts of town, she pulled off into the parking lot of a used-car lot, pulling the truck in neatly next to all the rest of the vehicles with price tags screaming from their windows.

"I take it we're stopping?" Wolfe asked as she cut the engine.

She nodded, opening the door and hopping out. "Yep. I don't know about you, but I could use a bed."

She walked to the back of the truck and grabbed her bag, tossing him his as he climbed out of the truck behind her. "Well, I suppose if you ask nicely," he drawled.

Her head whipped around, a faint warmth flooding her cheeks as she caught his slow glance up and down her body. Blushing was not something she did. She wasn't a poor little virgin, flushing at the attention of her very first boyfriend. Annoyed at her own reaction, her temper flared. She thought about giving him a quick check to the gut, but he wasn't worth it. Rolling her eyes, she said, "In your dreams."

He waggled his eyebrows as he slung his bag over his shoulder. "Yes, you will be."

With a huff, she spun away from him. She dropped the keys on the front seat of the truck and closed the door. Without a word, she began trekking into the city.

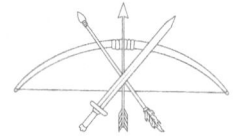

Chapter Nine

C OLIN COULD FEEL THE press of ancient history as they
walked through Istanbul. The city wasn't quite as old as
Themyscira, but unlike the Amazon homeland, it had managed to
keep up with the times and was now one of the biggest tourist
destinations in the world. The wars and regime changes had clearly
taken their tolls, but the history and beauty were still evident in the
massive cultural hub.

He spotted the Hagia Sophia in the distance, the size of the huge
building making it impossible to miss. The former Greek Orthodox
Church turned mosque perched on top of a rise overlooking the Sea
of Marmara, daring anyone to challenge it. He'd been there once
before, taking in the mosaics that had been there for hundreds of
years, the colors fading, but the artistry still evident. The attached
museum still housed some of the religious artifacts from the time
when it was a church, and Colin's fingers itched just thinking about
some of the beautifully jeweled pieces. He had no doubt that some

of his previous clients would pay handsomely for what was contained inside those stone walls.

He glanced at the back of Selene's head as she walked in front of him. It was tempting to try to slip her company and take off on his own, despite how appealing he found her. She was a puzzle he hadn't yet been able to figure out, and he was inclined to think he may never solve. Right now, she was standing between him and a potential gold mine, both here within the confines of the riches of Istanbul and with the treasure he was certain that Nyx and the soldier were going after.

The lure of gold and jewels was always tempting—and potentially worth millions—but Hippolyta's belt would be priceless. If he could really get his hands on something that no one believed truly existed, proving the experts wrong in the process, he could potentially gain something he hadn't realized he still craved, respect.

He'd gone into academia with the belief that he was going to become a world-renowned expert in ancient civilizations. He'd known that his research had been valuable and that he'd been on the verge of revealing information that others didn't even think possible. When he'd been kicked out of school, his reputation had been in tatters. No one would ever trust him again after he'd been accused of burglarizing his mentor's office and stealing his finds. He would never be the famous expert he'd once longed to be.

His new chosen profession was exactly the opposite. He lived his life in the darkness, skulking around museums and archaeological dig sites. The prizes he stole disappeared into the personal collections of people shady enough to pay someone to steal them in the first place. Nothing he did now earned him any sort of praise or glory, except perhaps in the criminal underground. Some of the jobs he'd pulled had earned him a reputation for carrying out impossible heists, securing him the moniker of "the Shadow." Apart from his nickname being on several white-collar crime detectives' most wanted lists, he was as far as he could be from the renown he'd expected.

Turning away from the stunning mosque, he refocused on his goal. He wasn't here to steal priceless artifacts out from under a snooty museum curator's nose. His prize was worth much more than that. Of course, he was going to have to figure out a way to escape from Selene. He had a feeling that once she knew what they were going after, there was no way she would let him just waltz off with it.

He had no idea where she was heading, but Selene marched ahead of him tirelessly, winding through the streets like she had the city memorized. He'd thought about suggesting they get a cab, but the tense hunch of her shoulders made him think twice. Just as he was about to break his silence, he happened to glance across the street.

"Shit." He reached out, grabbed Selene's hand, and yanked her into the alley they were passing, not stopping until they were hiding behind a dumpster.

She rounded on him, fist bunched. She opened her mouth, but he slammed his hand across her lips and narrowed his gaze. "Quiet," he said, practically hissing it under his breath. "The soldier from the jail."

She froze, her eyes widening. With a slight nod, she indicated she understood, and he removed his hand from her soft lips.

They crouched low, peering quickly around the corner of the metal dumpster. A hulking man with a military buzz cut and extensively tattooed arms strode down the sidewalk, inches from where they'd been standing. He didn't even bother glancing down the alley where they were crouched, so Colin was hopeful they hadn't been spotted. The soldier had ditched the all-black clothing that he'd been wearing in the jail, so clearly he'd managed to pick up a few supplies already.

Selene whipped out her phone and sneaked it around the edge of the dumpster to snap a few shots of the man as he walked by. He was heading in the direction they'd come from. Cautiously, Colin crept out of their hiding spot, Selene slipping out behind him. They walked back to the main street and peered around the corner of the building where the huge man had vanished.

"I thought you said they would be going to Mycenae," Selene whispered, stealing a quick glance around the building toward the man's retreating back.

Colin was just as baffled as Selene. If his research was accurate—and he prided himself on his accuracy—then the most logical place for Nyx to look for the girdle would be Mycenae. There was no logical reason that they would have come to Istanbul, unless it was for the same reason they were here. "Maybe they need supplies?"

Selene let out a quick hum, then darted around the corner. "Let's find out."

Colin realized that this was his shot. Selene had taken off and left him behind. Now was the perfect opportunity to make a run for it.

He could vanish and find the artifact on his own, and Selene would never even know what they were after.

But that meant leaving her to square off against that trained killer all by herself. The dude looked like he could do some serious damage, and Amazon or not, Selene might need help. With a slight squeeze in his gut at the missed opportunity, Colin took off after Selene, trying not to lose her in the crowds of people. Thankfully, there weren't all that many people in Türkiye with glowing red hair, so Selene's mane of glossy curls stuck out like a tracking beacon.

Luckily, their target also stuck out among the crowds. He was a full head taller than the people around him, and the colorful tattoos peeking out of his army-green T-shirt and fatigue pants made him even more distinctive. His enormous muscles also made it obvious he was someone you should think twice about messing with.

This was a bad idea. If Colin could get to Selene, there was a chance he could convince her that now was not the time to go after this dude, especially because they hadn't yet seen any trace of Nyx. For all he knew, Nyx was lying in wait somewhere, and this dude was leading them into a trap.

Selene was too far away from him to say anything. She was dodging in and out of crowds like a pro, completely ignoring Colin as she got farther and farther away from him and closer to their prey.

Their target suddenly turned into an unmarked doorway, the faded turquoise paint of the frame not giving any clues about what sort of place it might be hiding. Selene followed mere seconds behind the soldier, sliding out of sight before Colin was even in shouting distance to tell her to stop.

His heart slammed into overdrive, blood pulsing in time with his breath. He had to get to her before something bad happened. Breaking into a run, he forced his way through a crowd of people who muttered at him as he shoved past. He reached the doorway and ducked inside, then dropped to his knees after he heard gunfire.

Turquoise wood splinters rained down on him as he hit the paving stones of a small courtyard. The sound of his racing pulse rushed through his ears, making it difficult to separate one sound from another as he deliberately tried to suck in long breaths and slow his racing heart.

He hated guns. He used them when necessary, but if he was doing his job correctly, guns weren't usually an issue.

Glancing around quickly, he saw Selene slumped over, leaning against a large planter. Her back was to him, and he could see blood pouring freely down her arm.

He had to get to her.

Steeling his nerves, he glanced quickly around the doorway into the courtyard beyond. From where he was lying on the ground, he couldn't see much, but it appeared to be an open area with fountains, planters, and benches for enjoying a relaxing afternoon. He didn't see the soldier anywhere. Of course, depending on what sort of training this guy had, Colin might never see him coming, but with Selene bleeding just a handful of feet from where he was crouched, he needed to act.

He couldn't let her die.

Colin launched himself from his hiding spot, bracing for the barrage of bullets he was expecting to hit him. He landed next to

Selene with a thud, all the air forced out of his lungs by the impact. Not wasting any time, he sat up next to her, his hands racing over her, trying to find the source of the bleeding.

Her right arm had a bullet graze, which was the source of the blood he'd first noticed. The bigger problem was a through-and-through shot to her left shoulder. Blood was soaking her skin and her tank top as it oozed from the torn flesh.

Her eyes fluttered open as he ran his hands over her. Her green eyes were hazed in pain as she bit her lip to keep from crying out. "Don't worry about me," she said. "I'll be fine." Her voice was weak, and he swore under his breath.

"Sure you will," he said. He didn't have any first aid supplies with him, so he ripped open his bag and grabbed a long-sleeved shirt, tearing the thin fabric at the seams. He tied one of the arms of his shirt around the bullet graze, pulling tight enough that she swore like a sailor. The shoulder wound would be much harder to wrap because of its location.

He did his best, wadding up the other arm of his shirt and tying it in place, hoping the pressure would slow the bleeding long enough for her to get to a hospital.

She watched him work, her eyes narrowing as he tied the final knot on his makeshift tourniquet. He patted his pockets, looking for his phone, forgetting that she'd confiscated it before they'd started. He had no idea how to get help.

"Where's the shooter?" she asked, her voice somewhat stronger than before.

Colin glanced around the planter but wasn't shocked to find the courtyard empty. He'd assumed when he hadn't been shot while trying to get to her that the soldier had taken off. "Gone," he said, grabbing her bag and starting to rifle through it.

"You don't need to call for an ambulance." She sat up straighter, making herself more comfortable against the concrete planter. "I promise you I'll be fine."

He rolled his eyes. "Sure, you can just heal from a couple of bullet wounds." He kept digging.

"Yes, I can."

His hands froze as he was digging through her surprisingly lacy underwear, still unable to find his phone. He glanced away from the bag he was ransacking and looked at her face. Her already pale skin had been ashen when he'd first found her, any natural color drained from her cheeks. Now, however, mere minutes later, a healthy pink glow was already starting to return. *What the hell?* He examined her more closely, confused by what he was seeing. "What do you mean you can heal from bullet wounds?" he asked warily.

She shrugged, something that should have been incredibly painful given the shoulder wound he'd seen. "Exactly that." She reached up and untied the sleeve he'd tied around the bullet graze. After a brief struggle with the knot, she managed to get the material free.

Despite all the blood that still covered her arm, the wound was gone.

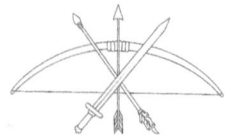

Chapter Ten

S ELENE PUSHED TO HER feet, catching herself against the wall as her head spun with dizziness. She sucked in a deep breath and pushed off from the wall, studiously avoiding looking at Wolfe. She knew what she would see on his face if she did—fear. It wouldn't be the first time or the last.

Usually she wasn't stupid enough to get shot in front of strangers.

The commando shouldn't have known she was following him. She made her living by getting to people who otherwise couldn't be touched. Sneaking up on people was practically in her job description, not that her organization used anything resembling a job board. She needed to catch the bastard just so she could figure out how he'd known she was coming.

With a sigh, she glanced around the courtyard. The guy had disappeared. There was no way to track where he'd gone. She'd lost their best lead at getting Nyx back.

She started to walk toward the doorway she'd come through but was pulled up short by a hand grabbing her elbow.

"Hands off," she snapped, her eyes darting to Wolfe's before she quickly glanced away.

"Are you okay?" he asked hesitantly. He glanced at her now-healed arm, then at her shoulder, which was still bleeding, though not much more than a cat scratch. "How is that possible? People don't heal that fast."

She sighed. "You're right. *People* don't." She tried to tug away from him, but he held fast. She could easily have broken his grip if she wanted to, but she didn't need to be saddled with a useless companion with a fractured wrist.

His fingers gently grabbed her chin, forcing her to look at him. Surprisingly, there was no fear in his eyes, only concern. "So it's an Amazon thing then?" His eyebrows rose. "You people are cooler than I imagined."

One of the unwritten rules she'd always lived by was that she never talked about herself. She didn't like people poking into her business. Plus, it wasn't her place to spill the secrets of her people.

There was something about Wolfe that made her want to break that rule. His touch on her arm had gentled, his thumb rubbing small circles along the recently healed skin. His sexy-as-sin mouth was curved in a laughing smile that almost tempted her to join him.

"It's a me thing," she said before her brain could stop her. She dropped her gaze to his chest, unable to stand his intense stare. "All Amazons heal faster than humans. I heal faster than other Amazons."

"Seriously?" he asked.

"You saw how beat up Sam looked, right? Well, he and Kalli were attacked on the same day, less than a week ago."

Colin let out a low whistle. "She didn't have a scratch on her."

"The queen doesn't heal as instantly as I do, but she heals fast enough."

"So what makes you so special?" he asked, crossing his arms over his chest and causing his muscles to bulge distractingly.

"Not a damn thing," she said, turning away and heading out of the courtyard.

They were silent the rest of the walk to her favorite hotel. In a stroke of luck, they had exactly one room left. They would have to share, which would allow her to keep her eye on him.

Upstairs, she waived the card in the direction of the reader and opened the door. She paused in the entryway to take it in. Their room was nicely appointed, if on the small side. There was tasteful commercial art on the beige walls, and she knew from experience that the linens were incredibly soft. The only downside that she could see was that there was only one queen-size bed.

Crap. They would have to share.

It was shocking how small the bed looked when she could feel the heat of Wolfe's body mere inches behind her. It wasn't like she was a blushing virgin or anything, and she'd slept with men platonically in the past. It was Wolfe that was going to have to be careful, she assured herself. She was absolutely fine. Or at least she would be once she was clean.

She'd thrown on a jacket over her bloody tank top, but the siren song of a shower was calling her name. She might heal quickly, but that didn't get the blood off her skin. It was drying and starting to itch.

Without a word, she dumped her duffel on the floor and strode into the bathroom, turning the water on as hot as it could go. Slipping under the water, she could only wish it would wash away her memories with the blood.

Colin watched Selene as she retreated into the bathroom. She hadn't spoken since she'd walked away from him on the streets of Istanbul, and to his surprise he found he missed her sarcastic wit. On one hand, she was sort of moody and bossy, exactly the type of woman he would never have picked for himself. On the other hand, she kept him interested and intrigued, doing ridiculous things like running after a soldier without any backup and getting herself shot.

He still hadn't processed everything she'd told him. It didn't seem possible that she was able to heal as quickly as she had. If he hadn't seen the proof of it happening in front of his own eyes, he would have said it was bullshit. Fortunately, or unfortunately as the case may be, he had seen it. She'd proved exactly what she was capable of, and he was dying to know more.

He debated following her. He couldn't get his mind off what her tempting body would look like in the shower, but he knew she wasn't looking for that. Not right now, and not from him. That didn't stop him from imagining her there. The water sluicing over her perfect form, her nipples puckering under the onslaught. His groin hardened at the thought, and he tugged on his jeans as they began cutting off his circulation.

He sat on the only chair in the tiny hotel room, dropping his head into his hands. He could do this. He had the capacity to spend the night in a hotel room with a gorgeous woman in a completely nonsexual way.

He just had to keep convincing himself of that.

Just when he'd thought he'd gotten his mind out of the gutter, the bathroom door opened to reveal Selene wearing nothing but a towel and a scowl. She'd left the bathroom door open, revealing her bloody clothes piled in a heap on the white-tile floor. She ignored him as she rifled through her bag, pulled out clean clothing, and retreated to the bathroom. He closed his mouth, surreptitiously trying to make sure he wasn't drooling. Selene had no idea how unbelievably attractive she was. If she did, she never would have walked in front of him in nothing but a tiny scrap of terry cloth. At least not if she was trying to stop him from jumping her bones.

There was no way he was sleeping tonight.

The door opened again, and she came out of the bathroom wearing tiny shorts and a tank top that hung low enough that if she breathed the wrong way it might give him a bit of a peep show. He wiggled in the chair again. He watched her as she dragged a comb through her long, curly locks. Tucking the comb back into her bag, she turned and walked to the far side of the bed.

"Don't even think of trying to sneak out. I'm a light sleeper." With that, she pulled back the comforter and climbed underneath, letting out a contented sigh as she closed her eyes.

Colin thought about trying to join her but didn't relish the idea of being trapped next to her body all night and not being able to do anything about it. Rising, he grabbed his red notebook out of his bag and brought it back to the chair before flipping it open. If he wasn't going to get any sleep, he might as well be productive.

Hours later, he'd managed to make it only halfway through his notes, but the exhaustion weighing him down forced him to call it quits. Snapping the book closed, he tugged off his shirt, undid his pants, and let his clothes drop onto the floor by the side of the bed. He slipped under the covers—staying as far away from Selene as he could—and immediately fell asleep.

Chapter Eleven

S ELENE WOKE FEELING MORE rested than she had been in a long time. She felt safe, warm, and comfortable. Snuggling farther underneath the covers, she wiggled slightly, settling into the warmth that ran the length of her back.

The warm arm that settled around her waist froze her in place. Her eyes snapped open, taking in the bland hotel room decor and her bloody clothes, which she could just make out in a crumpled heap on the floor. Everything came back in a flash.

She was snuggled up against Wolfe.

Before she could think it through, she launched herself out of bed, landing eight feet across the floor, her breath coming out in pants and her eyes wildly circling the room.

Wolfe's head lifted groggily off his pillow, his eyes cracking open slightly. "Where's the fire?" His voice was a sleep-roughened rumble that went straight to her libido.

Now that she was no longer snuggled up against his far-too-comfortable body, her mind was clearer. She must look ridiculous standing in the middle of the floor, staring at him. She had no problem sleeping in the same bed as him when she'd gone to bed, but here she was acting like a prude in the morning. She needed to snap out of it.

"Nowhere. Nothing, just some excess energy," she said, rolling her head to loosen her neck. His deadpan blink made it obvious she hadn't fooled him for a second.

As casually as possible, she walked to her bag and grabbed a pair of jeans and a tank top. She headed into the bathroom to change. One glance in the mirror reminded her of how much of a wreck she was. Her long, curly hair was a massive, messy halo around her head, and she had slight purple shadows beneath her eyes. She might feel rested, but clearly her body didn't agree.

She glanced at her arm and shoulder where she'd been hit the day before. The scars were slightly whiter than the skin around them, but the wounds were completely healed. If anyone saw them, it would look like she'd gotten them years ago rather than hours.

She'd been stupid to get injured, even more shortsighted to do it in front of a civilian. Super-accelerated healing powers came in handy, but she didn't like advertising her abilities. It just invited questions. Not even Ambrose knew what she could do.

Yet Colin knew.

Here she was, trapped with a man she wanted to hate, yet she found herself enjoying. It was easy to dislike him for what he did for a living and for what he had done to Sam. He was a thief and had stolen from one of the only men in the world she trusted implicitly.

In the harsh glare of the bathroom light, she was forced to admit to herself that the reason she wanted to dislike him so much wasn't because he was a criminal. It was because he reminded her of herself.

Was she really any better than he was? Her current choice of career—really her entire modern-day life—revolved around working outside the law to do things that the authorities couldn't or wouldn't do. She'd hurt people, she'd stolen from them, hell, she'd even killed them. In fact, during her life as an Amazon—before she'd been exiled from Themyscira—she'd killed more people as a part of doing battle than Colin could ever have thought about hurting.

What she did now was different from what she'd done all those years ago. As an Amazon warrior, she'd done what she was supposed to do, what she was commanded to do. She'd always been a soldier as a part of a unit, and they had been doing what needed to be done. Now, however, none of that was true. She operated with impunity. She reported to no one but herself. There were no checks and balances, and no one to rein her in. She'd become someone her fellow warriors wouldn't recognize.

The person she had become was no longer fit to be called an Amazon.

Selene turned on the cold water and splashed it on her face. Whatever her current job title was or wasn't, she was on a mission. Her friend and queen had asked her to figure out what Nyx and the soldier were up to, and that was what she was going to do. If that meant working with the man in the other room, maybe that wasn't such a bad thing.

When she left the bathroom, Colin was sitting on the bed in nothing but a pair of navy boxer briefs. Her eyes trailed down his tanned, muscular chest, lingering far too long on the bulge in his shorts. With a shake of her head, she yanked her gaze up to his face.

He must not have noticed her stare, because a look of concern clouded his eyes. "Feeling better?"

She nodded. "Much," she lied. He didn't need to know what was going on in her head.

"How are your injuries?" he asked, nodding to her shoulder.

She rolled her shoulders and flexed her fingers. "Good as new, as advertised."

With a nod, he stood and crossed the floor to his own duffel. She tried not to drool as he tugged on a pair of jeans and a snug black T-shirt. He glanced around and caught her staring, a knowing look crossing his face. "See anything you like?"

Selene rolled her eyes. Yes, but she wouldn't tell him that. "Just waiting on you." She grabbed her bag off the floor, quickly shoving her belongings back inside. "Where to next?"

He sent her a sinful grin as he tucked his notebooks back into his bag. "Well, we could blunder around Istanbul looking for them, or we could head to their next step." He shrugged nonchalantly. "I still think they're heading to Mycenae."

Selene crossed her arms over her chest and stared at the man across the room. He was gorgeous—there was no question about that. But, she couldn't read him. He would make a killing at the poker tables.

"You need to give me something more than that. What are they searching for?" she asked, her exasperation simmering just below the surface.

She could see him hesitate. "What sort of assurances do I get that if I tell you what they're after, you won't take off and leave me?"

She rolled her eyes again. "Please. If there is anyone in Themyscira that wants to see you behind bars, it's me. I wouldn't dare miss out on the opportunity to catch you doing something nefarious and lock you up again." Her stomach balked slightly as she said the words. She was saying the right things, but her heart wasn't in it anymore. She didn't want to examine her reasons too closely.

He ran his fingers through his hair, making it stick out at odd angles. His hazel eyes flashed, and he nodded absently. "All right. I believe that Nyx and her errand boy are after an Amazonian artifact. One with important cultural significance." He paused, his eyes narrowing. "I think they're looking for the girdle—well, belt, really—of Hippolyta."

Selene took a stunned step back, her hand coming to rest on her stomach. A buzzing started in her ears, drowning out everything else. He couldn't be right. There was no way they could be going after the belt. Not after all these years.

"But it's gone," she said, making her way to the edge of the mattress and perching on it gingerly. "It was stolen thousands of years ago."

Colin crossed the floor and sat next to her on the edge of the white comforter. "I know. One of Heracles's twelve labors was to retrieve the belt of Hippolyta, the queen of the Amazons." He paused and she nodded. "The myth is that Hippolyta was willingly going to give the girdle to him, but the idea angered the goddess Hera. She spread a rumor that Heracles planned to kill the queen. The Amazons rose to the occasion and attacked Heracles and his men, but Queen Hippolyta was killed in the fight. Heracles escaped and took the belt with him."

Selene nodded as if in a trance. His words were clinical and cold, but his simple recitation of facts sent her spinning. She remembered that day as if it were yesterday. She could picture the bright-red blood spilled all over their beach, the coppery smell an assault to the nose. She remembered seeing their beloved queen Hippolyta cut down by a sword through her torso, her body bucking with the force of the blow. Her unlimited life span hadn't prevented her death in battle. They were immortal, not invulnerable.

Selene could still picture the triumphant smile on Heracles's face. The Greek warrior of legend and myth accomplished his task and left, not caring what his efforts had cost her people. He and his men had sailed away from their shores, leaving the Amazons to suffer and mourn their dead.

Shaking her head to clear out the dark memories, she brought herself back to the present. No need to dwell on what the girdle cost her people more than three thousand years ago. "Your version of the story is accurate enough." A thought bubbled up from the recesses of her mind, a tickle of an idea as to why Nyx might be interested in the belt. "The girdle was supposed to provide the wearer with power."

"Really? That's interesting. None of the references I've seen have ever mentioned that." His lips pursed. "What sort of power did it have?" He grabbed his notebook out of his bag and started scribbling inside.

Selene wasn't certain if she should be sharing what she knew. She looked at his face, his eyes alight with curiosity. Colin was an outsider, and someone she didn't fully trust. But he'd taken a risk and told her what they were chasing. The least she could do would be to meet him halfway.

"The Amazons have more than just strength and speed. We have enhanced abilities." She gestured to the fading scar on her arm. "My ability is to heal, but others have different ones. Kalli, for instance, can talk to the gods."

"The gods?" he asked, his rising voice betraying his disbelief.

Selene nodded. She could understand his skepticism. "Queen Kalliope is the one that asked the gods to hide Themyscira from the outside world. It remained hidden for twenty-five hundred years, until four days ago. Kalli called on the power of the gods and removed the veil that protected the city. It's the only reason you were able to find it."

Colin nodded slowly, rubbing his hands over his jeans. "Okay, assuming I believe all of that, what does it have to do with the girdle?"

Selene flopped back on the bed, her hair billowing around her face. "The girdle was created to enhance the wearer's natural abilities. Think of a body builder that becomes as strong as Superman, or someone with telekinesis who can suddenly fly, that sort of thing.

The Greeks would never have known about its purpose, because it only works on a true Amazon. It wouldn't have worked for them."

Colin slowly lay down next to her on the bed, turning his head to look at her sideways. "So what would happen if Nyx got ahold of it?"

A sour knot formed in Selene's stomach. She sighed. "Nothing good. It was Nyx that staged the coup that overthrew Kalli. She's brutal and power hungry and has an unnatural affinity for weapons. She also has a level of charisma I've never seen in anyone else, which is how she manages to convince people to follow her. I can't imagine how much more tyrannical she would become if any of her gifts were strengthened."

She stared at the white ceiling, her eyes tracing patterns in the stucco-like texture. This was seriously bad. If only they'd located Nyx before she'd escaped. She deserved to be in jail for the harsh treatment and starvation she'd inflicted on the Amazons during her reign of terror. If Themyscira hadn't been invaded when it had, Kalli could have dealt with Nyx properly.

Of course, if Themyscira hadn't been invaded, she, Zoe, and Kalli would never have been back in Themyscira in the first place, but that was neither here nor there. She needed to call Kalli and warn her about what was going on. If Nyx got ahold of the belt, there was no telling what she would do or how far she would go. Nyx had always hated Kalli, so it was a fair bet she would come back and use her newly enhanced gifts to finish what she started and retake Themyscira. What if she didn't stop there? Would Nyx go so far as to try to conquer more than just Themyscira?

"It looks like we have our work cut out for us," Colin said, glancing in her direction.

He was offering to stick with her and go after the belt. He was probably doing it for purely selfish reasons—he was a thief, after all—but it was still somewhat of a surprise that he wanted to tough it out after what she'd just told him about how the belt would affect Nyx. Of course, if she was any sort of real Amazon, she wouldn't let him come. He was a civilian, not a soldier. There was no place for someone like him in this fight. Stopping Nyx was her responsibility.

Despite all of that, she was glad he was there. She was more than capable of going after Nyx and her minion on her own, but she'd gotten used to working with a team over the last decade. She might be the leader of her little band of renegades, but she usually worked with others to carry out their missions. It was nice knowing that someone had her back.

She glanced into his gorgeous hazel eyes, already knowing what she would tell him. "Yes, I guess we do."

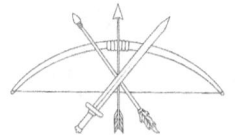

Chapter Twelve

C OLIN WATCHED SELENE AS she paced back and forth across their hotel room. She'd been on the phone for half an hour already and didn't seem to be losing any steam. First, she'd called Zoe and explained what they were after. He couldn't hear Zoe's end of the conversation, but from the narrowing of Selene's stunning green eyes, he couldn't imagine it was anything good.

As soon as she'd hung up with Zoe, she'd immediately called someone else. This time he had no idea who she was speaking with, but she appeared to be arranging a supply delivery and transportation to Greece.

The woman in front of him was fascinating. She was fierce, motivated, and dedicated to her cause, but something felt off about her. She talked about the Amazons like she was talking about someone else, some other civilization that she wasn't a part of, despite her genetic makeup.

It was the way she'd talked about the girdle that gave it away. She'd made it a point to emphasize that only a *true* Amazon could wear it. She hadn't been talking about Nyx—that much was obvious when the look of determination had crossed her face when she'd talked about what would happen if Nyx were ever to get ahold of it. No, he had a feeling she was talking about herself. What he didn't know was why.

Why didn't she feel like an Amazon?

There was no way that he could ask her. She'd never admit to it, and, knowing her, she'd punch him just for asking. No, if he wanted to know anything about her, he was going to have to be sneaky.

Good thing he did sneaky for a living.

"We're all set," Selene said, pushing the END CALL button on her iPhone. "We leave for Athens in two hours."

"I guess we'd better get to the airport then," he said. There was plenty of time to dig into her background later. After all, they were going to be stuck with one another for a while.

As they walked through the airport, Colin's eyes snagged on a series of display cases along one of the walls. The contents didn't look like something you would normally find in an airport. He casually maneuvered sideways until he could see what was inside.

It was a temporary exhibit from one of the museums in town. He slowed his pace, his eyes hungrily taking in the contents of the cases. The small statues and pottery didn't look all that impressive, but his trained eye knew exactly what he could get for them. He instinctively assessed the security features of the case. The glass looked to be about an inch thick, and while he noticed a few security cameras pointing in his direction, there didn't appear to be an alarm on the case itself.

Child's play.

His fingers tingled and he slipped them inside his bag, looking for his small tool bag and lockpicks. There was nothing inside his duffel but his notebook and a small pile of clothes.

"Looking for something?" Selene's overly sweet voice cut through his haze.

Right. She'd raided his bag in Themyscira and taken all his tools.

He watched as she raised one impeccably arched eyebrow, a dry smile on her face. "You wouldn't be getting into any trouble, now would you?"

How could he have forgotten where he was and who he was with? Granted, it had been a while since he'd stolen anything, but it wasn't like he was an addict. He shouldn't need a fix.

"Of course not," he said, clearing his throat. He pulled his gaze away from a series of small clay figurines and looked at his companion. "I was just admiring the craftsmanship."

She rolled her eyes and crossed her arms. "Yeah, sure." She gestured down the terminal. "This way, Shadow." She strode off.

Colin bolted after her. "What did you just call me?" There was no way she could know that name. It was impossible. Even if she knew he was a thief, she shouldn't have been able to connect him to his alias. He'd been extremely careful that there was never any evidence tying him to his crimes.

"I called you the Shadow," she said, her voice smug. "That's what they call you, isn't it?"

Apparently they had different definitions of impossible. He grabbed her elbow, tugging her to a stop. "How do you know that name?" If she could identify him—if she could tie Colin Wolfe the man to the thief that went by the Shadow—he was in a lot more trouble than he realized. Being imprisoned by Amazons was one thing, but the FBI and Interpol weren't too fond of the Shadow either. He couldn't let her turn him in.

Colin's eyes instantly scanned the airport, looking for the exits. They'd come through the main door, but there had to be smaller emergency exits around somewhere. They were in a crowded place. Surely Selene wouldn't make too much of a scene in front of all these people.

Spotting a bright-red door with the picture of a running man on it, Colin spun toward it, hoping he could make it before she realized what he was doing.

No such luck.

A steel band in the form of Selene's hand clamped around his biceps, stopping him. "Where do you think you're going?" Selene hissed under her breath.

He tugged at his arm, fruitlessly trying to break her grip. He wasn't sure why he'd thought he could escape her. She was preternaturally fast and strong. He had no hope.

"I told you what you wanted to know. You know what Nyx is after. You don't need me anymore."

She took a half step back, her eyes narrowing. "I don't get it. This morning you were all about coming with me. Why the sudden urge to bolt?" She glanced around, noticing that they were starting to get funny looks from the crowds of people milling around them. She loosened her grip, dropping her hand to grab his, lacing her fingers through his. Now it looked like they were just holding hands.

Colin had never been this close to getting busted before. He'd honed his craft and made sure that he'd never gotten caught on tape. No one, not even Interpol, knew what the Shadow looked like. Selene knew something about him that no one else in the world knew.

There was nothing he could do. There was no way he could get away from her, at least not right now. If she knew who he really was, he was at her mercy. She could turn him in, and he would have no way of preventing her.

He was screwed.

His shoulders slumped, his gaze dropping to the tile floor. "If you're going to call the cops on me, then just do it." Better to get this over with. He had no desire to go to jail, but he was skilled in getting in and out of places he wasn't supposed to be. Maybe he could manage to escape before it ever got that far.

Selene let out an exasperated huff. "If I was going to turn you over to the cops, I would have told Zoe what I knew before we left Themyscira."

First things first. "Who does Zoe work for?"

"Interpol."

Of course. It had to be Interpol. They'd been hounding him for years. He'd heard there was an entire task force dedicated to finding him, not that they'd managed to figure out his true identity. That raised the next question. "How do you know who I really am?" He narrowed his eyes at her, studying her intently. It had been obvious from the start that she had connections. One of them must have tipped her off. There was only one group that had ever come close to catching him. "What's your last name, Selene?"

Her expression froze, and she took a half step away from him, but she didn't let go of his hand. "I don't see why that's important."

He closed the distance between them, crowding her. "Because I would bet my considerable bank balance that it's Blackburn."

She dropped his hand like it had burned her. "I don't know what you're talking about." She turned and started walking away from him.

Everything suddenly made so much more sense. How she always seemed to have everything at her beck and call, why she was always armed to the teeth. It wasn't just because she was an Amazon. "You're the elusive CEO of Blackburn Industries—one of the foremost security companies in the world. And rumor has it, a front for a vigilante organization that has its own definition of justice."

She continued to walk away from him, not even bothering to look in his direction. "Yeah, right. Me a CEO. I don't exactly give off the boardroom vibe."

Colin glanced at her casual clothing and untamed mane of curls. She was certainly right that she didn't look like she was about to strut into a negotiation for a multimillion-dollar deal, but that didn't matter. She had something else, a gut instinct for protection and a keen eye for danger. "No, you don't, and that's why I'd wager you have a slew of people at your beck and call to run the day-to-day operations of the company. I bet the person everyone thinks is the CEO is just a front person. That leaves you to run the more clandestine side of the business."

She stopped abruptly, and he had to check himself before he plowed into her. She spun to face him, her nose an inch away from his own. "What do you want?" He had no idea what she was talking about, so he just stared at her. "For your discretion, what do you want? Will two million cover it?"

His head snapped back like she'd punched him. She was trying to buy his silence? Who did she think he was? He may be a thief, but even he had some standards. He wasn't about to out her secret to the world. Everyone deserved some privacy, including an Amazon/CEO/vigilante.

There was one thing he needed from her, but it wasn't money. "I'll make you a deal. You keep my secret, I'll keep yours." He stuck out his hand and waited for her to take it.

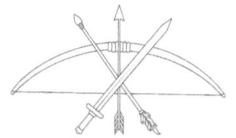

Chapter Thirteen

THE FLIGHT FROM ISTANBUL to Athens was short, and Selene spent all of it trying to figure out what had happened in the airport with Wolfe. She'd agreed to his terms but was still confused why he'd negotiated. Most people would have jumped at the chance to walk away with $2 million, but he'd looked offended at the thought and hadn't spoken to her since.

Had she read him wrong?

Wolfe was a thief, and if the way he was eyeing the display case in the terminal was anything to go by, one that had no problem making a quick buck. Most of the criminals she chased in her life wouldn't have even hesitated at her offer. They would have taken the money and walked. Yet here he was, smashed up against her as they lined up in the aisle to get off the airplane.

She was normally a great judge of character. A large part of her job relied on her instincts about people, and she prided herself on her keen insights. It baffled her that they would have been so wrong.

Even now, she could feel his presence behind her, almost pressing in on her. She had to admit—at least if she was being honest—she didn't get the same vibe from him that she did from the scum Blackburn Special Operations pursued. She'd originally chalked it up to his ruthless charm, which she'd been studiously ignoring, but maybe it was more than that.

Colin Wolfe now knew the two biggest secrets in her life. Ambrose, her right-hand man and stand-in at Blackburn Industries, was the only other person on the planet who knew she was the CEO of a multibillion-dollar security company. To everyone else, she was just Selene, the girl with the tough attitude and penchant for violence. It wasn't exactly like she could be the face of a company when she hadn't aged a day in the seventy years she'd been the owner.

She'd started Blackburn Industries in the 1950s as a physical security company, offering services like security guards for businesses and bodyguards for high-end clientele. With her weapons training and fighting skills, it had seemed like a natural fit. Then, as technology advanced, her company became the front-runner in creating and manufacturing advanced security systems. They secured contracts with hundreds of exclusive museums and galleries around the globe to monitor and secure their collections and respond whenever threats were detected. While she enjoyed the legitimate side of her business—protection was protection, no matter how it was delivered—the security company had always been a front for her. It gave her a cover story for her Special Operations unit and a way to fund her vigilante activities. Selene had dedicated her very long life to helping others, and Blackburn gave her not one but two different ways to fulfill that burning desire.

Before this mission, her professional life and her Amazon life had been completely separate. Wolfe was the only one who knew about both halves of her life, and it left her feeling vulnerable in a way she'd never felt before. She swallowed to relieve the burning in the back of her throat. As uncomfortable as she was, she also had a feeling that, despite his nefarious job description, Wolfe was a trustworthy guy. Surprisingly, if he said he was going to keep her secret, she believed he would.

The Athens airport was just as busy as the one they'd left. They made their way toward luggage claim to meet the person who would show them to their car but got stuck behind a large group of people who seemed to want to walk at a glacial pace. Selene tried to rein in her impatience. Now that they were in Greece, she wanted nothing more than to be in Mycenae, hopefully arriving before Nyx and her soldier of fortune.

When they finally made it to luggage claim, the first thing Selene noticed was a tidy-looking woman in a suit and a driving cap, holding a sign with the name Blackburn on it. The second thing she noticed was that directly behind the woman was a slim man in his midthirties with spiky dark-blond hair. He was wearing a medium-gray suit, complete with vest and tie, though he had the suit coat dangling by one finger over his shoulder. She acknowledged the driver and held up a finger for her to wait.

"Ambrose," she said in exasperation, before she leaned in to give the blond man a long hug and a kiss on the cheek. "What are you doing here?" She tried to ruffle his hair, but he saw it coming and sidestepped, avoiding her fingers. She hadn't requested backup, and Ambrose didn't normally invite himself along on her trips.

The man glanced from her to Wolfe and back, his eyebrows going up. "You seem to be getting into all sorts of trouble on your own. I figured I would come check on things," he said in a crisp British accent. He turned to Wolfe, who was watching the exchange with interest, and stuck his hand out. "Ambrose Moretti."

"Colin Wolfe." He shook the outstretched hand as he sized up the newcomer, his hazel eyes sharp, taking in every detail.

"I know. I ran your background check," Ambrose said as he turned back to Selene. "My, my. The sort of company you're keeping these days." He waggled his eyebrows.

Selene rolled her eyes. She'd known Ambrose for twenty years. He knew more about her than anyone else on the planet. Well, except for Wolfe. Her stomach twinged at the thought. How was it possible that a man she'd met only a few days ago knew more secrets about her than someone she had lived with for years?

A throat cleared behind them, startling Selene out of her reverie. "Are you going to take the car or not?" the woman with the sign asked.

Ambrose beat Selene to the punch. "Of course. I'm so sorry to have caused you a delay." He smiled charmingly and sent the driver a wink. The originally stiff-backed woman softened and visibly fluttered under his gaze as she began walking to the car.

Selene watched in amusement as Ambrose had the woman eating out of his hand in moments. Sometimes she envied that gift. She was far too rough around the edges to ever charm her way into anything.

They arrived at their large SUV, and Selene watched the other woman write her phone number on a piece of paper and slip it in with the paperwork she handed Ambrose. He gave her a devastating grin before turning back to Selene and Wolfe. "Shall we?"

With a shrug, Selene climbed into the passenger's side of the vehicle. She wanted to give Ambrose an earful for surprising her, but this wasn't the place. She'd save it for later.

⤙⟫⟫⟩ ⟨⟨⟨⟨⤚

From his position in the back seat of the SUV, Colin watched Ambrose and Selene with curiosity. The way they talked and moved and touched—not to mention the hug and kiss inside the airport—implied a level of intimacy that he doubted Selene had with many people. After scolding Ambrose for coming, she settled into a rapid-fire conversation with him, clearly catching up on everything she'd missed while being gone from her company. The blond man answered everything just as fast as she fired it at him, never missing a beat.

Her hand settled on Ambrose's arm, and Colin saw the other man give a secret smile that he doubted Selene noticed. She was too busy giving orders and digging for more information on their ongoing investigations to be sidetracked with anything else. However, the way she tried to ruffle his hair like she'd done it a thousand times sent a pang of wayward jealousy zinging through Colin's body.

Apart from absentee CEO and employee, he wondered what else they were to each other. He'd never given thought to Selene's personal life before but now found himself somewhat obsessed with the idea. How did an immortal warrior from a notoriously man-hating culture approach the modern dating scene? If Ambrose's reactions were anything to go by, she clearly had no problem finding men, even with her somewhat acerbic behavior. Hell, Colin had been lusting after her for days, and her sharp tongue only seemed to turn him on more. Apparently he wasn't the only one.

From what he overheard, Ambrose was the head of something called Special Operations, which appeared to be the cover for the Blackburn Industries' vigilante ops. Selene asked about one bad guy after another, some of which were well known enough that Colin had seen stories about them on the news. He was just starting to tune them out when the sound of his own name caught his attention.

"So what is Mr. Wolfe doing here?" Ambrose asked, casting him a suspicious glare in the rearview mirror.

Selene sent Colin a sideways glance from her position in the passenger's seat, before turning back to look at Ambrose's well-chiseled profile. "He's helping me on my current case," she said somewhat vaguely.

Ambrose's fingers tapped on the leather steering wheel. "And what sort of case are you working that involves getting into bed with known criminals?"

"We're not . . . ," Selene sputtered, then changed course. "We're tracking down a pair of very dangerous people." A slight blush crawled up her cheeks, fascinating Colin. He never would have pictured her as a blusher.

"Ah, yes. The photo you sent. His name is Quinton Duran, and he's not someone you'd like to meet in a dark alley." Ambrose smirked and cast a sideways glance at Selene. "Well, maybe you would. He's a mercenary that hires his services out to the highest bidder. He's been linked to genocide in Africa and appears to have raped and murdered his way across the Congo. He's been involved with drug-running in South America, illegal arms deals in the United States, and good old-fashioned blackmail in the United Kingdom."

"Sounds like a real charmer," Colin muttered.

"He's definitely not," Ambrose replied, glancing at Selene with a worried look. "He's the main reason I decided to join you. I know you can take care of yourself, but a little bit of backup never hurt anyone, especially when it comes to Duran." Ambrose reached out and squeezed her hand.

Selene squeezed back before making a noncommittal noise and turning to look out the passenger-side window.

"Who's the other person you're after?" Ambrose prompted, clearly trying to draw her attention once more.

"A woman by the name of Nyx," Selene said after a pause.

"Need me to run her?" Ambrose asked.

Selene shook her head, her curls bobbing as she did. "No. We have history. She might not have raped her way across Africa, but genocide wouldn't be out of the question." She waved vaguely in Colin's direction, not even bothering to glance at him. "Wolfe has intel on where they might be going."

"And what sort of information would a known thief have about the location of these people?"

The skepticism was grating on Colin's nerves, not to mention the snooty British accent.

"Oh, not much. Just their destination," Colin said helpfully as he leaned forward and stuck his head over the center console. "Which is where we were headed before you came along. So chivy along and drive us to Mycenae." He deliberately put on a fake British accent and earned the expected glare from Selene.

The blond man didn't rise to the bait. "Why Mycenae? It's nothing more than a cultural ruin, right? What could they possibly want there?"

Uncertain how much Selene had told her employee / possible boyfriend, Colin decided to play it safe. "They're looking for something. An object of great cultural and monetary value. I believe it's in Mycenae."

Ambrose's eyebrows shot up toward his hairline. "What sort of criminal would hide their goods in a place that's visited by thousands of tourists every year?"

Here came the tricky part. He glanced at Selene, and she gave a slight nod. With a shrug, he jumped right in. "Around thirteen hundred BCE, the king of Mycenae, a man by the name of Eurystheus, sent Heracles on twelve labors."

Ambrose cut him off in the middle of his story. "Don't you mean Hercules?"

Colin barely restrained his exasperation. Ambrose might be some sort of businessman by day, vigilante by night, but Colin had lived and breathed history for a decade. He knew what he was talking about. "I meant what I said. Hercules was the name the Romans gave him, but his original name was Heracles."

Ambrose grunted under his breath, his fingers rapidly tapping the steering wheel. "What does some mythological figure have to do with anything?"

Taking in a calming breath, Colin continued his story. "As I was saying, Heracles was sent on twelve labors. The ninth labor was to retrieve the girdle of Hippolyta, the queen of the Amazons. It turned into a battle, and Heracles killed Hippolyta and stole it. He sailed back to Mycenae and turned the girdle over to the king."

"Are you implying that Duran and Nyx are heading to an ancient ruin to try to find a belt stolen by a mythological hero from a race of women that never existed?" Ambrose asked dryly.

"I'm not implying anything. I'm stating it."

That shut Ambrose up nicely, the prick. Colin leaned back against his chair, satisfaction coursing through his veins. What did Selene see in someone as pretentious as this guy?

It was Selene who finally broke the silence. "So you think the belt is somewhere in Mycenae because of King Eurystheus? That he somehow stockpiled all the things Heracles acquired?"

"It's the only thing that makes sense. Heracles wouldn't have kept the girdle for himself. His labors had been tasked as a form of penance for killing his own wife and children in a fit of madness. The penance wouldn't have had the same effect if he'd kept the bounty of his tasks. He would have been forced to give everything to the king," Colin concluded.

"Wait, you're not saying you believe him?" Ambrose finally spoke as he glanced disbelievingly at Selene.

Colin waited with interest, wondering what she would say. "I do." She nodded once.

"What the hell happened to you in Türkiye?" Ambrose asked. Turning in the seat, he faced Selene and grabbed her hand. "You've been gone for less than a week, and when I see you again, not only are you on the tail of one of the worst guys we've gone after in a long time, but you've brought along a known criminal who has you believing in fairy tales."

Selene's shoulders pulled back, her spine straightening. Anger snapped in her green eyes. "Ambrose, I know what I'm doing."

The blond man sent an unflattering look of disbelief in Colin's direction, but Colin thought it wise not to jump into the conversation. "Maybe you've been working too hard. You know you never take vacations. What about taking a couple of weeks and going to a sandy beach somewhere?" Ambrose's voice turned pleading.

Images of Selene in a skimpy green bikini flashed in front of Colin's eyes, and he tried not to drool. He wouldn't mind taking her to that sandy beach, but it looked like he was going to have to fight this asshole for the pleasure.

Selene scoffed, popping Colin's fantasy with a pin. "What on earth would I do at the beach? Ambrose, you know me better than that."

The other man dropped her hands in frustration. "I thought I did. You're acting stranger than usual."

She crossed her arms and leaned away from him. "That may be, but right now I'm pulling rank. We're going to Mycenae, whether you're coming or not."

Ambrose growled under his breath and slammed the vehicle into drive. "Fine. But only as long as you remember I advised you against this."

That teased a smile out of Selene. "Noted." She reached across the console and squeezed Ambrose's arm quickly before retreating again.

Ambrose grimaced and pulled into traffic heading west.

At least it was a win that Selene trusted what Colin was saying. She didn't have a lot of reason to. He could be leading them on a goose chase across Europe for all she knew.

But he wasn't. He wanted that belt as much as she did, if not more. If he could find something that culturally significant, he might not even sell it. Maybe he could clear his own name in the academic world.

First, though, he had to find it.

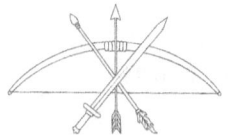

Chapter Fourteen

THE DRIVE FROM ATHENS to Mycenae took about an hour and a half. The ancient ruins sat atop a rocky hill that dominated the flat landscape surrounding it. Selene was somewhat surprised by the expanse of the ancient city, which was many times larger than Themyscira, even though they were approximately the same age.

The ruins were a popular tourist destination, and people were crawling all over the site like insects. Ambrose parked the SUV, and the three of them stared out of the windshield at the crowds.

Ambrose broke the silence first. "Look at this. There is no way that there's some hidden treasure trove in this place. It would have been found decades ago, if not centuries."

Privately, Selene was tempted to agree. If not for Wolfe's unwavering belief that this was the right place, she would suggest turning around and trying something else, maybe even asking Zoe to tap into her police resources to see if she could track Nyx.

"This is the place," Colin said, pulling out his infernal red notebook. He skimmed through a few pages, then tucked it into his back pocket and got out of the vehicle.

Ambrose seemed reluctant to follow, so she punched him lightly in the arm. "You're the one that invaded our mission, remember? This is what you signed yourself up for."

"How silly of me to assume you would be chasing bad guys that were at least from this decade," he snarked. "This should be loads of fun," he added under his breath as he opened his door and got out, slamming it louder than was necessary.

Selene jumped out of the vehicle and crossed to his side. Her temper, always close to the surface, flared. "You're the one that gave me the information about Duran. If you can't wrap your brain around what we believe Duran is after, at least remember that scum like him need to be taken off the map."

Ambrose nodded once. "You're right. I'm sorry." He glanced at Wolfe, who was already making his way toward the crumbling stones. "It isn't like you to make friends with criminals. Use them for information, perhaps, but not spend time with them. How do you know you can trust Colin Wolfe?"

That was a tricky question to answer. She was fairly convinced he had an ulterior motive for wanting the girdle, and it was pretty obvious what it was. Plus, Ambrose didn't know about her past life, so she couldn't exactly tell him that she'd caught Wolfe trying to steal from the Amazons and put him in jail for it. If he couldn't believe in the existence of the belt, there was no way he was going to believe she was four thousand years old.

Even if Wolfe did have an ulterior motive, Selene was starting to trust that she could rely on him. So far, he hadn't betrayed her. In fact, her little stunt in the airport that morning had been more of a betrayal on her side than on his. She didn't dare tell Ambrose she'd tried to bribe Wolfe to keep his silence. There was no telling what he would make of that.

"I just know," she finally said.

He rolled his eyes. "You're in charge." He turned and strode off toward where she'd last seen Wolfe.

Was she being unreasonable?

Her entire business, both the legitimate side and the illegal side, was built around protecting people from those who wanted to do them harm. During her time running Blackburn Industries—and her time as an Amazon—she'd had to rely heavily on her instincts about people. She was able to size up a situation in an instant, knowing who had good intentions and who had bad ones.

What was it about Colin Wolfe that threw her for a loop? He was gorgeous, but then again, so were a lot of men. He was a criminal, as were most of the men she hunted. Despite his career choice, however, she didn't get a negative read off him. He talked a good talk, and certainly had some less-than-honorable intentions, but even with all of that, she couldn't lump him with the usual delinquents she chased.

Glancing around, she realized that she'd lost sight of both Ambrose and Wolfe. With a sigh, she trudged off to make sure they were playing nice.

⋙⋙ ⋘⋘

Colin was in love.

He approached the famed Lion Gate with awe. The arched doorway was part of a wall that had long since partially collapsed. On top of the stone opening, built into the wall, stood a carved image of two lions standing on a pedestal and facing one another. Sadly, age and war had taken their toll on the famous sculpture, and both lions were missing their heads.

In all his travels around the world, most of which had involved stealing some sort of precious artifact or another, he'd never been to Mycenae. Parts of the city dated back to 1600 BCE—though the outskirts dated back at least five hundred years earlier—and the city had expanded under each generation of ruler. By the time Eurystheus was ruler, the city was the height of civilization and had a large palace where Eurystheus lived and entertained guests. Most of the walls were damaged or missing completely, but the ruins at least hinted at the grandeur that once stood there.

Colin's heart squeezed with the same mix of joy and sadness he always got when surrounded by ancient treasures. The miracles that ancient civilizations were able to accomplish never ceased to amaze and astonish him, and the harsh treatment those artifacts suffered broke his heart. It was part of the reason he was able to justify to himself what he did for a living. Perhaps if someone had taken down these poor lions years ago, they would now be intact in someone's vault.

With one last look at the lion carving, he made his way through the archway, trying to find his way to a high point that would allow him to look over the ruins from above. Spotting a likely option, he climbed a small rise and gazed down on the once-great city, everything spread before him like a map of history.

Footsteps coming up behind him alerted him to the fact that he was no longer alone. "Where do we start?" The question didn't surprise him as much as the fact that it was Ambrose asking it. Maybe he'd decided to cut the snark.

Glancing at the other man, Colin had a swift kick of pleasure when he realized that he was ever so slightly taller than him. It wasn't much, but in this one small way, he had Ambrose beat. Then Selene came walking up to join them and stood right next to Ambrose, nudging him playfully with her elbow. Their carefree interactions and light touches made Colin realize that in the most important way, Ambrose was still light years ahead of him.

He swallowed down a surge of jealousy and answered the man's question. "That's what I'm trying to figure out. I came up here to get a better lay of the land."

Turning away from where Selene's hand tugged playfully at Ambrose's sleeve, Colin studied the piles of rocks that used to be fortress walls and buildings. He could picture exactly how they would have laid out the city, where the major roads would have been, and which direction everything seemed to be pointing. What he wouldn't give for unlimited time to explore the remains at his leisure. Sadly, now wasn't the time.

After a few moments he pointed toward rectangular structures in the middle of the site and said, "That's where the palace once was. We start there." Without waiting for the lovebirds, he stalked off in the direction of the remains of the palace.

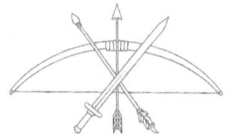

Chapter Fifteen

SELENE HAD NO CLUE how Wolfe had any idea what they were looking at. To her, it all looked like rubble with a few walls that were still standing, hinting at the fact that this was, at one point, a city. He seemed totally confident that they were now standing in what used to be the palace.

She was having trouble meshing the international criminal she knew he was with the history nerd that was currently pointing out the most likely places for the central hall, the bedrooms, the kitchen, and the throne room. He was lit up in the same way Sam had been when he'd finally gotten the opportunity to explore Themyscira. As different as the two men seemed now, four years ago they might have been mirror images of one another.

"Fan out and look for anything that might indicate a hidden cache or buried chamber. We need to figure out where King Eurystheus would have hidden his treasures," Wolfe said quietly enough to not be overheard by the nearby tourists.

She knew Ambrose was still dubious about what they were searching for, but at least he'd quit bitching about it. He knew her well enough that once she made up her mind, she was going to follow through, no matter what.

After two hours of searching the ruins, she was ready to admit defeat. Ambrose had been right. There was nothing to be found here that wouldn't have already been found by archaeologists. The sun was starting to drop, making it increasingly difficult to search. Most of the tourists had long since left.

What if they were wrong? Wolfe seemed dead set on the fact that Nyx and Duran were coming here to this site, but they hadn't seen any sign of them. Maybe Wolfe was wrong. If he was, she'd lost most of the day in her search, which wouldn't make Kalli and Zoe happy. She'd have to call them once they found a hotel and update the queen with their progress or lack thereof.

"Hey, why don't we—" she started.

"Get down!" Wolfe cut her off midsentence as he grabbed her arm and yanked her behind one of the crumbling walls. "Duck, you wanker!" He hissed at Ambrose when he didn't immediately do as he said.

"What's going on?" Selene whispered, peeking out from behind their hiding spot. Within seconds she had the answer to her own question.

"Nyx and Duran just showed up," Wolfe said.

From the waistband of his pants Ambrose pulled a gun, which had been tucked under his suit coat. Selene reached into the top of her boots and pulled out her small pistol. "Do you think they saw us?" she asked, trying to get a good look at their targets. She was forced to drop when a bullet hit the stone wall in front of her, sending chips of stone toward her face. "I guess that answers that."

"Split up," Ambrose said, barely sparing her a glance before he shuffled sideways along the wall, heading away from where she and Wolfe were hiding.

"I don't suppose you happen to have a spare one of those, do you?" Wolfe asked, nodding at her gun as she started heading in the opposite direction that Ambrose had taken.

"Not on me." She pulled out a small knife and handed it to him. She looked from her small gun to his smaller knife. When they got out of this, she seriously needed to stock up on weapons.

"What's the plan?" he whispered, crawling behind her as they made their way over the uneven ground.

"Try not to die," she said, risking a glance over the top of the wall. Duran was much closer than the last time she'd looked, though from the way he was spinning in circles, he didn't know where they were hiding. Nyx was nowhere to be found.

The crack of gunfire made her whip around, and Selene spotted Ambrose crouching behind a pile of rubble and firing at the black-haired dominatrix holding a whip and gun. Nyx was too fast. Her hand flicked her leather whip out, and it wrapped around Ambrose's wrist before he had time to react.

Duran smirked cruelly and took aim at Ambrose's head with his nine-millimeter pistol.

"No!" Selene yelled, launching herself over the wall at Duran.

Duran's arm changed direction mid-aim, swinging around to point at her. Selene tucked and rolled, aiming for his legs. She wasn't fast enough, and he jumped out of her way. The momentum carried her into a crumbling rock wall, but within seconds she leaped to her feet and faced Duran.

They squared off, guns leveled at each other. She heard scuffling behind her but didn't dare turn around to see what was happening. At least she hadn't heard any more gunfire.

"Nyx said you'd be coming after us," Duran said, his voice sounding like moving gravel.

"She was right," Selene replied, starting to circle around her target. If she could get on the other side of him, she could see what was going on between Nyx and Ambrose.

"I'm curious how you found us. It took me a bit of research to figure out where we might start looking for that pretty little accessory everyone seems to care so much about."

Hearing such a precious piece of Amazon history referred to as a pretty accessory made her blood boil and her eyes narrow. As much as she wanted to put a bullet between his eyes for all the atrocities he was responsible for, the responsible thing would be to at least attempt to capture him alive. If that wasn't in the cards, she'd kill him and not lose a minute of sleep worrying about it.

She continued circling Duran, who didn't bother to move but did keep his gun trained on her. She had no idea where Wolfe had disappeared to but hoped he was smart enough to stay out of sight.

At last she could see the cause of the scuffling. Ambrose had managed to grab ahold of the whip Nyx had used on him and tugged her to him. He was trying to get his arm around her neck, but Nyx was strong and ruthless. However tarnished Selene's morals might be, at least she had some. The same couldn't be said for Nyx.

She needed to end this now, before anyone got hurt. "Duran, you don't need to do this. You're outclassed, and you know it."

"Honey, I like my chances, but if you'd like to offer some sort of trade, I might be willing to listen." His gazed raked over her, and he licked his lips, making her feel dirty.

Enough was enough.

She dropped to a crouch and sent a low kick in his direction, managing to sweep his legs out from under him. The move took him by surprise, and he dropped like lead, hitting the ground with a loud groan. Unfortunately, he didn't drop his gun. He squeezed the trigger.

She wasn't quite fast enough.

The bullet grazed her arm as she dodged sideways, kicked his wrist, and sent his gun skidding across the stone floor. She stood with her pistol pointed straight at his face. Satisfaction surged through her, and her finger itched to pull the trigger.

A gunshot cracked, making her think for a second that she'd accidentally followed through. A moment later, a pained masculine groan from somewhere behind her told her that it wasn't Duran who was hit.

"Ambrose!" she shouted, her gaze arrowing to where he was crumpled on the stones a dozen feet from her. Nyx was standing over him, lining up a second shot.

A second bullet split the air, startling Selene. Nyx stumbled backward, her gun arm going limp and dropping her pistol on the stones near Ambrose's hand. Blood blossomed out of her shoulder and poured down her black leather vest and arm, dripping onto the ground.

Selene whipped around and spotted Wolfe several yards away, crouched behind one of the crumbling walls and holding Duran's gun. Her stomach lurched at his menacing expression as he stared down Nyx.

Her distraction cost her. Duran whipped his leg out and slammed it into her wrist. A loud crunch merged with shooting pain that radiated up her arm as her hand opened reflexively, dropping her gun. Duran snatched it and launched himself from the ground, taking off in Nyx's direction. He grabbed Nyx's uninjured arm, and the pair ran toward the parking lot.

Selene instinctively grabbed her own arm, trying to steady the broken wrist as she raced over to where Ambrose had fallen.

"Ambrose, talk to me," she said, frantically trying to find the wound.

Wolfe made it to Ambrose's side a split second after she did, shoving her sideways and using his two unbroken hands to pat the man down. Colin flipped open Ambrose's jacket, and Selene swore loudly. Blood was seeping out of a bullet hole in his torso. He groaned as Wolfe poked around the wound.

This couldn't be happening. She'd known Ambrose longer than anyone else in her life, not including Kalli and Zoe. They'd been through too much together for her to lose him now. She wouldn't allow it. Tears started flowing freely despite her best intentions to hold them in.

"Hospital. Now," she said, trying to dig her phone out of her jacket pocket with her uninjured arm, not even noticing the pain from her broken wrist. Wolfe stopped her frantic movements and grabbed his own phone, calling for an ambulance. "He's losing so much blood." She put pressure on the wound, trying to stop the bleeding, but it just kept coming. If they didn't hurry up, she was going to lose him.

Chapter Sixteen

WHEN THE AMBULANCE FINALLY arrived, Selene insisted on riding in the back. She was probably in the way as the paramedic did what he could to stabilize Ambrose, but the thought of being separated from him was too painful to bear. At least this way, she knew exactly what was going on, even if it wasn't good.

Her tears had finally stopped, but now all she felt was an aching numbness somewhere near her heart. Ambrose meant so much to her. It would be impossible to fill the hole in her life if she lost him.

The ambulance ride felt like it took ages even though realistically it had only been fifteen minutes or so. After they arrived at the hospital in Argos, Selene was unceremoniously left in the waiting room—covered in Ambrose's blood—as they rushed him back to surgery. She stood frozen, unable to remember what she needed to do next. The smell of burned coffee mixed with the metallic tang of the blood on her shirt, a pungent scent that kept her grounded while her mind went wild with what-ifs.

What if he died? How would she keep doing what she'd been doing without her business partner and, more importantly, her person?

Gentle hands gripped her elbows and tugged her toward the chairs in the waiting room. The warmth of the touch started to seep through her skin, making its way slowly to the icy ball in the center of her chest.

She glanced sideways and saw Wolfe's concerned face, his eyes full of sympathy. In her hurry to rush Ambrose to the hospital, she'd forgotten about everything else. She'd forgotten about Nyx and Duran, the girdle, and, most importantly, Wolfe. Though, looking at him now, his devastatingly attractive face so full of emotion, she had no idea how.

The feel of hard plastic hit the back of her thighs as Wolfe pushed her into a seat, then settled himself next to her. Gently, he reached out and tugged back her jacket sleeve, revealing her swollen purple wrist.

She hissed in pain, suddenly remembering her own injury. She'd managed to hide it from the paramedics, wanting them to focus on saving Ambrose, but now that he was being taken care of, her mind began to clear, and the throb began to settle in.

"You should have them look at this while you're here," Wolfe said quietly.

She tugged her hand away from him, regretting the motion instantly when pain went shooting up her arm. "I'll be fine."

He rolled his eyes at her. "You're either the most reckless person I've ever met or a sadist. I can't figure out which."

That was uncalled for. "I'm neither. I'm a realist. I know my own healing abilities. This might be bad at the moment, but give it an hour or so, and I'll be fine."

He shook his head with a look of disbelief. "You may have these fancy healing powers, but one day your reckless streak is going to catch up with you. You're going to take a chance that costs you more than even you can heal from."

She thought about what he said but just as quickly wrote it off. She was an Amazon, however tarnished. Her strength, speed, and healing ability were the things that defined her as a person. She was always careful not to get in over her head, and she knew her limits. She didn't just throw herself into danger without thinking about the consequences.

Did she?

The hours ticked by with no sign of the doctors. Her mind insisted on replaying the fight over and over in her head, trying to figure out where it went so wrong and how they got hurt so badly. One image ingrained itself into her memory, drowning out all the others. Wolfe shooting Nyx just before she would have killed Ambrose. He was the only reason Ambrose was still alive.

Wolfe looked exhausted. He was currently slouched as far back as he could manage in the plastic chair, his long legs sticking out across the lobby and his head propped against the wall. His eyelids had drooped shut, and his breathing was deep and even.

Tentatively, she reached out her now fully healed hand and brushed up against his arm. He came instantly awake, bolting upright like someone had taken a cattle prod to his rear end. He realized who had woken him, and his face softened, melting into a small smile.

"Hey, there," he said, his voice barely audible.

Why did she have to find him so incredibly sexy? It made what she had to do that much harder. Taking a deep breath, she said, "Thank you."

A deep vee appeared between his brows, and he cocked his head. "For what?" He honestly sounded baffled.

She let out a small huff. "For saving Ambrose. I saw what you did. Nyx would have killed him if it wasn't for you."

A shutter went down over his eyes. The smile stayed on his face, but some of the emotion leached out of it. "I just did what anyone would have done."

That wasn't true. In her experience most people would not have picked up a gun and shot a human being, even to save others. It took a special breed of person to do that. There was more to Colin Wolfe than met the eye. She opened her mouth to correct him, but before she could, someone stepped into her peripheral vision.

"Ms. Williams?"

Colin sent a confused look in the newcomer's direction, then glanced at Selene. She caught Colin's eye and subtly shook her head. Now was not the time to discuss her aliases. Instead, she looked up to find a tall man with black hair and glasses. His scrubs and white coat told her he was a doctor. "Yes?"

"Mr. Moretti is out of surgery. He's still hasn't woken up from the anesthesia yet, but he should make a full recovery."

Relief poured through her, and her eyes fluttered closed. Ambrose was going to be all right. She took a calming breath, rolled her shoulders, and forced all her muscles to relax. She opened her eyes to look at the doctor.

"He'll be asleep for a while yet. It's probably best if you come back and see him in the morning." The doctor nodded to her, then Wolfe, before turning to leave.

There weren't any beds in the waiting room, but Selene had slept in worse places. She removed her bloody coat and balled it up to use as a pillow.

"Come on," Wolfe said, standing in front of her and holding out his hand expectantly.

She stared at it blankly. "What?"

Wolfe rolled his eyes. "We're getting out of here. There's no use sleeping on hard plastic chairs when a hotel with a hot shower and soft sheets is just a few blocks away."

He was probably right. Staying in this uncomfortable waiting room all night wouldn't help Ambrose. Reluctantly, she fit her hand into his and tried desperately to ignore the warm zing that shot up her arm at the contact. She took a step back and dropped his hand like it had burned her.

"Lead on."

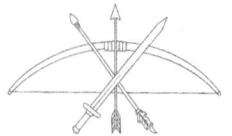

Chapter Seventeen

WAS HE SO REPULSIVE that she could barely stand to touch him? Or was she just that in love with her British boy toy?

Colin swallowed down his frustration and led the way out of the hospital and to their SUV, which he'd driven from Mycenae. He managed to navigate the unfamiliar roads to the nearest hotel. It wasn't five stars, but at least it wasn't far from the hospital.

He pulled their overly large vehicle into the parking lot, dodging a shiny black Mercedes that almost clipped his bumper. Yanking the wheel hard right, he managed to swerve out of the way just before he would have hit the stone wall that fenced in the parking lot.

"Idiot driver," he huffed, his heart rate slowing from the small rush of adrenaline. Before he could even take his seat belt off, Selene was out of the vehicle and running across the parking lot.

"Selene!" he yelled after her. She was already halfway across the pavement, so he had no hope of catching her.

"It's Duran!" she shouted back, not even breaking stride.

Not good. Colin took off after Selene, cursing his normal human speed. There was no chance in hell he could keep up with an Amazon running full tilt.

The Mercedes hadn't gone far. The powerful engine revved from where the car was crouched in the road, the headlights beaming in their direction.

He saw it happen almost in slow motion.

The sleek black car jumped as the driver slammed on the gas. The tires screeched in complaint against the pavement, the engine growling loudly as Duran floored it.

Straight into Selene.

Her body went flying across the road, her head smacking the cement with a stomach-twisting crunch. She lay unmoving as the Mercedes peeled away, tearing down the street and around the corner.

This could not be happening. Not to her. Colin's long strides ate up the remaining distance between them. His heart jumped to his throat when he saw the thick red blood pooling on the pavement, her curly red locks slick with it. He dropped down next to her, unwilling to touch her for fear of making any injuries worse.

For the second time that day, he fumbled in his pocket for his cell phone to call an ambulance. As soon as the operator picked up, he heard Selene moan, the pained sound tearing at his heart.

"You're going to be all right," he told her, praying it was true.

"Sir? What is your emergency?" The operator's brisk voice interrupted his train of thought.

"No," Selene said, her voice weak but insistent.

"What was that?" the operator asked.

Colin wanted to know the same thing. "What do you mean, no?" She clearly wasn't thinking straight. Of course she wasn't. She'd just smacked her head into the road. "We have an injured woman here. I need you to send medical attention," he told the woman on the phone.

Selene's bloody arm snaked out, grabbed the phone from his hand, and hurled it at the ground, shattering it into dozens of pieces. Her eyes weren't even open, but she had impeccable aim.

"What in the hell did you do that for?" His anger changed to concern as he glanced from his destroyed phone to the woman slowly sitting up in front of him. "Hey, no way. You need to stay put." He pushed on her shoulders but might as well have been pushing on the side of the hotel. She didn't budge.

"I'm fine," she mumbled, rolling onto her knees and slowly standing up.

Colin mirrored her motions, arms out to catch her if she fell. "I think the copious amounts of blood coming out of your skull would beg to differ. You need to sit down. Better yet, you need a hospital."

She glared at him, but her eyes gave away the pain she was attempting to ignore. "I told you before. I heal fast."

Colin shook his head and didn't bother to respond. Instead, he took a step closer, bent at the knees, and scooped her up into his arms bridal style. It was only her shock and dulled reflexes that let him get away with it, but it didn't matter. He was holding her—that was all that mattered. He would take what he could get.

Even in her injured and mildly dazed state she felt amazing in his arms. She wasn't some tiny damsel in distress, but her feminine warmth seeped into him as his long strides carried them across the street and back to their vehicle. He would have preferred to take her straight inside the hotel, but she probably would have attracted far too much attention covered in blood.

He yanked open the rear passenger door of the SUV and managed to climb inside with her on his lap. She slowly released her arm, which had curled around his neck without him even realizing it. She cleared her throat uncomfortably and slid back off his lap until she was seated next to him on the rear seat.

He dug around in the rear of the vehicle until he located the first aid kit that Ambrose had helpfully packed. He grabbed some antiseptic solution and gauze. "This is going to hurt," he said apologetically.

"Just do it," she said, not looking at his face.

To her credit, she didn't hiss or cringe as he mopped up the rapidly closing cut on the back of her head. Colin went through the entire supply of gauze and half the bottle of antiseptic before he was satisfied.

Now that the immediate danger was over and he could see for himself that she was going to be fine, anger rose within him like a giant beast. He placed the used gauze into a plastic bag and tied it shut, his movements slow and measured. He didn't want to lose his temper. Nothing good would come of that.

"That was foolish," he said through clenched teeth as he returned the rest of the supplies to the kit. "You could have been killed." He had no idea what he would have done if she'd been killed. He'd only just found this brave, gorgeous, somewhat infuriating redhead, and he wasn't ready to lose her yet.

Selene continued to stare out the window on the other side of the vehicle. "I'm not that easy to kill." She crossed her arms defiantly. He studied her profile as she diligently ignored him.

"Yeah? Well, I am. We can't all be Amazons," he bit out. "We're supposed to be in this together, Red. You don't get to go off on your own and get yourself shot or run over by a car or who knows what else." Maybe he was more interested in this partnership than she was. Ever since Ambrose had shown up, she'd been distant with Colin. Well, more than usual.

Her head whipped around, only a tiny wince giving away the pain it caused. "I've been living my life for a long time before I met you. Thousands of years, in fact. I've managed to survive so far. I think I know my own limits." She glared at him.

He turned his body to face her, arms crossing to mirror hers. "You're reckless. You charge into things before you have a chance to think if it's the right move. You count on your healing abilities to pull you back from the brink of death, but one of these days, it won't be enough." His face was inches from hers, his voice a harsh whisper in her ear. "What happens to me, to this"—he gestured between them—"if you die?"

She drew in a shuddering breath but stood her ground, not leaning away from him even an inch. He leaned back just far enough that he could see the confusion skate across her gaze. For the second time in ten minutes, he went for it. "Selene," he breathed out as his lips found hers.

For one hellish moment, Colin thought he'd guessed wrong. Just as he was about to pull back and make some contrived excuse, she pounced, her hand going to the back of his head to keep his lips locked against hers.

Thank God.

Colin couldn't believe he was finally kissing her, the hands-off goddess he'd been thinking about nonstop for days. Not only was he kissing her, but she was also returning the favor tenfold.

"Colin," she said between kisses, her hand raking through his hair and making him shudder slightly with pleasure. "We shouldn't be doing this."

Right. Of course, Ambrose. Colin couldn't believe he'd forgotten about her oh-so-attractive boyfriend. The one with the sexy British accent who was currently in the hospital after being shot.

He sat straight up, pushing himself as far away from Selene as he could get in the relatively confined space of the back seat. "My mistake." Of course she wouldn't want to get involved with him. What had he been thinking?

She looked like she was about to say something, but he cut her off. "We should get inside. It's been a long day and an even longer night. I could use some shut-eye." He grabbed his bag and rifled through it, grabbing one of his bulky hoodies and shoving it in her direction. "Put this on and pull the hood up. Hopefully it will cover the blood."

Without a backward glance, Colin pushed his way out of the vehicle. It was the middle of the night, and he was ready to pass out. With any luck, this place had a vacancy, and they could check in without having to try a bunch of different hotels first.

He heard Selene climb out behind him, but he didn't wait for her. He stalked to the lobby of the hotel and left her to trail in his wake.

Chapter Eighteen

SELENE FELT LIKE SHE'D been hit by a truck. Which, you know, she basically had. It wasn't that her healing powers weren't working. They obviously were or she wouldn't be up and walking around the way she was. But with everything that had happened in the last few hours, she felt flattened.

Ambrose was in the hospital, and it was her fault. The one person she'd been able to rely on for the last twenty years and he was injured because of her secrets. If only he'd stayed in London where she'd left him. He should never have stuck his nose into Amazon business.

Of course, he had no idea that it even was Amazon business, because she'd never told him about her past. He obviously knew something was strange with her—she hadn't aged a day since they'd met—but he'd never pushed for answers, and she'd never volunteered them.

Her body complained loudly as she hauled her small bag slowly after Colin as he charged into the hotel, obviously intent on getting away from her as soon as possible. Despite her aches and pains, one of her hands fluttered to her mouth, where she could still feel the soft, warm pressure of his lips.

She'd kissed Colin. Well, he'd kissed her first, but she'd definitely taken things to the next level. She couldn't believe she'd done that. First, he wasn't exactly her usual type, and second, they had far more important things to be worrying about, like the asshole who had mowed her down in his car.

That didn't mean she couldn't regret—just a little, of course—the fact that nothing else had happened between them.

By the time she dragged herself into the hotel lobby, Colin had already acquired a room key and was waiting for her, arms crossed and toe tapping impatiently. The clerk behind the desk gave her a somewhat disapproving look—probably spotting some of the blood—but Selene just tucked herself farther into the hood of Colin's sweatshirt and kept walking. If she happened to inhale a deep lungful of whatever spicy scent her criminal accomplice happened to have left on the cozy shirt, no one else needed to know that.

For better or worse, the room he'd reserved had two beds this time. Selene glanced longingly at the mattress but knew she had to wash the blood off before she could crawl between those bright-white sheets. With a sigh, she stripped off the delicious-smelling sweatshirt and headed straight for the shower. By the time she was done scrubbing off the evidence of her dance with the Mercedes, Colin was already fast asleep in the bed farthest from the door. With a mental shrug, she did the same.

The next thing Selene was aware of, sunlight was pouring through the window and directly into her eyes. She blinked groggily, trying to find the clock. It was 1:00 p.m., which meant she'd gotten ten hours of sleep. She couldn't remember the last time she'd slept that long.

A noise from the far corner of the room caught her attention. The shower was running. She glanced around and realized that the messy bed next to hers was empty. After pushing herself up, she swung her legs over the edge of the bed and was surprised by the deep-purple bruising that clearly hadn't faded yet. How was that possible? She'd recovered from bullet wounds faster than she was healing from her tangle with the Mercedes.

Something was wrong.

Before she could put much thought into it, the bathroom door opened, releasing a cloud of steam and a very sexy man wearing nothing but a towel and a startled expression. He froze where he was, hands tugging the knot on his towel slightly tighter.

"You look rough." His voice had no right to be as sexy as it was.

"Thanks, just what all the girls want to hear," Selene said as she stood. She stretched, which pulled the T-shirt she'd been sleeping in higher. Colin's eyes traced her legs from her feet on up, but his forehead wrinkled when he spotted the deep-purple bruises.

"You haven't healed yet." His hands twitched on his towel but didn't let go. Pity.

"So I've noticed." She took a tentative step toward where she'd dropped her bag when they had arrived, her muscles more sore than she would like to admit.

"What about your head wound?" Colin said. He crossed the floor to where she stood, reached for her head, and gently tugged her hair out of the way so he could inspect the injury. He used one hand to hold her in place while he softly probed the wound. The spot where he rubbed his finger was sensitive, but at least it didn't ache. His finger came away free of blood. "That's something at least."

Selene expected him to step back and release her, but he didn't. Instead, his second hand cupped her jaw and lifted her face so that she was looking him in the eye. She couldn't understand the conflict she could see in his expression, but finally it cleared.

"Selene," he said, exhaling her name like a whisper.

His lips closed the gap between them, his hands tugging her face to meet him.

With a slight moan, she leaned into him, sinking into the soft press of his lips on hers. The kiss was even better than the one from the SUV. It started out gentle but slowly slid deeper.

His tongue traced the seam of her lips, and she gasped, letting him in to plunder her mouth. She gave as good as she got, exploring his hot mouth and tangling her tongue with his.

His hands sank into her long curls, grasping the back of her head and keeping their mouths fused together. He gently pushed her head sideways and broke their kiss. Before she could protest, he began trailing kisses along her jaw to the side of her neck, slowly kissing downward until he was blocked by the neckline of her T-shirt. With an impatient huff he grabbed the hem of her shirt and yanked it over her head.

Once her arms were no longer trapped in her clothing, her eager hands went to the hot skin of his tantalizing chest. Starting from his shoulders, she traced his muscles, caressing his pecs, passing her fingertips down his ribs, and reverently sliding across the defined bumps of his abs.

He was far from idle. As soon as he'd yanked her shirt off, his warm hands landed on her ribs and slowly traced their way upward until he was cupping her firm breasts. He cupped one in each hand, feeling the weight of them before rubbing thumbs gently, but firmly, across her nipples, drawing them into tight peaks.

Colin took a step toward her, forcing her back a step until her legs hit the mattress she'd just left. With a gentle shove he pushed her down onto the soft surface. She sat down and was suddenly much closer to the tempting knot in his towel. With a quick flick of her wrist, the towel fell to the floor, and Selene was looking at his gorgeous cock.

She glanced at his face where fire burned in his gaze. She wrapped her hand around his hardness and stroked, watching as his eyes rolled in pleasure and his head tipped back.

"Selene," he practically groaned her name.

Encouraged by his response, she leaned forward and took just the tip of him into her mouth, running her tongue around his sensitive head. His fingers spasmed in her hair, but he didn't push her any further. She laved him with her tongue, starting at the base of his cock and ending by repeatedly circling his tip. She grasped the base of him and slid her hand up and down in time with her mouth.

"Jesus," he said as he pulled her off him. "You keep going like that and this is going to be over before it even gets started." Colin bent down and kissed her mouth, making her moan with pleasure. He put one of his knees on the bed next to her, leaning into her until she was lying flat beneath him.

Selene hadn't bothered to put on shorts to sleep in before she'd crawled in bed, but she happily lifted her hips as Colin's impatient hands tugged down her lacy bikinis. His fingers lightly traced her legs, hips, and torso as he came back up her body to lie down next to her on the bed. "You're incredibly beautiful. I want to worship your body," Colin murmured in her ear.

"You're not so bad yourself." Her hands began tracing the hard lines of his muscles once more. His ass was calling her name, and she reached behind him to squeeze it.

He moved back up to her breasts and fondled them, tugging gently on the peaks of her nipples.

She gasped as pleasure shot from her breasts to her core. Her hips moved almost involuntarily, desperate for more friction. She pushed Colin's shoulder until he was flat on his back, then straddled him. She pinned him in place with her hips, his hard cock nestling against her heat.

Colin's hand raced over her back, pulling her down until she was lying plastered across his chest. He fused their mouths together and swept his tongue inside once more. His hands came to rest on her ass, keeping her in place as she rocked against his shaft.

"I want you inside me," she whispered.

"I don't have any supplies with me. This wasn't exactly on my radar when I came on this trip." He smiled apologetically.

Selene pulled back slightly so she could look him in the eye. "Pregnancy isn't an issue, as we're infertile by nature. And with my healing abilities, diseases aren't a concern either. Does that about cover it?"

"It does indeed."

Selene planted one more quick kiss on his lips before she sat up. She gave his cock a few experimental tugs before she rose up and sank down on it, feeling him stretch her as she impaled herself on him.

Colin let out a deep groan as his hands came to rest on her hips. "You feel fantastic."

She winked mischievously. "You ain't seen nothing yet." With that, Selene started to move, setting a relentless pace that had them both gasping within moments.

Colin brought his hands up to cup her breasts as they bounced. One of his hands slid down her torso and into her curls before flicking her clit. He started rubbing back and forth in time with her movements. She threw her head back as sensations bombarded her. His hips lifted as he met her thrust for thrust. Seconds later she shattered, her orgasm ripping through her.

"Colin!" His name came out before she could stop it.

He thrust a few more times before practically levering off the bed with the force of his own orgasm. With a satisfied groan, he collapsed back on the mattress and tugged her down so that she was lying on top of him, his cock still inside her.

Selene couldn't remember the last time she'd felt this boneless and relaxed. She knew she should probably move—she wasn't exactly tiny—but the sensation of him gently tracing his fingers over her spine was amazing. It was odd, though, since she was normally a love-'em-and-leave-'em kind of woman. She didn't get snuggly with the men she slept with, and Colin wasn't exactly her normal type of guy. She froze, her whole body going stiff and his cock sliding out of her.

What was she doing? Colin Wolfe was a thief. He was someone who based his life around taking from others. He was the type of person she should be avoiding, not snuggling up in bed with. Besides, they were on a mission. Sex was just a distraction.

This couldn't happen again.

Holy shit. Colin could not believe that had just happened. In what world would a stunningly beautiful immortal warrior woman have sex with him? He wasn't exactly lacking in the looks or the ego department, but even he had to admit they weren't exactly on an even playing field.

He lay there, his heart rate slowly coming back down to normal. The tingling pleasure slowly fading from his limbs. That had been the hottest sex he'd ever had in his life, hands down. A small grin spread across his lips, and he turned to glance at the gorgeous woman in bed next to him.

"We should not have done that."

Her words stopped him cold, right as he was about to reach out and tug her against his side.

"We shouldn't have?" He paused, then frowned. "Oh, right."
Ambrose.

The name jolted through him. He couldn't believe that he'd forgotten that Selene was already taken. All the pleasure he'd been feeling fled. He sat up and turned away from her. He'd slept with someone who wasn't available. Of course she wasn't. Just look at her. She probably had a phone book full of men that she could call even if Ambrose wasn't already in the picture.

"I forgot." He threw off the covers and started rapidly glancing around for his boxers. Where the hell were they?

She pushed herself so she was leaning up on her elbow, the sheet tucked carefully around her breasts. "Forgot what?"

Finally locating his underwear all the way by the door to the hallway, he tugged them on and searched for his pants. "I forgot about Ambrose."

Her eyes narrowed and she sat up more fully, leaning against the headboard. "What about Ambrose?"

Was she playing coy? "You'll probably want to go see him." He tugged on his jeans and grabbed the first T-shirt he could find.

She shifted on the mattress, pulling her knees up to her chest and wrapping her arms around them. "I'm sure it can wait."

Shock zinged through him. How unfeeling was she? "It's cool, really. I'm sure you want to go see your boyfriend in the hospital." He was trying—and likely failing—to play it cool. Clearly he wasn't as good at this casual-sex thing as she seemed to be. He located his shoes behind his duffel bag and sat to tug them on his feet.

Her amused laugh stopped him in the middle of tying his laces.

"You think Ambrose is my boyfriend?" She chuckled again. "Is this jealousy? Or guilt?"

Finally finished tying his shoes, he turned to look at her. She no longer looked upset, and she definitely didn't look guilty. "Forgive a guy for being upset that he slept with someone that belongs to someone else."

She scoffed. "I thought I was the one from another era. I don't *belong* to anyone. And even if I did, it wouldn't be Ambrose. At least not the way you seem to think." She shifted closer to him on the bed, resting her hand gently on his forearm. "Ambrose is my ward. Or, at least, he used to be. Also, he's gay."

Ward. The word ricocheted around his brain, not quite settling down enough for Colin to process what she was saying to him. "Ward. As in your child."

She smiled. "Yes. I found Ambrose when he was fourteen years old. He'd been beaten within an inch of his life and left to bleed out in a dingy alley in London. His parents had kicked him out of their house, and he had been living on the streets. His mates, and I use that term lightly, didn't take too kindly to finding out he's gay. They decided to do something about it."

"Jesus. Those assholes." He ran his hands through his hair. As much of a prick as Ambrose had been, no one deserved that. Especially not a kid.

She nodded. "Yeah. He probably would have died from his injuries except I found him first. I took him to a hospital to get patched up and paid for his medical expenses. I haven't been able to get rid of him since." She smiled. He got the feeling it wasn't meant for him, but for Ambrose.

Everything he'd been thinking since Ambrose had popped into their lives the day before suddenly realigned in his head. Ambrose wasn't in love with Selene or vice versa. Ambrose was, however, unendingly devoted to Selene and would protect her with everything he had. Still a threat, just a totally different kind of threat. He could deal with that.

"But then why . . ." He trailed off, unsure if he wanted to finish his question.

She gave a small sigh. "Colin, look at us. You're a criminal. I'm a vigilante. I've spent thousands of years punishing men exactly like you for getting away with things they shouldn't be able to get away with. You literally broke into a museum my company was protecting and stole something right out from under our noses."

He sucked in a quick breath. He could barely enjoy the fact that she'd finally started to call him by his first name, because she wasn't wrong. They came from totally different worlds.

"Not to mention, we're in the middle of a cat-and-mouse game with the most dangerous immortal warrior in existence. It doesn't seem like a great time to get distracted."

He stood stiffly. "Of course, you're right." He walked over to his bag and grabbed his very tattered, now slightly bloody notebook and sat down on the only chair in the room. "I need to focus on figuring out where Nyx and Duran would go next, given that Mycenae was a bust. Plus, you probably should go check in on Ambrose. I'm sure he'll be awake by now."

She sent him an inscrutable look before nodding once. She shifted to the edge of the bed, pulling the sheets behind her. She seemed to debate for a second or two before she stood up, leaving the sheet behind.

Damn she was gorgeous. To think that only minutes ago his hands and mouth had been all over her peachy skin. The curve of her ass almost taunted him to go over there and see if she'd changed her mind in the last sixty seconds or so.

She tugged on her clothes, slowly covering the distracting view. She'd said it couldn't happen again. He had to keep reminding himself of that. He wasn't the type of man who would try to push himself on a woman who had said no.

No harm in looking, though.

When she was finally ready to go, she glanced in his direction. "You coming?"

It felt like a test for both of them. She'd obviously been reluctant to let him out of her sight since they'd left Themyscira. He understood why but hoped they had gotten past it at this point. Especially after what had just happened between them.

"I think I'll stay here and try to figure out our next move." He tapped his finger on his notebook.

"All right," she agreed. "I'll be back soon." With a quick flick of her hair over her shoulder, she was gone.

Small baby steps of trust. He'd take what he could get.

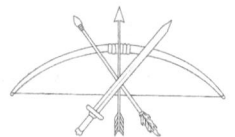

Chapter Nineteen

SELENE COULDN'T BELIEVE SHE'D walked out of that room and left him to his own devices. If he was planning to bolt, she'd given him the perfect opportunity. She'd had to get out of there, though. How could she have slept with him? They were working together. She didn't mix business with pleasure.

Flashes of his luscious lips and incredible body reminded her of exactly why she'd had sex with him. He was one of the most attractive men she'd ever met, and that was saying something considering how long she'd been alive. It was enough for her to wish, however quietly, that he didn't embody everything she'd fought her whole life against. Her getting involved with a thief was ridiculous.

Though she did have to admit, reluctantly, that he wasn't quite as awful of a human being as she'd imagined. Yes, he stole art and antiquities and sold them to the highest bidder, but that wasn't everything he was. During the fight the day before he'd been a real asset. He'd come to Ambrose's rescue when she'd been unable to stop Nyx herself. And, she recalled, she'd hopped right into the ambulance with Ambrose and left Wolfe on his own. If he was going to take off, he could have done it then.

But he hadn't.

Instead, he showed up at the hospital and waited with her, even when he'd thought she and Ambrose were a couple. When he had no reason to care about Ambrose and every reason to dislike him or distrust him. She could try to argue with herself that he was there for the belt, and there still could be some of that floating around in his head, but it didn't feel like that was his primary reason anymore. She didn't know what to make of it.

Selene glanced up, noticing that she'd arrived at the hospital without even realizing it. She headed inside and checked in at the front desk. Thankfully, she was sent right up to Ambrose's room.

She braced herself. Gutshot wounds were never pretty or quick to recover from. Ambrose had been in a lot of dangerous situations with her in the past, but it still got to her every time he was injured. Call it dormant maternal instinct or call it empathy, but every time he was injured, she wished she could somehow pass her healing gene to him so he would recover faster.

With a sharp inhale she pushed the door open and walked into the room.

"Took you long enough." The mildly annoyed British lilt was much weaker than Ambrose's usual voice, but it still sounded wonderful to her ears.

"Ungrateful little shit." She smiled at him and watched his lips twitch as he fought a losing battle against his own smile. She crossed the room and stood next to his bed. She wanted to touch him, connect with him in some way, but didn't want to make anything worse.

"But you love me anyway." He reached out slowly, and she grabbed his hand, squeezing gently.

"You know I do." She took in the wires, machines, and bandages. "So what's the prognosis?"

He shrugged, then groaned in pain. "They're going to keep me for a day or two and then reassess. It could have been much worse. The bitch somehow managed to miss all my major organs."

Selene released a breath she hadn't even realized she'd been holding. She couldn't have hoped for a better outcome. It could have been so much worse. She could have lost him.

Selene had lived a very long life. She'd loved and lost many times—romantic partners and friends, though never a child—and it never got any easier. She couldn't fathom how much more pain she would be in when she eventually did lose Ambrose for good. It was inevitable that she would outlive him like she did everyone else, but at least their time together wasn't being cut short by her sister Amazon's hand. She wouldn't know how to live with herself if ghosts from her past took Ambrose's life. He had no idea who she really was, and she wanted it to stay that way. It was safer for everyone.

"I'm glad that you're going to be all right. Though you know I'm going to have to leave you here to fend for yourself, right?" She squeezed his hand again and placed a gentle kiss on his forehead, trying to send comfort in the only way she could.

"What exactly are you and Colin Wolfe up to? This isn't our normal type of case. Not that Duran doesn't deserve everything you plan on sending his direction." His brown eyes narrowed as if he was trying to read her mind. "Is this some sort of secret Amazon vendetta going on between you and Nyx?"

Selene's eyes snapped to Ambrose's face. He smirked at her but remained silent.

"What on earth are you talking about?" She tried to play it off, but she could already tell it wasn't going to work. The flat lips, sideways eyes, and exaggerated slow blink were a dead giveaway.

"You do realize that researching things is literally part of my job description, right? Not to mention, you haven't aged a day since I met you twenty years ago. No one's genetics are that good. Unless, perhaps, they have a bit of help?" He asked it like a question, but it clearly wasn't.

"Whatever you think you know, you're wrong. I'm not an Amazon." It was sheer stubbornness that had her denying it. Clearly he already knew what she'd thought was her biggest secret. Apparently she'd been very wrong.

"Selene, I know everything. I know that Themyscira exists and that it's in Türkiye. I know that you're some badass warrior who heals injuries faster than should be physically possible. I know you're immortal." He whispered the last word, as if suddenly worried someone might overhear them.

She was floored. No one, in the thousands of years that she'd been alive, had ever figured it out. Well, except Colin Wolfe, but he'd had a rather abrupt introduction to her people. "How long have you known?"

He gave her a small smile that softened his normally hardened expression. "Mum, I've always known that something strange was going on with you. When I was fifteen, I saw you recover from a broken arm in less than an hour. But as to the rest of it, I finally figured it out with this trip. How are Zoe and Kalli, anyway? Oh, I'm sorry, Queen Kalliope." His smile turned into a smirk she wanted to wipe off his smug face. "It was the anthropologist that gave it all away, you see. If you want to stay off the radar, maybe don't travel with the world's most renowned expert in Amazons."

Ambrose hadn't called her *Mum* in ages—it wasn't exactly something they advertised at the office. Tears gathered in the corners of her eyes, but she tried to blink them back. Instead, she huffed and plopped down on the hospital bed next to Ambrose's feet. He groaned quietly, and she sent him an apologetic wince. "I don't even know what to say right now." It was the truth. She'd never been at this much of a loss for words.

"How about starting at the beginning and filling me in? Maybe together we can figure out a solution."

So she did. She explained the coup that Nyx staged thousands of years ago and how she, Zoe, Kalli, and Eris, along with several others, had been banished. She skipped most of the intervening years that weren't relevant to their current situation and jumped right to how Kalli had met Sam, then chased Eris halfway across the globe. Selene had to grit her teeth as she recounted the battle that had taken place less than a week before, during which she'd lost several of her sisters.

Or really her former sisters. She wasn't worthy of the title of Amazon anymore.

Before she could stop it, flashes of a ruined city being burned to the ground swam in front of her eyes, an ancient memory floating to the surface. Bloodied bodies of men, women, and children strewn about haphazardly. And one person standing in the middle like a conquering hero.

"Selene?" Ambrose prompted quietly.

She hadn't realized she'd trailed off. She shook her head, trying to clear the disturbing memories. She didn't have time to deal with them. "We threw Duran and his men in jail. According to Wolfe, Nyx sneaked into the jail and convinced Duran to join her. Who the hell knows what she promised him in exchange for his services."

"Why the belt, though? What does she think she's going to get for it? Is she going to sell it and use the money to pay Duran and set herself up for life?"

It wasn't a bad theory, but she didn't think that was the end goal. "I'm afraid it's worse than that." Selene explained how the belt amplified an Amazon's powers and that she and Colin thought she was going to find it and use it. Essentially, she could turn herself into an invincible warlord.

"So now an Amazon warrior/corporate executive and an international art and antiquities thief are going to stop a military dictator and one of the worst humans currently walking the planet before they take over the world and enslave the rest of humanity," Ambrose said, summing it up.

"Don't call me that," she responded. "I'm no longer an Amazon. Now I'm just a simple vigilante with several thousand years' worth of disposable income at her fingertips. Invest early and often, folks." She tried to crack a joke, but it fell flat.

"Selene," he started, but she cut him off.

"No."

He dipped his head in acknowledgment and left it alone. "So what's next? I mean, I'd offer to help you out, but"—he gestured limply to the hospital gown and monitors softly humming away around his bed—"should we call in a team?"

Selene stood and shook her head. "I'm not dragging anyone else into this." She lifted her hand to cut him off before he even got a word out. "Yes, I know the team would drop everything to support me. That's not the point. They can't know what we're up against, and I don't send my people into the field without as much knowledge as possible. I'm definitely not sending them in when I'm deliberately hiding something this big from them. It's going to have to be me and Colin."

She crossed to the door but turned to face him when Ambrose spoke again.

"Mum? Don't worry. I won't judge, even if Wolfe is closer to my age than yours. If he played for my team, I'd have hit that too."

It was the eyebrow waggle that got under her skin. She wanted to throw something at him but remembered just in time that he was injured. With an irritated scoff she spun on her heel and left the room, the sound of Ambrose's laughter trailing after her.

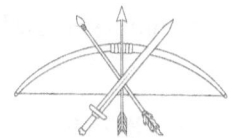

Chapter Twenty

A FTER SELENE LEFT, COLIN gave himself exactly two minutes to think about their bedroom escapades before forcibly tucking it to the back of his mind. As much as he was craving a repeat, it was clear she regretted it, so that was that. Time to move on.

Colin thought about suggesting they go back to Mycenae, since they hadn't been able to fully explore the site before Nyx and Duran had showed up, but his gut was telling him that the belt wasn't there. As much as he didn't want to admit it, Ambrose was probably right. So many people visited that site it was unlikely a cache of ancient artifacts had been overlooked.

He dove into his notebook, flipping from page to page, but he already knew what he was going to find. Nothing. None of his research had ever mentioned the belt or any of the other Herculean artifacts being moved from their resting place in Mycenae.

Hitting a dead end with his own research, Colin pulled out his laptop and did a little digging through the research he'd "borrowed" from Sam. Unfortunately, Sam hadn't done any digging—of the literal or research kind—on Hippolyta's girdle either.

Plan C. To the internet.

As with most things on the web, there were plenty of conspiracy theories, half-truths, and flat-out lies. Most of the resources he found were simply a recounting of the various Greek myths surrounding the belt but nothing serious about what would have happened after Heracles sailed off with it and presented it to the king.

Several pages into his search results, Colin found an intriguing link titled "The Fall of Eurystheus." Clicking the link led him to an academic paper written by a Professor Aleksy Kyrkos that was buried deep in the digital archives of Athens University.

Colin spent the next hour reading the original paper and diving into everything he could possibly find about the professor. The more he read, the more convinced he was that this guy had to know something. There was nothing conclusive in any of the documents online, but Colin's gut was screaming at him.

The click of the door opening startled him, pulling him out of his research stupor. He glanced up at Selene as she entered. "What's wrong?"

She blinked blandly at him. "Nothing's wrong. Why do you ask?"

It was hard to say. Something about her demeanor felt off. Like she was already defensive before he'd even opened his mouth. "Did something happen with Ambrose? Is he all right?"

Relief flooded into her eyes. "Yes, he's going to be fine. He'll bother everyone in the hospital for a while, then head home."

Colin's instincts told him that wasn't what she'd been thinking about when she walked into the room, but he didn't push. "I have a lead."

Her eyebrows winged up, and she parked herself on the corner of the bed closest to where he was sitting, wrinkling the pristine white duvet. "I'm all ears."

"We need to head to Athens University to talk to Professor Kyrkos."

She leaned back on the bed, propping herself up on her hands. "I'll bite. Why do we need to talk to this professor?"

Colin explained about the paper he'd found and the research he'd been doing. "This guy's whole field of study is about where Greek myth meets Greek history, and he studied King Eurystheus extensively. If anyone is going to know where the belt is, it's him."

Selene tipped her head sideways as she stared at him. Then, shocking the hell out of him, she jumped to her feet and said, "That's only an hour-and-a-half drive. Let's go."

He smirked. "As flattered as I am that you believe me, we have a bit of a problem." He nodded to the window, which revealed the darkened street outside. "It's nighttime. The professor isn't going to be at the university right now."

She glanced at his smug face and then the window. He could tell she was fighting a battle between logic and letting him win. "Fine." She huffed and sat back down. "We'll leave first thing in the morning."

It definitely wasn't awkward *at all* as they got ready to sleep and climbed into their separate beds. Colin kept wanting to come up with something to say that would take things back to the way they'd been before they fell into bed together, but everything he came up with just sounded trite. With a final huff, he gave up, rolled over, and attempted to get some shut-eye.

He woke with a startled yelp when Selene smacked his shoulder. "Get up. We need to head out."

Colin blinked several times, trying to get his eyes to focus. A quick glance at the hotel window showed it was still dark outside. "The sun isn't even up yet. Why on earth are we leaving right now?" His voice sounded rough even to his own ears.

"Night is generally the best time to do things that are illegal."

His eyes popped wide open. Selene was standing next to his bed, fully dressed in her uniform of jeans and a dark tank top. She had her hands on her hips and her head cocked sideways like she was going to start tapping her toe impatiently any second.

"What are you talking about?" Colin sat up, the duvet sliding down his chest and pooling in his lap. Selene's eyes traced the motion of the bed linens before snapping back to his. Clearly she wasn't immune to him, despite her insistence that sleeping together was a mistake. He sent her a cocky grin.

She rolled her eyes and crossed her arms. "We need to pick up supplies of the munitions variety. Generally frowned upon by much of polite society."

Ah. That was what she was talking about. She wanted more weapons. After their encounter with Nyx and Duran at Mycenae, he wasn't going to argue. Maybe she would finally trust him with a gun.

"What are you smiling about?" she asked.

"Absolutely nothing, Red." He threw off the covers and stood, which brought him within inches of where she was glaring at him. He stretched and reached his arms for the ceiling. If his pecs happened to brush her breast in the process, it was her fault for standing so close, right?

She let out a disgusted huff—which was *not* reflected in the interest he saw in her gaze—and spun on her heel to walk away. "Get dressed. We leave in ten." With that, she grabbed her bag and stalked out of the room.

Congratulating himself on rattling her, Colin dressed quickly and tossed his stuff back in his bag. He was out the door less than two minutes after she was.

Selene was already waiting in the SUV—the driver's seat, obviously—when he made his way out of the hotel. He tossed his bag into the cargo area and climbed in beside her. "Where to, boss?"

She glanced at him out of the corner of her eye but didn't comment on the new nickname. "You'll see."

She pulled out of the hotel parking lot and turned right, heading toward the edge of the city. Several minutes later, Selene pulled the vehicle off the road and into a construction site for some sort of enormous warehouse or office building. There were piles of gravel and concrete blocks everywhere and a rough structure built out of huge steel I beams with towering concrete columns that would probably turn into staircases or elevator shafts at some point.

Selene parked the SUV in the corner of the dirt lot but didn't immediately get out. They sat in silence for at least ten minutes before there was a quick flash of light from the direction of one of the towers.

"Stay here," Selene said before slipping from the vehicle and stalking in the direction of the flash of light.

Normally he would have pushed back against being left in the vehicle like a child—not that anyone would bring a child to an illegal arms deal—but he figured maybe her source was twitchy or something. It wasn't like Selene couldn't take care of herself.

He saw her slip into the doorway of the concrete shaft and disappear from view. Several minutes went by, and he started to get a bit worried. Not that she needed him to worry about her, but he hadn't heard a peep. He stared intently, squinting against the dark to try to make out any sense of movement.

The snick of a hammer being pulled back made Colin's head whip around. Standing next to his door was a middle-aged bald man who was absolutely stacked with muscles. In his hand was a semiautomatic pistol pointed directly at Colin's head. The dude smirked, then gestured with his gun for Colin to exit the vehicle.

How in the hell had this dude crept up behind him? With only a small knife in his back pocket, Colin didn't have a lot of options.

He put his hands up to show he didn't have a weapon. When the guy nodded, Colin slowly opened the door and got out, careful to always have his hands in view.

"Who the hell are you?" The gun was once again pointed at Colin's head.

"Um, nobody?" Colin tried.

"I'm sure. Just a random person who chose this particular lot to take a quick nap in?" The guy grunted out his disbelief.

Colin glanced around quickly, looking for anything he could use to get himself out of this mess. There was some heavy construction equipment behind the guy that he might be able to use as cover, but he'd have to get around him.

Maybe he could try another way first. "Look, I have no idea who you are. I'm supposed to be meeting a woman. She told me she was going to meet me here for a quick blowie before work, you know what I mean?" He winked at the dude and put his hands down.

The dude glared at him. "A woman?"

"Yep. I totally get it if you're not into that sorta thing. Dudes can be pretty hot too sometimes, am I right?" Colin leaned back against the SUV, his hand slowly creeping toward his back pocket.

The wall of muscle took a step closer, and Colin froze, wondering if he'd gone too far.

"I'm not interested in men."

"Okay, that's cool. I'm sure the ladies all love you, right? All those muscles?" He traced his eyes from the top of Baldy's head to his toes, checking him out with a slow grin and a waggle of his eyebrows.

The man's forehead creased, and his eyes narrowed. Fortunately, his arm also relaxed, giving Colin the opportunity he needed. Colin's hand snapped out, grabbed the dude's wrist, and shoved Baldy's arm so the gun was no longer pointing at Colin's chest. Since the gun didn't immediately go flying out of the other man's hand, Colin stepped closer and turned his body, twisting the other man's arm and forcing him off balance. Colin pinned Baldy's arm between his elbow and his armpit, immobilizing him.

"What was your next idea?" Selene's droll question came out of the darkness behind him. "He outweighs you by a least sixty pounds." She slowly walked around them until both Colin and the trigger-happy dude could clearly see her.

Colin didn't move and didn't let go of the other man's arm or the hand holding the gun. "I've got moves. You don't know all my secrets."

The corner of her mouth twitched up. "Sure you do." She turned her gaze to the man Colin was holding immobile. "Nikos, I presume?"

The man blanched, looking from Selene to Colin and back again. "You're who I'm here to meet? There's no way." The skepticism was clear in his voice.

Selene rolled her eyes.

"I told you, man. I'm just here for a woman." Colin winked and made the guy scowl again.

"Can we do business, gentlemen? Or are we all going to stand around being misogynistic assholes?" She crossed her arms and cocked her hip, the perfect picture of boredom.

"Fine by me," Colin said as he let go of the dude's arm. Colin could practically see the thoughts running through Baldy's head before he lurched toward Selene, the gun swinging in her direction.

Selene's hand whipped out and gripped Nikos's wrist to immobilize him while her other arm wrapped under his armpit and around his shoulder. She pivoted in place and threw him over her shoulder flat onto his back. She stomped on his gun arm and towered over the dude as he let out a pained moan that he clearly tried, but failed, to muffle. "Are we done with the dick-measuring contest?" Her clipped tone clearly conveyed her frustration.

Nikos nodded from his prone position. "We're done."

"Great. Now lead on." She stepped back but didn't completely move out of his personal space.

Nikos got to his feet and took a hasty step back, tucking his gun back into its holster. "This way."

They followed Nikos to his black SUV and watched him lift the tailgate. Three large bags were lined up in a neat row. Selene rapidly unzipped each of them, did a quick visual inspection of the contents, removed one small box, and closed them up. She handed the box and one large bag to Colin to carry and grabbed the other two herself.

"Tell your boss that the payment should be in his account in the next five minutes. Also, be sure to convey that my organization will not be doing business with his again until such time as his men learn to show a little respect."

Nikos grimaced, clearly not looking forward to passing along that message.

Without another word, Selene turned back to their own vehicle and began loading the newly acquired gear in the back, not even bothering to watch Nikos drive off. With the weapons tucked away, they climbed back into the SUV and started driving.

As they pulled out of the construction area, Colin finally looked at the box he still had in his hands. It was a cell phone to replace the one she'd shattered. *Sweet.*

"Are you expecting to start a small revolution?" Colin asked as they finally hit the highway.

She didn't even take her eyes off the road. "No, I just like the idea of being prepared. The situation at the ruins could have gone very badly. I refuse to be that unprepared again."

"Fair enough." They lapsed into silence, and Colin watched the landscape as the sun slowly rose over the horizon.

They were almost to Athens when Selene finally asked, "A blow job? Really? Is that the best you could come up with?"

Colin froze, unable to read her tone. He glanced sideways at her out of the corner of his eye. Luckily for him, the corner of her mouth was twitching slightly, like she was trying not to laugh. He breathed a quiet sigh of relief. "He seemed like the kind of guy that would go for that sort of thing." The full implications of her words finally sank in. "Wait, you heard that? You were there the whole time and didn't step in?"

The grin finally spread across her face. "I wanted to see what you would do. I would have stepped in if I felt you couldn't handle it."

As far as backhanded compliments went, that one took the cake. It was good to know that she had some faith in him while simultaneously admitting that she half expected him to fail. "Gee, thanks."

She chuckled. "You did fine. I may even reward you with your very own Beretta for your troubles. As entertaining as it was to see you flirt with the arms dealer, it might have been easier if you'd been armed instead."

They arrived in Athens, and Selene navigated the streets in their overly large SUV until they arrived at the university. She parked in the lot closest to the professor's office.

"According to the schedule I dug up online last night, Professor Kyrkos is supposed to have office hours from nine to eleven," Colin said. Despite their early-morning rendezvous with Nikos, they'd arrived just before nine o'clock.

"Then let's do this."

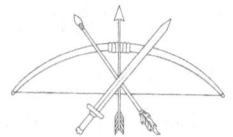

Chapter Twenty-One

A THENS UNIVERSITY WAS LESS than two hundred years old, but the buildings were designed to look like those of ancient times. The large stone columns rose majestically, drawing the eyes to the peaked roofs and the statues of famous classic Greek philosophers perched on top.

Selene watched Colin as he strode confidently across the campus, somehow seemingly at home in a place he'd never been before. It was hard to remember that Colin had not always been a thief. Briefly, he'd been an academic and would have fit right in at a place like this, where students sprawled out on the bright-green lawns with books open in front of them. He seemed to naturally fit among the stone architecture and the prestigious atmosphere in a way she never would.

The slight bump in his waistband from the pistol she'd just slipped him reminded her that while he may have been an academic at one point, he was clearly no longer that person. Now he was something much closer to herself. Not the same, mind you, but they were both on the wrong side of the law. The difference was that she did it for noble reasons, and he did it for personal gain and money.

Selene tried to shake off her wandering thoughts as they approached the history department. She automatically assessed everyone they passed for signs of a threat. It wasn't that she was expecting danger, but it was always a good idea to be alert and pay attention. Who knew what trouble would find them next?

Colin carefully navigated the hallways that thankfully weren't yet packed with students. Most of them were probably still asleep, trying to take classes as late in the day as humanly possible. They arrived outside of the professor's door, and Colin rapped on the wood with a sharp crack.

A muffled voice called out something in Greek.

"He said we're welcome," Selene helpfully translated.

Colin rolled his eyes at her. "Yeah, got it, thanks. I know both Greek and Latin. Did you forget I was literally getting a PhD in anthropology and Greek mythology?"

She shrugged. Sometimes that was very easy to forget.

Colin entered the office as instructed and paused in front of a man who was probably in his midfifties. He had large dark slashes for eyebrows, a receding hairline, and a bushy mustache all set into a rather squarish-looking face.

"Professor Kyrkos, I presume?" Colin asked, with a slight bob of his head in acknowledgment.

The professor's eyes narrowed as he took in Colin's jeans and leather jacket. His gaze bounced to Selene, who had taken up residence just inside his office door, then returned to Colin. "Yes, how can I help you?" he asked in lightly accented English, his gaze mildly suspicious.

Colin turned on his high-wattage smile and extended his hand. "My name is Colin Wolfe, and I'm studying under Dr. Samuel Treadwell of Georgetown University. I'm in the country doing some research for my dissertation and was wondering if I could bend your ear for a few minutes if you have some time."

The cloud of suspicion cleared somewhat. "Dr. Treadwell, yes, lovely man. Interesting areas of research too. We met at a conference in New York several years ago."

Selene admired Colin's acting skills. His blazing smile didn't give a single hint that everything he said was a lie.

"I'm sure you two had quite a lot to discuss. That's part of the reason why I'm here. I recently came across your paper titled 'The Fall of Eurystheus' and thought you might be able to help me with a research project that I've been working on."

At the mention of his research paper, all remaining doubt cleared from the professor's eyes, and his whole face brightened. "Of course! Eurystheus is one of my passions! Such a misunderstood part of Greek history and myth. In fact, most of my colleagues didn't agree with my findings that Eurystheus was real and not just a story, but Professor Treadwell was one of the few people that agreed it was possible."

Colin sat in one of the chairs facing the professor's messy desk and perched on the very edge of the seat. There was a sparkle in Colin's eyes that Selene wasn't sure she'd ever seen before. He started diving into the details of what his "research project" was all about, some of which were true and most of which were a very hand-wavy version of reality.

She let the two men geek out over their chosen field and surveyed the room. It was exactly what she pictured a professor's office would look like. Every surface was covered in papers, file folders, books, and maps. An entire wall was filled floor to ceiling with bookshelves, each one crammed so full that books were lying sideways on top of the neatly aligned rows and the bottom shelves spilled onto the floor.

Selene kept an eye on the nutty professors when Kyrkos started rifling through his desk. He yanked out a tattered book and ran his finger down the text to point out to Colin things that honestly bored her to tears. She'd live through history once. She didn't need to repeat it again.

She began to wander around the small space, taking in the trinkets he kept mixed with his books and the items he felt important enough to display on his walls. She stopped in front of a large replica of an old-looking map, one that showed the approximate layout of the ancient world. Most of the major sites from Greek history were listed, though only a few had pins sticking out of them. The obvious ones were Athens and Mycenae, but for some reason, there was also one random pin stuck in the southwest corner of Rome, right on the Tiber River.

"What's this?" Selene interrupted their animated discussion and pointed to the pin on the map.

Colin turned to look at her, his hazel eyes glowing with excitement. "That, Red, is exactly what Aleksy and I were just discussing."

He was already on a first-name basis with the professor? Of course he was. "And what's that?" she prompted when he didn't continue.

Colin stood, clearly reluctant to be drawn away from whatever it was that the professor was showing him in the text. "It's Professor Kyrkos's theory that at some point long after Eurystheus died, the spoils that Heracles collected for him were moved."

"Moved where?"

Colin nodded in the direction of the map. "To Rome. Specifically, to the Temple of Hercules Victor. It was built in the second century BCE by Romans, but it's built from Greek marble. The professor has a theory that the artifacts were collected from Greece and moved after the Roman temple was finally completed. He believes that the final resting place of every Herculean artifact is in that building."

It sounded too good to be true. "That seems a little too on the nose. Why wouldn't someone have found them by now? It doesn't look like that big of a structure, and there's a whole modern city built around it."

The professor was nodding. "You are right, of course. The building was added to the World Monuments Fund almost thirty years ago. Restoration efforts have been conducted to preserve its history. People have been over every square inch of the place."

Any budding hope Selene had vanished. There was no way the professor could possibly be right. She looked at Colin, whose hazel eyes sparkled with excitement. It was quite cute if she was willing to admit it to herself. "Clearly I'm not following. You just told me that that entire building has been searched, yet you're also telling me there's a cache of artifacts there that no one knows about."

Colin jumped to his feet and began to excitedly pace the small office from one messy bookcase to another. "Exactly. The professor believes the artifacts are under the temple, not inside it."

Selene rolled her eyes. "So we just go talk to the Italian government and ask if they'll pretty please let us dig up their historical monument to recover artifacts no one in their right mind believes are real?" She crossed her arms and leaned back against the wall. This whole excursion was starting to feel more and more like a wild-goose chase. The only reason she wasn't giving up right this minute and heading back to Themyscira was because of Nyx and Duran. As long as they still believed that the belt existed, they would tear through the entire ancient world looking for it. They needed to be stopped.

Colin stopped pacing and cocked his head at her before letting out an exasperated huff. "No, of course not. Aleksy thinks there's a chamber under the building. The key will be figuring out how to access it."

"Oh, is that all?" Selene was only mildly relieved that they weren't talking about a hole in the ground covered in hundreds of tons of marble. They were just talking about finding an access point into an underground chamber that no one has managed to find in over two thousand years. No big deal. It would probably be a walk in the park.

Colin smirked at her. "Come on, Red. What's life without a little adventure?" His wink did naughty things to her that she'd rather not think about.

"I have plenty of adventure in my life," she grumbled under her breath. It was too much to hope that he hadn't heard her, because he chuckled.

Selene didn't like feeling out of her element. She was well versed in weapons and combat. She knew how to use all the vast array of technology she had at her disposal, both to protect things and to break into places she wasn't supposed to be. But she'd lived through the ancient times these men were discussing with such reverence. She knew how harsh and chaotic things had been and knew exactly how awful any documentation or recordkeeping would have been back then, if it even existed at all. Relying on records that were several thousand years old to find something that may or may not still exist in the here and now seemed foolish.

A throat cleared loudly behind her, pulling her from her thoughts. "Ticktock, time's a wasting." Colin was standing by the door to the professor's office. He gestured with his head toward the hallway.

She nodded at the professor, then followed Colin into the hallway. Maybe it was time for some trust. If Colin believed he was on the right track, who was she to question him? His information had gotten them this far.

They made their way back to the rental car and climbed inside. Selene pulled out her phone to start making arrangements. She'd just loaded up on weapons, so they wouldn't be flying commercial. Lucky for them, she was rich. With Ambrose still in the hospital, she would have to ask someone else to make the arrangements, but this was what they did. Her company could get her access to anything she needed, legal or otherwise. A private jet to bounce from country to country in Europe was a snap.

"A plane will be waiting for us at the airport in two hours," she said as she hung up the phone.

"They're just going to look the other way when we show up with a small arsenal?" Colin asked incredulously.

"They'll be paid to look the other way." It wasn't the first and wouldn't be the last time she'd done something like this.

"And people don't catch on that Blackburn Industries occasionally does some stuff that's not quite on the up-and-up?"

She turned to look at him head-on. He knew more about her than almost anyone else at this point, save for Ambrose. What was the harm in telling him the rest? "Our Special Operations department, which Ambrose runs, is very good at what they do. Blackburn Industries is the legitimate legal company that funds and supplies our less-than-legitimate endeavors."

His eyes narrowed and his head cocked sideways. "Yeah, I got that from listening to you and Ambrose on the way to Mycenae. But why do you take the risk? You have a billion-dollar company that protects some of the most priceless art and antiquities in the world. You know those customers would drop you immediately if they found out some of the stuff that your Special Operations department does. You're an Amazon, for God's sake. A do-gooder from way back. I just don't understand why you do the things you do."

She felt like he'd stabbed her straight in the heart. No one else in her life had ever called her out like this. No one had enough of her backstory to do it. Somehow this anthropologist turned thief had stripped her bare and poked at her raw spots in a way that left her exposed and vulnerable. She wanted to rage. She wanted to punch something. Instead, the truth poured out of her.

"Because I'm not! I'm not an Amazon. I'm not a do-gooder. I'm tainted and not worthy of any of the delusions of grandeur you have in your head. I'm a trained fighter, someone who has the power to try to help others who can't help themselves. People who have been screwed over by circumstance or hurt by others."

For the second time in two days, she felt tears welling behind her eyes. She blinked to try to keep them from falling. No way was she going to cry in front of this man.

His hand hesitantly reached out and settled on her arm, rubbing small circles. "Red, I don't have a clue where this is coming from. Yes, you might be one of the most terrifying people I've ever encountered, but that doesn't mean you aren't a good person. It definitely doesn't mean you're not an Amazon. Those other chicks might be scary, but you have them beat hands down. You're good at what you do, and you look rather sexy doing it, if I do say so myself." He winked at her. "I can't imagine anything you could have done in your incredibly long life that would make me or anyone else think any less of you."

Her head fell back against the driver's seat. Here it came, her biggest failure in life. She closed her eyes and took a deep breath as pain welled up inside her. If she had to look at him, she never would have been able to confess her sins.

"Thousands of years ago, when Kalli was queen the first time, there was this village in Greece called Akalia that I stumbled on during one of our adventures. The people were so desperate. They had no food, no protection. Someone had been intercepting their trade caravans and raiding their food stores. As if that wasn't enough, the person kept coming back and demanding payment in exchange for not attacking them. At first they refused to pay. Then warriors came in the middle of the night. They slaughtered some of their farm animals and kidnapped several of the women, who were never seen again. After that, the villagers were scared not to pay even though they couldn't afford to.

"When I found them, they were desperate for any help they could get but, understandably, they didn't trust an outsider to help them. It took a while to gain their trust, but I eventually did. I declared myself their protector. I made it my job to try to fix their situation. The problem was that they didn't know who their tormentor was. Apparently the person in charge never showed up themselves, always sending underlings to do their dirty work. I made it my life's mission to figure out who was blackmailing them and stealing their food and coin.

"One day, I was called away to a neighboring city to assist with a mission for Kalli. The mission went sideways, and I was ambushed, barely escaping with my life. After reporting my failure to Kalli, I headed back to Akalia. Only Akalia wasn't there anymore. The town had been razed to the ground. Homes were burned, crops destroyed, bodies strewn about. No one had been left alive, not even the children. And there, standing right in the middle of the destruction—her sword dripping with blood—was Nyx. Not only did I disappoint my queen by not completing the assignment, but I utterly failed Akalia in every way possible. Nyx was never held accountable for what she did, because shortly thereafter Nyx staged a coup and overthrew Kalli, exiling her and her closest friends from Themyscira. The next time I saw Nyx was six days ago."

Silence settled heavily, and Selene took a deep breath. Someone else finally knew about her biggest failure. The reason she did what she did. She hadn't been able to save the people of Akalia from Nyx's horrific treatment, but she could damn well save people today. No one deserved to live in fear, and she made sure they didn't have to.

"You know that's all bullshit, right?" Colin's voice broke the tension.

Selene's eyes flew open, and her head whipped around. How dare he question her story? He hadn't been there. She had.

"Calm down," he cut her off before she could say anything. "I'm not doubting your story, only your sense of blame. What happened in that village was awful, no argument there. What's bullshit is the fact that you're blaming yourself for it. You are not the one that attacked them. You are not the reason they died. The blame for that lies one hundred percent at Nyx's feet."

It wasn't anything she hadn't tried to convince herself of in the past. "Yes, but . . ."

"But nothing. You tried to help them. You did what you could. In fact, it wasn't even your fault that you weren't there the day Nyx came calling. Kalli sent you on a mission, right? Do you blame her for sending you away that day?"

Her stomach clenched at the very idea. "No, of course not. She's my queen. I would bow to her every request."

Colin was nodding like he expected that answer. "Right. Of course you would because that's who you are. You're a good person who believes in the difference between right and wrong."

She opened her mouth to speak and was interrupted yet again.

"Amazons don't have last names. It was something I noticed while in Themyscira." She shook her head at the abrupt change in topic, but he barreled on. "That means that no one else gave you the last name Blackburn. You chose it for yourself, didn't you?"

She nodded numbly. "It felt like it described me appropriately. Black and charred to a crisp." It came out quietly, but he clearly heard her. His hand slipped from her forearm to slide into her grip and squeeze.

He leaned across the center console of the large vehicle, his soft voice soothing her rough edges. "Red. Selene," he corrected, "you are not the monster you think you are. I understand why you do it now, why you take the risks that you do. You will never be able to help everyone, but I'm sure those you are able to help will be forever grateful for what you did for them. Even if, as I suspect, those victims never find out who was responsible for making their lives better. You risk your life to help people every day. I kind of think that's a textbook definition of an Amazon, don't you?"

Some of the cracks in Selene's soul started to fill. What pull did this man have on her? No one, in more than twenty-five hundred years, had been able to soothe the rough patches she held close to her heart.

What was it about him? He was hot as hell, obviously, but that wasn't it. He was a thief and a historian, but clearly there was more to him than just his outward profession. If all he'd wanted to do was steal something and sell it for the money, he could have vanished a long time ago and saved himself from the trouble that they were currently in. And, yes, he was obviously interested in the history and the myth behind the belt they were chasing, but that didn't explain everything either. Underneath it all, he was a good person who was trying to help stop Nyx from taking over the world or whatever her grand plan was. Wolfe may still be "the Shadow," but he was also just Colin, the man helping her stop something terrible from happening.

His hazel eyes searched her face as if he was trying to read her thoughts. His concern for her was obvious in his wrinkled forehead and hesitant smile.

With a quiet moan she leaned across the center console and captured his lips in a searing kiss. He hung back for a few seconds before his hands came up and speared through her hair, holding her mouth against his as he deepened the kiss. His hands shifted as they lightly traced her jaw and slid down the side of her neck.

She grabbed his shoulders and tried to tug him closer to her, but the awkwardness of their positions in the vehicle made it impossible for her to get as close to him as she wanted. She settled for running her hands up and down his muscular shoulders and biceps. The waistband of his pants was calling to her. She slid her hands down his ribs and up under the bottom of his shirt near his lower back, reveling in his warm skin. She traced around to his front and began tugging at the button of his jeans.

"Selene, wait," he said between kisses that were progressively lighter and more teasing. He pulled back, resting his forehead against hers.

"Why are you stopping?" she asked, her desperation obvious even to her own ears.

"Red, did you forget where we are?"

Her eyes opened to the sight of the interior of the SUV and, through the windows, the grassy quad, where undergrads sprawled to enjoy the sun as they studied. Right. Not exactly a great place for jumping someone's bones.

"Right. Of course." She pulled back to the driver's seat and reached for the keys to get the vehicle started. "We have to go meet the plane anyway." She tried to hide her disappointment, but it seeped through nevertheless.

"Oh, don't you worry. This isn't over." Colin leaned back in his seat, a knowing smirk on his lips.

"It isn't?"

"Not a chance."

Well, in that case . . .

Selene revved the engine and peeled out of the parking lot.

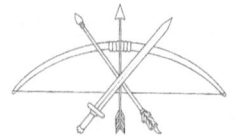

Chapter Twenty-Two

COLIN HAD TO HAND it to Selene. When she said her people were very good at what they do, she wasn't lying. They pulled into the back side of the airport, where the smaller personal planes were. Sitting outside one of the hangars was a small jet with the steps already down and waiting for them to board. Standing practically at attention was a well-built man dressed head to toe in black tactical gear. As soon as the SUV pulled up, he snapped into action, meeting Selene at the driver's-side door and opening it for her before she had a chance to do it herself.

"Thank you, Marcus," she said as she slid out of the vehicle. "Please make sure our supplies are loaded and stowed appropriately."

"Yes, ma'am." He practically snapped his heels together before heading to the rear of the SUV.

"Ma'am?" Colin snickered, and Selene gave him a side glare.

"Most of my guys are former military. They prefer a clear organizational structure," she said primly. Her nose wrinkled and she frowned. "I hate it, though. I don't care how old I am. *Ma'am* makes me feel ancient."

Colin laughed again as his hand naturally came to rest on her lower back as he urged her toward the steps. "You are ancient."

"Yes, but I don't need anyone to point it out to me."

She pouted, and Colin had the urge to plant a kiss right on the tip of her nose. He refrained himself, however, not wanting to embarrass her in front of her employee. Smothering his laughter, he followed her up the steps into the small, but very nicely decorated, plane.

His jaw dropped slightly as he took in his surroundings. He'd known that Selene was well off—hopefully anyone who had been alive for four thousand years would have had the foresight to invest some money for the future—but this was over the top. The jet had a small kitchen, a seating area with seats covered in buttery gray leather, a bathroom that included a shower, and a bedroom all the way in the back. Their flight to Rome was only a couple of hours, but Colin had every intention of making the most of their time.

He followed Selene to a pair of seats that looked a lot closer to recliners than they did plane seats. They strapped themselves in and watched as Marcus bound up the steps and then closed and latched the plane door behind him. He nodded in their direction before making his way into the cockpit and closing himself inside with the pilot. Within minutes they were taxiing down the runway and shooting into the sky.

"So when we land in Rome . . ."

Colin cut off Selene's question by planting his mouth on hers. She let out a startled noise before relaxing into the kiss.

The soft press of her lips on his was like a drug. The rushing of the plane engines and the swooping sensation of them climbing up to cruising altitude faded into the background as he lost himself in her. He brought his hands to her neck and slowly slid them into her glorious hair, holding her mouth against his own as they traded kisses.

Her hands landed on his shoulders and then slid down his biceps, her nails gently scratching his skin as she traced her way up and down his arms.

He tried to draw her against his chest but was stymied by their seat belts. He came up for air just long enough to verify that the FASTEN SEAT BELT light was off before undoing both of their belts and tugging Selene to her feet. They stumbled their way to the bedroom at the back of the plane before crash-landing on the bed, lips still locked together.

He lifted himself up on his elbows enough that he could look into her lust-drunk green eyes. Her pink lips were kiss-swollen, and a slight blush crested her cheeks.

"God, you're beautiful," he whispered as he planted tiny kisses on her forehead, cheeks, and chin. "I feel like the luckiest man alive to be here with you." He planted gentle kisses down her neck, then moved the strap of her tank top so he could kiss her shoulder.

"Colin," she breathed his name out on a sigh. The blatant desire in her tone caused a warm swooping sensation in the vicinity of his stomach.

Almost of their own volition, his hands landed on Selene's stomach, inching her shirt upward as his hands traced her ribs, brushed the side of her breasts, then tugged her shirt from her completely. He leaned down and worshipped at the altar of her stomach, gently tracing her lightly muscled abs with his fingers. He reached behind her and undid the hooks of her bra, then tossed it in the general direction her shirt had gone.

His hands skated over her velvety-soft skin as he skimmed her ribs, then finally cupped her breast. His thumb captured her nipple, rubbing back and forth until he'd coaxed it into a tight peak. He leaned down and sucked the bud into his mouth. He flicked his tongue back and forth, making her gasp.

Her hands latched on to the back of his head, holding him in place as he lapped at her breasts, moving from one to the other to make sure they got equal attention. Her head thrashed on the pillow as her fingers raked through his hair. She moaned softly, making him smile around the nipple in his mouth.

His hand slid down her torso until it reached her waistband. He tugged gently on the button and then pulled down the zipper. She helped him by lifting her hips, and within moments her pants were on the floor. Her lacy bikinis soon followed, leaving her bare to his hungry eyes.

"This is pretty one-sided, you know," she teased as she tugged on his shirt.

Colin whipped off his shirt and shucked his pants and boxer briefs in record time. They came back together, his hot skin against her silky-smooth body. He groaned as they touched from their chests to their toes. She arched up into him, pressing them even closer together.

He slid down her body, brushing kisses on every inch of her skin. Once he reached her toes, he started making his way back up a little bit at a time, ensuring he hit all the sensitive places, like the arches of her feet and the backs of her knees.

He reached the apex of her thighs and gently nudged her knees apart to give him access to her most intimate places. Her head popped off the pillow as he spread her folds and licked her core. A filthy moan came out of her mouth, and she squirmed under his ministrations. He caught himself smiling as his tongue flicked her clit relentlessly. She bucked her hips forcibly enough to dislodge him, so he clamped one of his arms around her to hold her in place as he tormented her with pleasure.

Her fingers pushed into his hair, restlessly tugging at the strands with her fists. The slight sting only drove him on as he did his best to drive her out of her mind.

"Colin, I . . ." She couldn't finish her thought. When her words failed her, she tried another way. Her hands clamped around his upper arms as she forcibly tugged, dragging him up her body until they were face-to-face. "I need you inside me, now."

Only too happy to oblige, Colin lined himself up with her entrance and pushed forward until he was fully seated inside. He let out a guttural moan there was no possible way he could have held back.

The warm clamp of her inner walls around his cock felt like nothing he'd ever experienced. He'd had sex with plenty of women, but none of the rest of them were Selene. He had no idea if she had some Amazon gift that made sex just that much better, but he doubted it. It was just her. She was amazing and, at least for the moment, she was his.

His eyes met hers as he pulled himself almost completely out of her, then slammed back home. Her pupils blew wide with desire, and her eyes rolled back with pleasure.

Colin pounded into her with a rhythm that drove them both wild. Her legs came off the bed and snaked around his waist, holding him to her and allowing him that much deeper into her body.

Unable to ignore the tempting feast in front of him, he latched his mouth onto one of her nipples and sucked it deep into his mouth.

Selene keened a high-pitched noise as she came, bucking beneath him has he pounded into her a few more times before his own orgasm ripped through him, making his whole body go rigid. He collapsed on top of her with a slight "Oomph."

She chuckled slightly, her fingers tracing unknown patterns on his damp back.

"I'll move, I swear. Just give me a minute to regain feeling in my limbs." His offer was muttered somewhere in the puddle of her hair, where his head had landed.

He could hear the smile on her face when she responded, "Take your time. I'm not breakable."

That might be true, but that didn't make it any less rude to collapse on someone and cut off their ability to breathe. With more effort than it should have taken, Colin rolled off her, landing next to her on the mattress.

He had no idea what he'd been doing with his romantic partners in the past, but if this was what sex was supposed to feel like, they'd clearly been doing something wrong. Sex with Selene was on a whole different level.

And once he regained the ability to speak, he was going to tell her that. Probably.

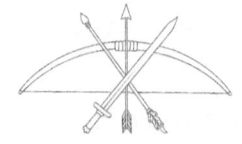

Chapter
Twenty-Three

"SO HOW DOES A geeky PhD student somehow become one of the most wanted thieves in the world?" The sweat hadn't even dried on their skin yet. Selene traced her finger through the light sprinkling of hair on Colin's chest, her head using his shoulder as a pillow.

It wasn't that she didn't understand his motivations for getting back at Sam. In Colin's eyes, Sam had ruined his life, and therefore Colin was bound and determined to get back at him for it. Her brain had a hard time reconciling the notion of a history buff suddenly deciding to brush up on their lockpicking and hacking skills.

Colin sighed, his arm wrapping around her naked shoulders and keeping her in place, snuggled up against him. "It's a long story," he finally said.

"Where am I going to go? We're on an airplane."

The silence stretched on for what felt like an eternity. She was about to tell him not to worry about it when he finally started speaking.

"My story isn't particularly unique." He traced patterns on her upper arm as he spoke. "My dad was a bastard that used to rough up my mom whenever the idea popped into his head. One night—I have no idea what was different than any other—she decided to fight back. She'd been in the middle of cooking dinner, and he came in with some drummed-up excuse of a complaint. He grabbed for her, but she still had the kitchen knife in her hand. She lashed out. Her aim wasn't great, so it wasn't like she killed him or anything, but she did give him a nice deep gash down one of his arms. In retaliation, he flung her across the kitchen. Her head smashed into the cabinets. She stopped moving, but he didn't care. He called her a stupid bitch and stormed out of the house, leaving the door wide open behind him when he left. I don't know why that part of the memory is so distinct, but it is. I could feel the cool breeze across my cheeks as I sat there next to my mother, hoping she wasn't dead." His voice trailed off.

"How old were you?" Selene asked, almost wishing she hadn't started this conversation in the first place. The pain in Colin's voice was evident with every word he spoke.

He cleared his throat. "Five." He took a deep breath. "Eventually I grabbed the phone and called 911. They took her to the hospital. Thankfully apart from a minor concussion, she was fine. Equally thankfully, we never saw my prick of a sperm donor ever again. But that left my mom as a single parent with no real job experience who suddenly needed to support a five-year-old kid. We made do for a while, but as the years went on, it seemed to get harder, not easier. We moved around a lot, most often when my mom couldn't make rent on whatever shitty apartment we were living in. The older I got, the more bitter I became."

Selene wrapped her arm more fully around his torso and gave him a quick squeeze. She felt for his younger self. She'd met far too many kids through the years in similar situations. It was never easy to live through trauma at such a young age.

His hand stopped tracing doodles on her arm and began to rub up and down, almost as if he was trying to keep her warm.

"From there you can probably guess what happened. I met a guy named Ian from a similarly shitty background, and we bonded over our shared crappy childhoods. We fell in with a bad crowd and started getting into trouble. Little stuff at first, you know? Shoplifting, pickpocketing, that kinda stuff. Eventually we escalated to boosting cars to make a quick buck."

Selene propped her chin on Colin's chest and finally looked him in the eye. "So what changed? How did you go from aspiring kingpin to anthropologist?"

Finally, a true smile crossed his face. He brushed a stray red lock away from her face, his fingers tangling in her hair. "Mr. Peterson. He was my world history teacher in eleventh grade. He saw something in me that no one else ever had. He sort of took me under his wing and helped me realize that there was another option for me."

Selene was grateful that Colin had had someone like his history teacher in his life. Yes, in the end, he still became a thief, but he still had someone who believed in him, someone who convinced him he could strive for more. Things could have gone so much worse for him had he not had that positive influence in his life when he did.

"So you went off to college and eventually grad school," she prompted.

He planted a swift kiss on the tip of her nose. "Yep. I worked really hard to turn my grades around, went to a community college until I could transfer to a better school. Then wound up in the PhD program at Georgetown." He trailed off.

Right. Colin had been working on his PhD under Sam. "What really happened between you and Sam?" she finally asked when he didn't continue.

Colin sighed and squeezed the arm that was wrapped around her, like he was trying to bring her closer even though they were already plastered together as tightly as they could be.

"It was during my second year of the program. I hadn't been studying under Sam for very long, so we didn't know each other all that well, but I was doing my best to impress him. I thought that if I could get him and his impressive academic credentials on my side, I would have an even better shot of getting what I wanted out of life.

"One afternoon I went by Sam's office to see him. He wasn't there, but the office door was open, so I went inside to wait for him. That's where Dr. Jonathan Aldridge found me." He practically spit out his name, venom lacing his tone. "Dr. Aldridge was, and may still be, Sam's coworker in the history department at Georgetown. Unfortunately for him, he also had a hobby that involved losing lots of money at the poker tables. Aldridge had apparently built up quite the pile of gambling debts and was looking for a quick score to settle his IOUs."

"How did that involve you?" Selene asked.

"In the worst coincidence in the history of coincidences, Dr. Aldridge went to grad school with Mr. Peterson. Apparently they'd been friends for years. As Mr. Peterson was helping me straighten out and apply to various colleges, he was also sharing with his friend all about the teenage thief who was turning his life around and getting ready for university. He was quite proud of me, according to Aldridge." Colin's eyes unfocused slightly, as if he was getting trapped in the past.

Selene could see where this was headed but didn't interrupt. He needed to get it out.

His gaze zeroed in on her face as he snapped back to the present. "When Aldridge found himself in a heap load of financial trouble, naturally he thought of me. Me and the precious gold-and-emerald necklace that Sam had unearthed at one of his digs in Greece."

"What did he do?" Selene asked quietly.

"He demanded that I steal it and give it to him. He told me that if I didn't, he would ruin any chances I had of making it in the fields of history or anthropology." Colin let out a short laugh, but it was clear he didn't find any of this funny. "I didn't believe him. I told him no. I had gotten out of that life and had no intention of going back to it. I thought he was bluffing. The next day I found out that the necklace was missing and that Aldridge told Sam he saw me sneaking out of his office with it."

"Did you ever get to tell your side of the story?" Selene snuggled closer, her face settling in the crook of his neck.

"Yes, but it didn't matter. Sam believed his friend and colleague, whom he'd known for years, rather than some grad student he barely knew. The dean took his side, and I was expelled the next day." He shrugged, but Selene could tell it was anything but casual.

"So how did "the Shadow" come to be?"

"I was not in a good place mentally after getting kicked out of school. It had been my one escape plan from my old life, and I'd had it yanked out from underneath me. I wound up back in Chicago, licking my wounds, and reconnected with my old pal Ian. He'd never gotten out of his old ways and had escalated into breaking into houses and stores and stealing stuff he could fence. It didn't take much for me to fall back into the life. I thought I had escaped, but the Aldridge situation pushed me over the edge. If people were going to accuse me of stealing, I might as well do it and make a quick buck in the process, you know? But I also had this need for revenge. Sam and Aldridge had ruined my life, and I wanted to reciprocate. I paid Aldridge back years ago by whispering in just the right ear that I knew where a certain mob family could find a lowly professor who owed them a decent chunk of change. I guess they felt he paid off his debts with a few broken bones and a mild concussion. From there, I took the skills I had honed helping Ian and turned them toward Sam's archaeological digs and museums rather than jewelry stores and high-end houses."

Selene sat up, tugging the sheet to cover her nakedness. "Including the Winthorpe Archives."

His eyes narrowed and he sat up, leaning against the headboard. "Yeah. But how did you know that?"

"Blackburn Industries is in charge of security at the Winthorpe. We were never able to figure out exactly how someone had gotten in and stolen Hatshepsut's diamond."

Colin had the nerve to chuckle. "That's one of yours? The truth comes out. Let's just say it had to do with a gullible guard, a mini electromagnetic pulse, and a lot of luck."

"Wait, that's all you're going to give me?" Selene lunged at him, her fingers aiming for his ribs.

He laughed and tried to dodge her tickling fingers. He rolled over, pinning her underneath him and securing her hands to the bed near her head. She could have easily overpowered him, but where was the fun in that?

His mouth swooped down and captured hers in a searing kiss. By the time he pulled back Selene was breathless and craving more. "I can't tell you all my secrets, now can I?" He winked at her before hopping off the bed. "Now if I'm not mistaken, we'll be landing soon, so we should probably get dressed."

She knew he was probably right. The flight from Greece to Rome wasn't that long, but she was still sad to see all that sexy tanned skin get covered up with his plain old jeans and a T-shirt. With a small huff, she rolled off the bed and tugged on her own clothes.

They buckled back into their seats just as the pilot announced their descent into Rome. The wheels of the plane bounced down on the runway, and they taxied to a hanger some distance away from the main terminal of the airport.

Marcus came out of the cockpit, glanced from them to the messy sheets that were just visible through the open door of the bedroom, and sent a knowing look in their direction. Whatever. Selene wasn't ashamed. Colin noticed Marcus's smirk and leaned over the armrest and gave her a quick kiss near her ear. Marcus nodded at the gesture, then turned and opened the plane door, allowing them to disembark.

Yet another dark SUV was waiting for them. They climbed into the front seats—Selene driving, as usual—and waited for Marcus to see to their luggage and the weapons before venturing off into the city of Rome.

Selene had ensured they had a hotel room booked at the hotel directly across the street from the Temple of Hercules Victor, requesting a room with a view that overlooked the temple itself and the river on which it sat.

"So what's the plan?" Selene asked as she plopped down on the bed closest to the window. She glanced outside and saw the swarms of people wandering the streets of Rome, including throngs of tourists with their giant cameras and smartphones on selfie sticks, taking hundreds of photos of every little thing.

"Well, I don't know if you've noticed or not, but there's a fence surrounding the temple." He nodded to the window.

Selene glanced outside and squinted toward the round building diagonally across the street. There was a black, six-foot fence surrounding the temple itself. A minor inconvenience in the grand scheme of things, but still an annoyance. "Right."

"For now we can go play at being tourists for a few hours. We can scope out the park the temple is in, check out the surrounding area, that kind of thing. Then after dark we can hop that damn fence and check out the building itself."

The plan sounded as good as anything she would have come up with, so she nodded and bounced her way off the bed. "Lead on."

Colin gave her a small smirk and headed to the hotel room door, which he opened and then waved her through. She rolled her eyes at his gesture of chivalry and left the room. As they made their way through the hotel lobby and out onto the sidewalk, Colin snagged her hand in his.

She glanced at him in surprise, but she didn't pull away. His small smile warmed something inside her that she hadn't felt in a long time. Maybe ever. She couldn't remember the last time she'd walked down the street holding a man's hand. Her life didn't lend itself to casual romantic strolls. Flying bullets and dirty knife fights were far more common in her reality than being able to leisurely spend time with a romantic partner.

Because that was what he was, much to her astonishment. They may not have known each other long, and they may have come from totally different places, but something had changed in the last few days. They were involved now, even if they hadn't put a name to whatever it was that they were doing. She wasn't dumb enough to press him on it either. She was over four thousand years old. The term *boyfriend* sounded so childish when compared to the hundreds of lifetimes she'd lived through. Besides, she didn't want to think too hard about the fact that Colin was only twenty-eight. It made her feel like a cradle robber.

They crossed the street from their hotel to the small park where two temples stood. First, they paused in front of a small rectangular building featuring crumbling columns and surrounded by a metal fence that prevented them from getting too close. There was nothing particularly noteworthy about the temple, but they feigned interest nevertheless.

"What are you thinking about so hard over there?" Colin asked, a slight teasing note laced through his question.

"You. Me. Us," she answered after a moment's hesitation. His eyebrows winged up, but she plowed through. "When we first met, did you ever think this is where we would end up?" she asked, gesturing between them with her free hand.

"I mean, I always hoped we would wind up in bed." He winked. "But no, I didn't give it much thought beyond that. You?"

She couldn't stand being the sole focus of his piercing stare, so she headed toward the round temple across the park, the one they had actually come to see. Since she still had a grip on his hand, he followed. "No, I can't say I did. In most people's eyes, you and I wouldn't make any sense." One of the most obvious reasons floated to the top of her mind. She was immortal. Colin was not. If Selene did commit herself to some sort of relationship—romantic or otherwise—with Colin, she was going to have to live with the idea that she would inevitably lose him. Whether it was in some freak accident during a heist a year from now or sixty years in the future, ultimately, he would pass, and she would live on.

"Maybe not. But if you haven't figured it out by now, I'm not someone who really cares what other people think. Most people thought I wouldn't amount to anything other than a thief, and I proved them wrong, at least for a while. When my life went to shit again, I adapted. Maybe not in a way most people would approve of, but that's just more evidence that I never gave a crap what other people thought."

She made a noncommittal noise as they glanced at the outside of the relatively small temple the Romans had dedicated to Heracles. Time had ravaged the structure, carving large chunks out of several of the columns that surrounded the circular building. The temple had obviously been restored over the years, with metal bands securing several of the columns. In addition, a large glass window and door that led inside the building were clearly modern.

Nothing about the building screamed that there was a hidden chamber underneath that held treasures and artifacts. The grass and trees in the surrounding park showed no signs of hidden entrances, staircases, or even a sewer grate. They maintained their casual stroll, eventually winding up at the other end of the park in front of the Fountain of the Tritons, which was shaped like an eight-pointed star. The fountain had two intertwined sculptures of Triton—a lesser god of the sea—holding a basin from which water poured.

"Where to next?" Selene asked, glancing at Colin out of the corner of her eye. "Should we move to another location?"

He brought her hand to his lips and brushed a soft kiss over her knuckles. "Are you always this impatient?" He was smiling as he asked, taking away the mild sting of his words.

The answer was no. She wasn't. When she was working a case, she could focus intently for as long as she needed to. She could sit still in unmoving silence for hours while she was stalking one of her prey. So what was it about this situation that was different?

The answer came more easily than she anticipated. It was Colin. It was their hands, which were still joined, and the soft smiles he sent her way. None of those were things she would have been doing if she were with Ambrose or any of the rest of her team.

It wasn't like she didn't spend time with men. She was a sexually active person. What she wasn't was a relationship person. Is that what was happening here? Were she and Colin in some sort of relationship? Did she dare ask? Did she even want to know the answer?

It was like she had an itch she couldn't scratch right between her shoulder blades. She tried her deep-breathing technique, taking a long inhale and then slowly blowing it out as she rolled her shoulders and relaxed each muscle. It didn't do any good. She was tempted to try to reach her hand up behind her to see if she could contort her way into reaching the area, hoping that would relieve the sensation.

Beside her, Colin stopped walking. Since they were still holding hands, Selene was tugged to a stop. Colin gave a small yank on her hand, bringing her around to face him on the sidewalk. "Just stop." He grabbed her other hand as well, linking them together in a small circle. "There's no need to crawl out of your skin, or whatever it is you're trying to do right now. Whatever this is between us, we'll figure it out and move at whatever pace you're comfortable with. Right now, this is just us. Two consenting adults enjoying each other's company. You're still you and I'm still me. You could still crush me like a bug if you chose to, though I sincerely hope you won't." He winked at her, and the knot she hadn't even noticed forming in her stomach started to unwind.

He was right, of course. They weren't committed to each other in any way. There was no reason for her to be freaking out, and there was no reason she couldn't enjoy a lovely afternoon in Rome with a gorgeous man. She let out a deep breath, her shoulders dropping from where they had crept up around her ears.

"There we go."

She nodded at him. "Thanks. I'm not sure what that was about."

He let go of one of her hands and started walking again. "It's okay to be nervous around someone as attractive as me. Don't worry. You'll get used to it." He sent her a roguish wink as they circled the back side of the park.

They made a circuit around the entire park, then branched out down some of the streets that led away from the temple. It was halfway across the Ponte Palatino bridge—which spanned the nearby Tiber River—that Colin spotted it. Strategically placed in the stone walls that paralleled the road above and held back the river below were several archways built directly into the stone.

"Bingo."

"What am I looking at?" Selene asked.

Colin smiled with a catlike grin. "Our way in. Allow me to introduce you to the ancient Roman sewer system."

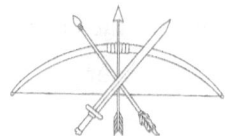

Chapter Twenty-Four

RECONNAISSANCE HAD BEEN COMPLETED. The quick circle he'd taken around the temple with Selene had showed him everything he'd needed to know about the building. There was only one way in and out, and it was covered by security cameras and motion sensors. All of that was, of course, after having scaled the fence that was put there precisely to keep people away from the ancient structure.

He didn't honestly believe that the entrance to the vault was going to be as simple as a trapdoor in the middle of the floor of the museum. If it was that easy, it would have been found years ago, and he would have heard about it. While it wasn't likely that what they were looking for was in the temple, they still needed to be thorough. With any luck, they could be in and out quickly.

He had a good feeling about the sewer system, though. He often had to think on the fly in his line of work, so he trusted his gut. While the Roman sewers were a known archaeological remnant of an ancient civilization and had likely been explored before, they were also still in use today. The likelihood that people would just randomly, or even deliberately, go wandering into a sewer system for fun was low.

Now he just had to worry about getting them in and out without being detected or damaging anything. No sweat, though, because this was what he did. Selene may have all the money and resources she could want at her fingertips, but he was the Shadow. Getting in and out of places he wasn't supposed to be was sort of his specialty.

The museum would probably be straight forward. He didn't see any security measures nearly as advanced as anything provided by Blackburn Industries, so some of the more old-school tricks should work. Some dark clothes, a lockpick kit, maybe a signal jammer, and they'd be good to go.

Colin was more worried about the sewers. If they were really the entrance to a hidden underground vault full of treasures, then what awaited them down there? Why would no one else have found them in the two-thousand-plus years since the Romans hid them? There had to be some sort of trap or trick to it.

What he needed was information. Lucky for him, one of the most famous libraries in Rome was a twenty-minute walk from their hotel. The Lincean Academy, also known as the Library of the National Academy of Science, dated back to the sixteen hundreds and had once counted Galileo Galilei as one of its prestigious members. The history fanboy in him couldn't wait to see it with his own eyes.

Before he set off, he made a quick shopping list of supplies and gave it to Selene to do her thing. He was sure she would be able to acquire whatever he needed for their nighttime of breaking and entering. He grabbed his trusty notebook, shoved it in his back pocket, and headed off into the streets of one of the oldest cities in the world.

A beautiful stone exterior and countless arched windows greeted him when he finally arrived. The academy and the library were tourist destinations, much like many of the buildings in Rome. Despite several disasters over the centuries, parts of the library's collections dated back hundreds of years.

Colin wandered around, glancing at scrolls and early books that were carefully preserved in glass cases. His anthropologist heart was singing in his chest at the beautiful collection, while his thieving fingers tingled. Some of the pieces in the collection were priceless, which was exactly the sort of thing the Shadow usually targeted. In his world, there was no such thing as priceless. Someone always had money they were willing to spend to acquire yet another feather for their cap or a one-of-a-kind piece that they knew they wouldn't be able to show off to their friends even though they desperately wanted to.

He shook off the sensations. He wasn't here to rob the place. The artifacts in the library were where they were supposed to be. He didn't need the money, and even if he did, it would hurt his soul to steal such antiquities. He wasn't here for himself. He was here to stop Nyx and Duran.

Glancing around the space, he found a librarian and dusted off his rusty Italian to ask if she could point him to any resources that would detail the ancient Roman sewer system. He was pointed to a section that contained works on architecture, and he dove in, doing his best to become an expert in the short time he had before they closed for the day.

Several hours later—his head swimming with facts that may or may not help them in any way—Colin made his way back to the hotel room to find Selene. Just as he was about to step into the hotel lobby, Colin's phone buzzed in his pocket. He tugged it out and glanced at the name on the screen.

Ian Getty.

Why on earth would Ian be calling him? Colin hadn't spoken to the other man in months. Despite Ian being the reason he'd gotten into a life of crime, he'd never wanted to involve him in any of his larger heists. Part of that was to protect Ian from any consequences that might happen if they'd gotten caught, but more importantly, he'd felt like his arts and antiquities thefts were more of a personal vendetta. It was something he'd needed to do alone. Sort of a giant middle finger not only to Sam but to the world at large that thought he wouldn't make anything of himself.

He was reluctant to take a call from Ian while he was in the middle of the adventure he was on with Selene, going after the belt, but given how long it had been since they'd spoken, Colin couldn't help but feel like if Ian was reaching out, there was a reason.

Against his better judgment, he tapped the little green icon to accept the call. "Ian, long time no talk, man."

"Wolfie, my man." Ian's teasing voice rang through loud and clear. "You been avoiding me or something?"

Honestly, yes, but he couldn't tell that to his oldest friend. "Of course not. I've just been doing a lot of traveling lately." Well, that wasn't a lie, at least. Ian didn't know that he was the Shadow, and Colin intended to keep it that way.

"Good. That's real good. Because I got something that I think may interest you." The way Ian trailed off, it was clear that whatever he had to offer wasn't on the right side of the law. "The score should be off the charts. Enough to retire on, bruh."

Colin's mouth dried out, and he found himself having a hard time swallowing. A few years ago—hell, a few weeks ago—he might have jumped at whatever it was that Ian was offering, but something had shifted for him. The thrill of the steal and the high of the sale no longer seemed as appealing as they used to.

An image of Selene popped into his head, her red curls falling enticingly down her back, her mesmerizing green eyes narrowed in suspicion and accusation as she glared at him. She was strong enough to snap him like a twig, but it wasn't fear of her that was holding him back with Ian. She made him question his life. She made him want to be a better person, which was a shock to him. He'd had only one positive influence in his life, and that had been Mr. Peterson back in high school. He'd spent his life keeping people at arm's distance for a reason. Yet somehow Selene had slipped around his defenses and gotten inside. Much to his surprise, he wanted to keep her there. For however long he managed to keep her in his life.

"Sorry, man. No can do. I'm in Europe at the moment."

There was a long pause on the other end of the line. "Look, I need you on this one, Colin." There was no more teasing tone in Ian's voice. If anything, he sounded nervous. "I may have agreed to a job that I don't actually have the skills or the crew to pull off."

Colin leaned against the exterior wall of the hotel, closed his eyes, and pinched the bridge of his nose. Of course Ian had gotten in over his head. He shouldn't be surprised by that, yet somehow he was. "Who?" he choked out. "Who are you in deep with?"

Ian's sigh was evident even from halfway around the world. "Scolvetti."

"Damn it. You know better than to get involved with that rat bastard." Luka Scolvetti was a loan shark, slumlord, and all-around horrible person who had his fingers in just about every illegal deal in the city of Chicago. He wasn't a person you wanted to cross, and if you owed him something, he wasn't particularly picky about how his guys collected on that debt. "How much do you owe him?"

"One point two."

Colin's eyes flew open. "You owe Luka Scolvetti more than a million dollars? What the hell are you mixed up in?" There was no way that Ian would have that much money to pay off what he owed. No wonder he'd agreed to a job he wasn't able to pull off. He must have thought the payout would get him clear of his debt. There was just one problem. Ian Getty was a small-time crook. He didn't have the knowledge or the resources to pull off a job worth that much cash.

Colin pulled his phone away from his ear and started looking up flights. There was a plane taking off in three hours that he could probably make if he hurried. His finger was hovering over the button to book a ticket when Ian finally answered him.

"Does it really matter? I'm in deep, man. The least the Shadow could do is pull his best friend out of a jam."

Ian wasn't supposed to know that name. No one was supposed to know that name. How did this keep happening? Was it possible he hadn't been as careful as he'd thought he'd been? "What did you just say?" Colin asked as he put the phone back to his ear to make sure he didn't mishear.

"You heard me the first time, bruh. I'm the one that took you back in after you went off to rich-boy college and it blew up in your face. I helped you get started in this world, and then you left me behind and went after the big scores. The ones that would have set both of us up for life. You cut me out of the most lucrative jobs you've been pulling for the last four years. And I get it, you know. Every man for himself. You saw an opportunity to strike it big, and you did. You do you, man. But now I need your help. Think of this as payback for all the jobs you cut me out of. If you'd brought me with you, I wouldn't be in this deep with Scolvetti. You hearing me?"

A clarity he hadn't felt in a long time settled inside Colin. He knew exactly what he needed to do. "You're right, Ian. I'll help you."

Selene couldn't believe what she'd just overheard. It was painfully obvious that Colin had no idea he'd stopped to have his phone call directly below the open window of their hotel room.

It was also equally obvious that she had been right in the first place. Leopards didn't change their spots. Despite any change she thought she'd seen in him the last few days, Colin was a thief, and he probably always would be. And it wasn't like she'd forgotten that. Before he'd left for the library to do whatever research he'd felt he needed to do, he'd given her a list of supplies that included things like lockpicks, pry bars, and high-tech equipment that could override the museum's surveillance systems.

Then why did it still feel like such a betrayal? She was well aware that she was taking advantage of the skills he'd gained while being the Shadow. Somehow, though, since they were fighting for the greater good—stopping Nyx from whatever her evil plan was—Selene had convinced herself that it was okay. That there was nothing wrong with siding with a thief.

Maybe, even though she didn't want to admit it to herself, there was more to it than that. Despite her earlier freak-out, she could only continue to lie to herself for so long. She had feelings for Colin. She didn't fully know when they'd started or how she'd gotten this deep, but her heart was on the line now more than it had ever been. She hadn't known Colin long, but he'd managed to weasel his way inside. She cared about him. Maybe even more than cared about him. She couldn't quite bring herself to use the L-word—it was way too soon for that—but her emotions were definitely involved.

What would she do if Colin left her in Italy and ran off to help his childhood friend? Could she do what they were about to do without Colin? The actual breaking-and-entering part, almost assuredly. Just because she ran a security company didn't mean that she didn't understand how to circumvent the very things her company installed to increase security.

There was, however, the other side of what they were doing. The historical and archaeological part. Yes, Selene was over four thousand years old, and she'd lived through all the centuries during which the ancient Greeks and Romans were in power. But she would fully admit that she didn't know enough about them or their cultures to have been able to get as far as they'd already come. Plus, they weren't done yet. Who knew what lay ahead in the quest to locate the belt and keep it away from Nyx once and for all?

With a deep sigh, she came to the only logical conclusion. While she may not trust Colin as much as she had been hoping she could, she also couldn't do this without him. So for now they were still going to have to work together. She would use him for his skills and his knowledge and nothing else.

They'd only just gotten involved, so no matter how fast her heart had softened, she would just have to harden it all over again if he tried to leave. No more sleeping together. No more sex. Just two professionals working together to accomplish a mission.

The door to the hotel room swung open, and Colin stepped inside. His face lit up when he saw her sitting on the couch by the window. He immediately crossed the floor and tried to draw her into a kiss. In a moment of weakness, she let him, his soft lips caressing hers. She sank into the gentle connection, which he didn't try to take any deeper or push any further. Just a soft reconnecting after having been separated.

She steeled herself and pulled back, knowing she needed to stop this for her own protection. She couldn't let herself get pulled back into a physical relationship with him, no matter how much her body yearned for his. This was strictly business.

"Did you find what you needed?" she asked when her voice was strong enough that she believed it wouldn't waver.

The most adorable spark of excitement shone from his eyes as he described visiting the library and what he learned. She tuned out slightly when he started listing names of all the famous people who had apparently been members of the library over the years, but her ears perked back up when he started describing the sewers themselves.

"They were originally designed as an open-air canal system that, over time, was enclosed to increase efficiency. However, these aren't the sewers you'd think of in modern times. They're large enough for a grown person to walk in. They were also primarily used for directing water away from the major buildings of ancient Rome, not so much for sewage in the way we do now."

"So you're basically saying there's a labyrinth of relatively clean tunnels under the city, and that we can access them from right underneath the Temple of Heracles," Selene said, summing up his mini TED Talk.

He nodded once, a definitive bob of his head. "Yes."

"Works for me."

They agreed that they should still do a quick inspection of the museum, even though neither thought it was likely to have the belt inside or even easy access to the vault underneath. Just because they didn't think it was the right place didn't mean they still shouldn't do their due diligence.

While they were planning their approach, there was a knock on the door. Selene crossed the floor, her hand hovering over the knife strapped to her thigh, and peered out the peephole. When she saw it was Marcus, she opened the door and gestured for him to come in. Without saying anything, Marcus hauled in a box full of equipment and gear and deposited it on the small coffee table in front of the couch. He gave Selene a quick nod in acknowledgment and then left them alone once more.

Showtime.

Chapter Twenty-Five

S OMETHING WAS OFF. COLIN couldn't quite figure out what had changed, but Selene was acting strangely. Oh, she was still helping with every aspect of their caper. And she'd kissed him back when he came into the room, but it hadn't felt the same. Sadly, he didn't have time to figure out what was going on with her. They were minutes away from breaking into a historical site, and he needed to be on the top of his game to make sure they didn't get caught. He didn't particularly relish the idea of being sent to an Italian jail. Though it was probably at least nicer and more modern than the jail in Themyscira.

That made his mind spin right back around toward Selene. He hadn't been gone very long. What on earth could have happened in the few hours they'd been apart that would explain her suddenly frosty exterior?

It was fine. They were fine, he assured himself. Maybe after they had located the damn belt and stopped Nyx from her power grab, he'd offer to take Selene somewhere. Maybe a beach vacation or a mountain villa. Something relaxing for just the two of them. No work, no thieving, no vigilantism, just them. He smiled at the thought, then smothered it when Selene gave him a strange look. That was for later. This was now.

Colin dressed in the all-back tactical gear that Marcus had dropped off for them and loaded up his pockets with everything he would need. He slung a large knife over his shoulder and tightened the straps so they were snug to his chest.

"A machete?" Selene asked dubiously.

He shrugged. "You never know."

The sun had long since set, and the streets were empty of people. It was closer to dawn than midnight when he and Selene grabbed their gear bags and slipped out of the hotel into the cover of night.

Streetlights were never a friend to someone trying to stay out of sight. They dodged from the corner of one building to another as they made their way across the street. They entered through the back of the park, on the opposite side of the door to the temple. Hiding among the low trees and bushes there, Colin reached inside one of the pockets in his jacket and pulled out a small electronic device. With the tap of a few buttons, he turned on the signal jammer and mounted it to the fence in front of him. With any luck, the small device would override the wireless signals on both the security cameras and the alarm system.

He nodded to Selene, and as they'd discussed, she cupped her hands and made a step for him. He put his foot in her outstretched hands, and she used her superior strength to give him the boost he needed to get to the top of the anti-scaling fence, pull himself over the top, and land on the other side. She did one of her wicked parkour moves, pushing off a nearby boulder and launching herself over the fence to land lightly next to him.

They crept toward the entrance to the temple. Colin glanced at the security camera, which was pointed directly at the door, and was pleased to see the light was off. The signal jammer appeared to be doing its thing. He glanced around quickly to make sure there was no one around to see what was going on, then pulled out his handy-dandy lockpicking kit and got to work on the door locks. There were, of course, electronic locks as well, but with any luck the jammer was working on those too.

The lock opened with a barely audible click, and he tugged the door open. The alarm panel on the wall was still on, though not blaring any sort of alarm. He pulled out his multi-tool and cut the wires for good measure.

Selene was right behind him. She pulled out a small flashlight from her own pockets and clicked it on.

Since the temple wasn't open to the public, Colin hadn't been sure what they would find inside the building. It was a relatively small space, but there were several display cases that hugged the curvature of the walls. As quickly and as quietly as they could, Colin and Selene circled the space looking for anything that could point them toward what they were looking for.

The display cases included a sword that was purported to be that of Heracles himself. Colin glanced at it longingly. The history that the sword represented was simply astonishing. Most people thought that Heracles was a myth, a figure in a story that was everything you could want in a hero. However, the same was true for the Amazons, and yet here he was, ten feet away from the sexiest Amazon on the planet. Selene was alive and well and looked like she wanted to kick someone's ass.

After thoroughly checking every nook and cranny inside the temple, there was only one possible answer. The belt wasn't there, and neither was the entrance to a hidden vault.

Time to go.

They slipped out of the building the same way they came in. Colin even locked the door behind them, though there was nothing he could do about the cut lines in the alarm system. They hopped the fence in the same place as before, and Colin grabbed his electronic toy and slipped it back into his pocket.

They exited the back of the park close to the Tiber River. Across the street, next to the bridge, was a set of steps that led down to the river below. They jogged down quickly and headed to the huge archways that marked the entrances to the sewer. The first one they came to was completely walled over. There was no getting in that way unless they wanted to go back for a jackhammer or some explosives. Not the most subtle move they could make.

A few hundred feet down the riverbank was a second arch. This one was far less grand than the first, but that didn't matter. What mattered was that it was open. Colin led the way down the embankment and under the arch. Once he was deep enough in the tunnel that he wouldn't be spotted by anyone outside, he clicked on his flashlight and glanced around.

The sewer was plenty tall enough and wide enough that they could stand up straight, but they couldn't walk next to one another unless one of them wanted to be walking in the stream of water that was making its way to the river. The walls were made of uneven stone blocks that were damaged in a few places, allowing the root systems of enterprising plants and trees a chance to thrive in the dark and moist environment the sewer provided. The corridor's ceiling was arched and stretched as far as the eye could see. In the distance other tunnels intersected the one that they were in, branching off to other areas of the city.

Colin strode along the narrow sewer ledge, scanning the walls for any clue that might direct them toward a vault or something of the sort. He went several hundred feet and saw nothing. With a huff, he turned back around, making Selene jump.

He knew he was missing something; his senses were tingling. What could it be?

"Care to share with the rest of the class?" Selene said as she watched him walk back in the direction they'd come from.

Colin glanced down at the watch on his wrist, then looked at the ceiling directly above him. "It's right here." He muttered to himself, again looking at the walls around him.

Selene crossed her arms and arched an eyebrow. "What's right here?" She also looked around, seeing the same blank walls that he was.

He showed her the GPS coordinates on his watch "We're directly under the temple. If they were going to hide something down here related to the monument, it only makes sense if it's in this area."

She nodded to acknowledge his point and turned to search the walls.

There was nothing obvious. There were no doorways or archways or even nooks. Colin ran his gloved hands over the stones, trying to push on them to see if perhaps any were loose. No such luck. He moved a few feet over and tried again.

His glove snagged on one of the roots that clung to the wall. He tugged, but it had somehow gotten stuck. He used his other hand to remove the glove and left it dangling from the stupid tree. He grabbed the glove, intending to yank it off the wall and put it back on, but the root it was attached to moved when he touched it.

The tree root should have been climbing down a sturdy stone wall. It should not have given way when he touched it. He pushed on the root more deliberately. Once more, it gave.

"Holy shit." He pushed his fingers through the dense roots, and where he should have hit a solid surface, his fingers hit nothing but air.

There was a gap in the wall.

"I think I found it." His voice was barely above a whisper, but Selene clearly heard him anyway. Her head whipped around, sending her glorious red hair flying around her face.

"I told you that it never hurts to be prepared." Colin yanked the machete out of the sheath on his back and began hacking away at the roots. Selene pulled out her wicked-looking tactical knife and started on the other side. After several minutes of hacking and sawing, they had cleared enough of the roots that they revealed a small passageway. It was skinny enough that they would only be able to go through sideways, but Colin didn't hesitate. He sent Selene a giant grin, which she returned, and then he plunged into the dark.

The tunnel went back fifteen feet before it took a sharp turn to the right. Ten feet after the turn the passageway opened into a small round room. Leading away from the center of the room like the spokes of a wheel were a series of tunnels each slightly wider than the one they'd just come through. Colin moved to the center of the room and spun in a circle, his flashlight zooming wildly around the walls.

"Dear God, which one do we take?" Selene asked as she joined him.

He had no idea. Not including the opening they'd come through, there were twelve paths. Depending on how long each of the tunnels were, that could potentially be a lot of ground to cover. There had to be some sort of clue that would point them in the right direction.

The tunnels were shaped relatively identically, and each was made of the same stone blocks as the sewer walls. They were dingy, some covered in dirt or moss, but thankfully there were no tree roots this time around.

Colin took an emergency glow stick out of his pocket, cracked it, and tossed it in the tunnel they'd emerged from. No sense in getting turned around and being unable to find their way back out. He wandered the perimeter of the room clockwise, running his hand along the smooth stone as he went. It was painstakingly slow, running his flashlight around the entrance to each tunnel, looking for something that might distinguish one from the other.

Nothing was immediately evident. He didn't allow himself to get frustrated, though. He didn't need to wear his thief hat right now, the one that said get in and get out before anyone saw you. Instead, he had to rely on his archaeology brain. There was no rush. No one was trying to sneak up on them. He had to think logically.

"Let's split up. Look for anything that would indicate which direction we need to go. An arrow, a label, something."

They started at the archway they'd come through and circled the room in opposite directions, diligently searching every inch of the tunnel entrances, archways, and floors. The minutes crawled by.

Thirty minutes later, Colin was about ready to call for a break to grab a bottle of water and brainstorm new ideas. Maybe there was no key and they were just going to have to search each tunnel one by one.

"Is this . . ." Selene hesitated before she continued. "A deer?" Her voice was quiet, like she didn't trust her own eyes or her conclusion.

Colin rushed to where she was standing just inside the third tunnel she'd searched. She was squinting intently at one of the stone blocks halfway up the wall.

He could see why she wasn't certain. There was definitely something, but it was so damaged he couldn't tell if it was intentional or not. He pulled a small soft brush out of his kit and began to clear away the dirt and moss that clung to the small carving.

"I'll be damned." It absolutely was a deer. There was no mistaking it.

"What do you think it means?" Selene asked.

Colin's mind was whirling. "Let's see if we can find any others."

They split up again, heading down the adjacent tunnels. Within minutes, he'd found another. "It's a boar." He carefully brushed away the debris that had been blocking the ancient carving. It was possible he was the first human who had laid eyes on that overgrown pig in hundreds of years, if not thousands. The thought made him giddy.

"Here's another one!" Selene shouted from a few tunnels over.

Colin once again rushed to her side and watched her uncover a carving of a snake. But not just any snake. It was a multiheaded snake. A hydra. "It's the labors. Heracles's labors," Colin said as he walked back to the center of the room.

"What are you talking about?" Selene asked as she followed behind him.

"Look around us." He gestured broadly. "There are thirteen tunnels off this room. If you subtract the one that we used to enter, that leaves twelve. That's an awfully coincidental number when we're standing under the Temple of Heracles, who famously completed twelve labors."

Selene nodded. "I'm following so far."

"Then you have the images themselves. The one you just found in the second tunnel was a hydra. Heracles's second labor was to slay the Lernaean Hydra." He pointed to the third tunnel, where they had seen the deer. "His third labor was to capture the Ceryneian Hind. *Hind* is another word for deer."

He could see the excitement building in her eyes. It mirrored the rising thrill in his own gut. "That means," he continued as he counted around the room until he got to the ninth tunnel. "This one should lead to Heracles's ninth labor, the girdle of Hippolyta."

Colin crossed the floor, Selene hot on his heels. Colin glanced closely at the walls of the tunnel, examining the stones before finally saying, "I was right. This is it." There, staring at him plain as day, was a carving of what was unmistakably an Amazon warrior. She was wearing what appeared to be a large belt around her waist. "We found it."

Selene came up behind him and stared at the carving. "It even looks like her," she whispered.

He wasn't sure how she could tell, since the carving was so small, but he wasn't about to doubt Selene. He sent her a grin. "This is amazing." He walked back to the center of the room. "Just think of the amount of history down here. The artifacts and treasures. They're probably just sitting in their hidden caches, waiting for someone like us to come along and find them. Can you even imagine the value of the artifacts waiting at the end of these simple stone tunnels?"

His mind was scrambling, trying to put the pieces together to figure out what he was looking at. Many of Heracles's labors were to slay monsters like the hydra or beasts like the Cretan Bull. What trophy could possibly be waiting at the end of those tunnels? Was it the animal's hide? Or perhaps the head? Neither of those seemed like they would hold up very well to the thousands of years that had passed. Perhaps they were something else entirely. Maybe a carving or a representation of the monsters Heracles had slain.

Colin's fingers itched to find out. He took a step in the direction of the first tunnel, the one that would lead him to the treasure of the Nemean Lion, but was cut short when he heard a throat clear loudly behind him.

"Shouldn't we be going this way?" Selene asked pointedly as she gestured down the tunnel with the carving of the Amazon.

Colin shook his head. "Right. Of course." There was plenty of time to come back later and explore the rest of the site. Who knew what sort of history lay buried in this underground vault that needed to be excavated and shared with the world?

For safety's sake, Colin grabbed another glow stick out of his pocket, cracked it, and dropped it in the entrance to the tunnel that hopefully led to the belt, then followed Selene farther into the dark.

Fifty feet into the tunnel their way was blocked by a portcullis. Flanking the large gate were two stone statues, one on either side of the tunnel. The statue on the left depicted an extremely muscular man in full armor, including what appeared to be a metal sword in his outstretched hand. The statue on the right was clearly an Amazon warrior, obviously Hippolyta, given the depiction of the large belt around her waist. Unlike the sword on the other statue, the belt was part of the stone statue and wasn't metal.

It would have been too easy if the belt had just been wrapped around the statue, waiting to be removed.

"Now what?" Selene asked as she walked to the portcullis and shone her flashlight through the gaps in the gate. He joined her and tried to peer into the space beyond, but it was impossible to see with only the small beams of their lights.

"I'm not sure." Colin took a step back and looked around him. The portcullis appeared to be coming from the ceiling, but as far as he could tell there was no switch or lever on this side that would operate the mechanism used to lift the door out of place. Through the lattice of the gate, it looked like there were chains that might operate it, but they were on the opposite side of the gate from where he and Selene were. No help there.

What was he missing now? He ran his hands along the stone walls on either side of the gate but didn't find any buttons to push or loose stones. He got down on his hands and knees and scoured the floor, but the story was the same. No hidden pressure plates or latches to be found. As far as he could tell, the only things on this side of the heavy immobile gate were the statues.

The statue of Hippolyta was exquisite work by a very talented sculptor, but there was nothing special about it. It appeared to be one solid piece of stone and likely weighed thousands of pounds. There were no moving parts or hidden compartments that he could find.

Heracles was another matter. That statue was also made of several thousand pounds of stone. Once again it was all one piece, with nothing that stood out. With one exception.

The sword.

Colin ran his fingers along the blade of the sword to confirm what his eyes were telling him. It was metal instead of stone, and somehow, after more than two thousand years, it was still in perfect condition. The metal was shiny and unblemished, the cutting edge still sharp enough to slice through anything.

"This is impossible. There's no way a weapon this old that's been exposed to the elements, even in a semiprotected place like this, should still be this well preserved."

Selene shrugged. "I've seen it happen before." She came over to inspect the sword as well but didn't seem nearly as impressed.

"What do you mean you've seen this before?"

She shifted her weight from one foot to the other, like the conversation was making her uncomfortable. "When Kalli, Zoe, and I were exiled from Themyscira, Nyx handed us over to a group of Greek soldiers. They tossed us on a boat and tried to sail home. Unfortunately for them, they didn't realize who they were messing with. We overpowered them and took over the ship, but by that time we were outside the veil that protected Themyscira and couldn't return. We landed on the coast of Greece and made camp. Eventually, we decided we had too much weaponry to carry around, so we buried a cache of weapons inside a mountain in Greece—well, a volcano really." She shook her head like she was clearing her mind. "We dug them up two weeks ago."

Colin's jaw dropped. "And they were in good condition? After several thousand years?" It shouldn't be possible. Science backed him.

Selene stuck her hands in her pockets and shrugged. "Looked like new. Kalli had asked Hephaestus, the god of blacksmiths and forges, to protect them for us. I guess it worked."

His brain spun. Colin made his way to the wall and leaned against it. Believing in a race of immortal warrior women was one thing.

He was staring at the proof of that with his own eyes. Believing the Greek gods were real was a step beyond.

Ultimately it didn't matter, though. He could process the Greek gods being a real thing later. That didn't affect him now. Now, the only thing he had to worry about was the puzzle in front of him. There was a locked door, figuratively speaking, and he was on the wrong side of it. He'd been over everything on this side of the gate, and the only remarkable thing was the metal sword sitting in the stone statue.

"I wonder . . ." He walked to Heracles again and reached to where the hilt of the sword was clasped in the cold stone grip of the mighty warrior. "Sorry, my guy." Colin patted the statue's shoulder and then gave a slight tug on the sword.

"What are you doing?" Selene asked.

Colin wasn't sure if he was surprised or not when the sword easily slid free of the statue's hand like it was meant to be removed. He was by no means an expert in weaponry—he'd never had the need to learn to sword fight in his line of work—but even he could tell that the sword he was holding was exquisite. It felt far lighter than it should have given its size. He gave a few experimental swings, and it felt almost natural in his hands.

Turning back to the portcullis, he stared at it blankly. He had no idea how to use a sword to open a gate. He was confident he was on the right path, but the last piece of the puzzle just wouldn't click into place.

He glanced at the statues, studying them. Heracles was on the left, and he was lunging forward, the sword extended in front of him.

Across the hallway was Hippolyta, her sword arm raised, but not in a position to block the blow that her foe was about to land on her.

"Damn it." It couldn't be. He had to be wrong.

"What?" Selene asked. "What did you just figure out?" She came to stand next to him, staring at the statues the same way he was.

It was wrong. Disturbing. And evil enough that he could see some centuries-old game master chortling with glee about how no one would ever be able to solve his puzzle.

"Selene, how exactly did Heracles take the belt from Hippolyta?" His voice was strained, and he braced for the answer he knew was coming.

She narrowed her eyes at him. "You know the answer to that. You told me about it days ago."

"Humor me."

She huffed and crossed her arms. "He stabbed her and took the belt off her body."

Hoping that his conclusion was wrong, Colin had every intention of trying any other solution before attempting the one his gut was telling him it truly was.

He turned toward the statue of the former Amazon queen. He took a few experimental swings at it, but each time the sword glanced off the stone with a clang, causing a few dull sparks.

"It wasn't a slashing blow. Try stabbing her stomach," Selene said, her voice trailing off quietly.

He did as she asked and tried to stab directly at the statue's torso. The impact sent shock waves up his arm, forcing him to drop the sword. It hit the stone floor with an ungodly clamor. Colin shook his arm to relieve the tingling sensation.

Selene glanced at the sword, which had fallen between them on the floor. She stared at it for a while before her head whipped around and she looked at the statues again. He could see the moment everything became clear in her mind. She'd clearly come to the same conclusion he had. It was like, suddenly, everything they'd been through in the last week made sense. She turned to him, her shoulders slumped and her expression resigned. "You have to stab me."

"No." Sick twisted puzzle or not, there was no way he was going to stab her. She may be a hotheaded and stubborn woman who thrilled him and frustrated him in equal measure, but she was his. There was no way he was stabbing her, even if she was the only living Amazon anywhere around. "No, that is not happening. We'll find another way." Colin grabbed the sword from the floor and crossed back to the Heracles statue to return the sword to where he'd found it.

"There is no other way, and you know it." Selene grabbed the sword from where he'd put it in the warrior's stone grip and handed it back to him. "You can bet your ass that if Nyx and Duran showed up here, he wouldn't hesitate to stab her. And she'd not only let him but encourage him."

Hope fluttered in his gut. "That's it. We'll lure Nyx here, and then I can stab her and not you." As much as he didn't like the idea of stabbing anyone, he'd much rather stab the wannabe dictator than the woman he was rapidly falling in love with.

Oh dear God, he was in love with Selene. The sword dropped from his hands once again and clattered loudly on the ground. He stumbled backward until he hit the wall, then slid down it until he was sitting on the floor.

This was not the time for this. He was in a dingy tunnel with barely enough light to see ten feet in front of him. There was a mercenary and a warlord on their trail, and he was currently staring at the woman he'd fallen in love with, who was looking at him like he was off his rocker.

He wanted to laugh. He'd never thought he would fall in love. His lifestyle wasn't exactly conducive to having a partner, let alone a girlfriend or a wife. He wasn't sure he'd ever thought about the word *wife* before without some sort of snide comment attached to it. But suddenly he could picture his life with Selene. They would make an amazing team. He would happily stop thieving if it meant he got to be with her. His skills would probably even come in handy on her vigilante missions.

A soft smile graced his lips. He would change for her. He had already changed for her. A week ago, he wouldn't have hesitated to fly across the world to help Ian out of his mess. Instead, he'd chosen to stay in Rome with Selene, who was currently looking at him like he'd finally cracked.

With newfound confidence, he stood and tugged Selene until she was plastered up against him. He kissed her gently and could feel her surprise before she opened and settled more fully into the kiss. It was Colin's silent promise to her that they would figure it out. Together.

"What was that for?" she asked when he pulled away.

"Just for you." He reached down and picked up the sword from where it had fallen against the stone floor. "Okay, so we'll set a trap and lure Nyx to meet us here. Then I can stab her, and hopefully us re-creating the trial that Heracles had to go through will make this damn gate open and allow us access to the belt."

Selene nodded. "Makes sense. Except for one thing. Nyx is a warrior that has, give or take, about four thousand years more experience with sword fighting than you do. How do you plan on besting her in a fight?"

The question was asked lightly, but Colin's stomach sank. She was right. There was no way that Colin would be able to take Nyx.

"Maybe I could stab her?" Selene asked.

Colin was already shaking his head before she finished her question. "It has to be me. Heracles wasn't an Amazon. It only makes sense—as much as any of this makes any sense—if the person doing the stabbing isn't either." He paused to think. "What if you restrained her somehow?" He was grasping at straws, and he knew it.

A sad smile crossed Selene's face. "You're also forgetting one more thing. I have the gift of healing. If you stab me, I'll just heal."

He had forgotten about that, but he still didn't like it. Selene's healing magic seemed to have gotten weaker even in the short time he'd known her. He didn't want to rely on her being able to recover from a wound he'd inflicted on her.

"Selene, I can't," he said quietly, his forehead bowing slightly to rest against hers.

"Sure you can. I'll help you." She reached out and carefully grabbed the extremely sharp blade and rested the point on her stomach, right below her ribs. "Just take a deep breath and shove."

Panic clawed its way up his throat, threatening to strangle him. There was no way he could do this. "Selene . . ."

"Colin, do it now!" she screamed, then pulled his face down to plant a searing kiss on his lips.

God help him.

He shoved, the blade sliding into her more smoothly than he could have imagined.

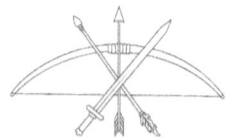

Chapter Twenty-Six

S ELENE HAD FORGOTTEN HOW much it hurt to get a sword thrust through her torso. Sadly, enhanced healing didn't prevent the injuries from causing extreme pain. She slumped forward, resting most of her weight on Colin's shoulders.

"Oh God! What have I done?" he asked frantically. He reached his shaking hand toward the hilt of the sword, but she lifted her own arm to block his.

"I've got this," she said, though it came out much weaker than she thought it would. The painful groan of rusty metal shifting and clanking rumbled nearby. "Besides, I think you need to go deal with that." Her hand flicked weakly in the direction of the portcullis slowly rising into the ceiling.

"What? No." Colin glanced briefly at the lifting gate before he looked back at her. "Baby, you're bleeding. Quite profusely I might add."

The concern in his eyes almost did her in. She was a warrior. She'd been injured thousands of times. Over the years, she'd had plenty of people around her when she was injured, but none of them had looked at her with worry and affection in the same way that Colin was.

It was enough that she almost forgot the conversation she'd over-heard between him and his partner back in the States.

That brought reality splashing back down on her head. She re-leased the death grip she'd had on Colin's shoulders and instead braced herself on the wall.

"Go. This is what we came for. Hopefully whatever's behind that gate will make this all worth it," she said as she wrapped her own hands around the hilt of the sword and yanked. The blade came free of her body with a sickening squelch.

"But," he protested again, his hands flapping in place like he didn't know what to do with them.

She handed him the sword but stayed where she was, leaning up against the wall, allowing it to support her full body weight. "Just go!" she practically yelled, then groaned at the effort it took. She could definitely use a speedup in the self-healing department.

Colin looked her up and down, his eyes narrowing in on the blood seeping out of her stomach, but eventually he did as she asked and walked into the hallway beyond the gate. She watched as he made his way in the dim glow offered by their flashlights. Slowly, so she didn't jostle her wound any more than necessary, she followed in his footsteps, using the wall as a crutch to help her.

The hallway ended about twenty feet farther in, widening into a small nook. In the center of the nook was a stone pedestal, and draped dramatically over the altar was a sight she'd never thought she'd see again: the girdle of Hippolyta.

The girdle, much like the sword, was in pristine condition when it had no logical reason for being so. The leather band with shiny bronze accents was wider than any modern belt. In truth, it was closer to a corset than a belt and would have covered most of her torso from her hips to below her breasts. In the center of the belt was a purple gem with an intricately carved symbol. A bow crossed with an arrow, a spear, and a sword.

The symbol of the Amazons.

Selene slowly sank to the floor, the pain of holding herself up finally overcoming her excitement at finally finding the thing they'd been searching for. As much as she wanted to be across the room with Colin, the pain was overwhelming.

A small not so easily ignored part of her brain was worried about how slowly she was healing the sword wound. When she was at her usual levels of healing, it would have been mostly healed by now. Instead, blood was still oozing slowly out of the gash and being absorbed by her shirt. She had no idea why her healing was slower than usual, but it didn't bode well. Unfortunately, she didn't have time to focus on it. They had a belt to save and a wannabe warlord to stop.

Colin was still standing in the middle of the room, reverently holding Hippolyta's belt. He was running his fingers over it as if it were the finest silk or the most valuable jewel he'd ever seen, and knowing some of the artifacts and artworks he was purported to have stolen, that said a lot.

It had been painfully obvious that Colin had been desperate to go down the other eleven tunnels off the main room. He clearly wanted to see what sort of artifacts remained from each of Heracles's other quests. The real question, however, was what he would do with them if he found them.

Over the last week or so that they'd spent together, Selene thought she'd seen a different side of Colin, a softer side. One that didn't just look at the world through the lens of how much money it could make him. She was curious what he saw when he looked at the four-thousand-year-old artifact in his hands. If he had the choice, would it go back to the Amazons, into a museum, or into the hands of someone who could add a nice stack of padding to what had to be his enormous bank balance?

"Can you believe it?" he finally whispered as he balanced the belt between his hands and turned to face her. "We found it. I'm not sure I believed we would actually do it."

Selene insides warmed at the awe she heard in his voice. Maybe he really had reformed. "I never would have gotten this far without you." She told him honestly. Even if she'd known back in Themyscira what Nyx was after, she would have had no idea where to even start. She had all the modern tracking software she wanted at her fingertips but that could only tell her where Nyx and Duran were, not where they were going. She wouldn't have been able to get ahead of them and beat them to the punch. Especially not while injured.

A shy smile crossed Colin's soft mouth. "Well, you can vice that versa. I probably wouldn't have survived that first battle in Mycenae if you and Ambrose hadn't been there."

Selene shifted, trying to sit up more fully so she could see the belt better. The movement sent liquid fire racing across her torso, and she let out a small yelp.

Colin crossed the floor and crouched at her side. "I don't know why you aren't healing as fast as normal, but it can't be a good sign. Is it possible that you've overtaxed your gift lately? In the past week alone you've been shot, stabbed, broken your wrist, been practically run over by a car, and been in several fights. Or maybe the sword was poisoned?" Colin asked, worry obvious in his tone.

Selene shook her head. "I'll be fine. It's already better than it was." It wasn't a lie, exactly, but it wasn't the full truth either. She had no idea why her healing gift wasn't working the way it normally did. He gave her a dubious look, but she brushed it off.

He shrugged. "So what's our next step? Where do we go from here?"

"Your next step is to walk over here and hand me the belt," a smug voice said from just inside the small room.

Selene's head whipped around toward the voice, the movement agitating her wound and making her let out an unintentional moan. There, standing near the portcullis, were Nyx and Duran. They weren't alone. Sandwiched between the aspiring evil overlord and her well-muscled companion was a head of spiky blond hair and a familiar set of brown eyes, laced with pain. Ambrose.

Damn it.

Selene tried not to wince when she saw that he was paler than usual, his skin shining with a fine sheen of sweat. He'd been shot three days ago. There was no way he should have been up and about, much less trekking underground on some ridiculous treasure hunt that had nothing to do with him.

"Selene, I must admit, you aren't looking so good," Nyx taunted from across the room. "What have you been up to during these last twenty-five hundred years? Babysitting our good-for-nothing queen?"

With a roar of rage, Selene pushed herself up off the cold stone floor, but before she could even attempt to lunge at Nyx, Colin stood up and held his hand out to stop her.

"Don't. Going off half-cocked isn't going to solve anything. Think of Ambrose," Colin said quietly, but it was clear from Nyx's laugh that she heard him anyway.

He wasn't wrong, but that didn't make it any easier for her to hold herself back. Nyx's smug face needed to be rearranged, and she knew just the Amazon to do it. With any luck, Nyx didn't know who Ambrose was to her. If she knew that Ambrose was her son, Selene couldn't even imagine how much worse this situation could get.

The stabbing pain in her gut reminded her, yet again, why she shouldn't be doing much of anything at the moment, no matter how much she might want to. She didn't want to look weak in front of Nyx and Duran, but her injury wasn't giving her much choice. She couldn't help Ambrose if she was too injured to move. Selene leaned against the wall for additional support and to take pressure off her wound.

Colin turned to face their unwanted guests. "Why should we give you the belt?"

Nyx's eyes practically rolled out of her head, and she let out a heavy sigh. "Because if you don't, I'll kill the lackey. Obviously." She gestured to Ambrose. "Honestly, is this your first time being threatened?"

Lackey, that was good. If Nyx was calling him snide nicknames, she clearly didn't know their actual relationship.

Colin glanced at Selene with a look of warning, then took a few steps in Nyx's direction with his hands open in front of him, making it clear he wasn't holding a weapon. "And if we give you the belt, how do we know you won't just kill him anyway?"

Duran snorted and sent a knowing look in the direction of Nyx, who returned it. "I guess you will just have to take my word for it." She smirked.

Nothing good could possibly come from Nyx getting her hands on the belt. From what Selene had seen of the state of her sister Amazons—who had spent the last twenty-five hundred years under her iron fist—the busty, raven-haired woman across from her should never be allowed to rule anyone ever again. The brutal methods she had for keeping people in line should never be used on anyone.

If the stories about the belt's power were true, the moment Nyx put it on, her own Amazonian gifts would be amplified. The charisma she had to bend people to her will would increase. Her merciless tendencies would only escalate. Lives would be ruined or lost, and it would all be because of the vicious woman in front of her.

Selene felt like her soul was being torn in two. On one hand, Nyx couldn't be allowed to carry out whatever horrible agenda she had in mind. On the other hand, Nyx was holding Ambrose hostage—the only person Selene had ever loved as a mother and a caretaker. She'd protected thousands of people over her long life, but she'd only mothered one of them.

She looked into Ambrose's pain-filled eyes. She made the only decision she could. He would have to understand.

"Colin, don't give it to her," Selene said. There had to be another way.

Ambrose slumped slightly, but she knew that he would have made the same call had their positions been reversed. As much as they loved one another, the greater good came first.

Duran shoved the muzzle of his pistol harder into Ambrose's temple, which pushed him sideways slightly. Ambrose let out a small moan of pain that he clearly tried, and failed, to keep in. A dark pool of blood spread slowly on the front of his white shirt. His stitches must have ripped. He needed to get to a hospital so they could repair the damage.

"Selene, think about what you're doing. This is Ambrose." Colin smiled sadly. "We both know what he means to you. There's no way in hell I'm letting that bitch take him from you, even if it means handing over the belt. We'll find another way."

She watched in distress as Colin crossed the small room and held out his hand, offering the belt to Nyx. With a cruel shove, Nyx propelled Ambrose farther into the small room, causing him to stumble and fall painfully to the stone floor. He groaned but didn't move from where he'd landed. Selene tried to make her way over to him, but the going was slow.

With a feverish look in her eyes, Nyx snatched the belt from Colin's outstretched fingers. He squeezed his hands into fists but let them fall to his sides rather than attacking her. "Now if what a certain Greek history professor told me is true, this is where things get interesting."

Greek history professor? Selene froze in place and slowly turned to look at Nyx.

"Oh yes, we located your wonderful professor Kyrkos before we hopped on one of those marvelous inventions I believe are called planes. Wonderful things, those. Anyway. The darling professor was extremely forthcoming about everything you discussed with him. Or at least he was with a little persuasion." Nyx pulled a knife out of a sheath on her belt and started using it to clean her nails.

Dear God. They'd not only located the professor but had likely tortured him for information. Colin looked at her in panic. She understood his alarm. She and Colin had brought Professor Kyrkos into this mess, and it might have cost him dearly.

Nyx glanced from Colin, who was standing no more than an arm's length away from her, to Ambrose, who hadn't moved from where she'd thrown him, and finally landed on Selene, who was using the wall to support her weight while she clutched her stomach. "In addition to helping us find you, Kyrkos mentioned a few other wonderful pieces of lore before he was sadly too . . . damaged to be of use. As soon as the belt leaves this room, that lovely metal gate is going to close behind me, trapping anyone who might still be inside." She focused her gaze on Colin and smiled cruelly. "You, my love, are going to have a choice to make. Are you going to come after the two of us and try to get the belt back? Or are you going to try to save dear, sweet Selene and the hapless sidekick?"

The panicked look on Colin's face was likely reflected on Selene's as the truth of what Nyx was saying sank in. Not only had they likely killed the professor, but Nyx was planning on trapping them down here where no one would ever find them.

"Ticktock," Nyx practically sang as she stepped over the room's threshold and into the hallway.

As promised, the portcullis started slowly descending, the chain rattling loudly. A wild look crossed Colin's face as he dashed across the room to Selene's side. He wrapped an arm around her, grabbing her hip and trying to support her weight as he walked them toward the exit. "Hey, wanker! Let's go!"

Ambrose made a valiant attempt to get to his feet, but Selene could already tell that between her injury and his inability to move, they weren't going to make it.

Colin's gaze bounced frantically from the lowering gate to Selene, to Ambrose, and back. Without a word or a backward glance, he dropped his arms from around her, sprinted across the floor, and dove under the portcullis seconds before it clanged harshly against the stone floor.

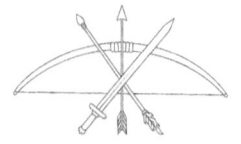

Chapter
Twenty-Seven

H E'D CHOSEN THE BELT over her.

Selene stood in the center of the room, clutching her stomach, and stared blankly after the man who had just fled. The man she had started to trust. Possibly even the man she'd started to love. It was obvious now that he didn't deserve that.

How could she possibly have been so stupid? In what world would he possibly be willing to give up his lucrative, if illegal, career for her? Instead, he'd run after his precious artifact with only a few seconds' hesitation, leaving her and Ambrose trapped underground in a cell that no one would ever find.

Snapping out of her shock, Selene limped to Ambrose's side. He had finally managed to roll over so that he was in a seated position, but his hand was clutching his stomach. She clutched his biceps tightly and lowered her forehead to his shoulder. She took several deep breaths to try to settle her racing heartbeat.

"What do you see in that dick?" he asked weakly.

Selene choked out a muted laugh before glancing up to take in their surroundings. The situation was bad. Like, really bad. They were in a small stone room that was no more than ten feet square. The only way in or out was blocked by an incredibly heavy metal gate that was not only shut tight but had taken some form of magic in order to open in the first place. Plus, the sword that Colin had used to stab her was on the other side of the gate. Not that she wanted to be stabbed again, considering she was still healing from the last one.

Ambrose slowly climbed to his feet, but the effort made him wobble slightly. Selene grabbed his shoulder to steady him, her knuckles white as she tightened her grip. He tipped his head sideways to rest it against hers. "Did he really leave us down here?" Ambrose stared at the portcullis as if he couldn't believe what he was seeing.

Selene sighed heavily. "It would appear so."

"What are you going to do about it, warrior woman?" Ambrose asked, lightly poking a finger into her rib cage.

Ambrose's question kicked her mind into high gear. Wolfe may have left them trapped underground, but she wasn't helpless. She was a damn Amazon, after all. She could figure this out.

She extended her arm to help stabilize the man at her side, and together they walked to the exit. Selene used the meager light from her flashlight to investigate the walls around the portcullis, looking for some sort of switch or lever that would operate it. Sadly, nothing jumped out at her.

The metal chain that moved the gate up and down was on this side of the door, which was an advantage they didn't have when trying to get into the room. Selene crossed the few short feet to where it was hanging against the wall and gave it an experimental tug.

Nothing. Not even an inch.

"Here," Selene said, handing Ambrose the light. "You keep looking for some way to lift the gate."

"What are you going to do?" he asked hesitantly.

"Try the hard way."

What she had in mind probably wasn't a good idea, especially not for the wound on her stomach, but she didn't see that she had much choice. Colin Wolfe, the conniving bastard, had left them to rot underground. Nyx and her pet mercenary were getting farther and farther away from her with every passing second. She was the only one aware of how bad the situation was, and it wasn't exactly like she was going to get a cell signal to call in backup—either from Kalli or Blackburn Industries—while trapped in an underground stone box.

Trying to ignore the tugging of her slowly healing wound, Selene walked right up to the portcullis. She braced her feet, bent her knees, and with a deep grunt used her enhanced strength to deadlift the gate. With an eardrum-shattering screech, the gate lifted.

About six inches.

Her muscles started to quiver, and beads of sweat popped out on her forehead. Her palms began to sweat, and she lost her grip on the ancient metal. With a clang that had a serious chance of causing hearing loss, the portcullis smashed back into the stone floor of the hallway.

Selene stumbled back a few steps, clutching her stomach, and came face-to-face with the wide eyes and slack jaw of her cellmate. Right. Ambrose had seen her do some pretty impossible things before, but perhaps not deadlifting a several-ton metal gate.

"So that almost worked." She breezed past any questions or concerns he might have. "Maybe if we can find something to wedge under the gate, we can get it propped up enough that we can slide under it."

Unfortunately for them, the room they were trapped in was almost completely empty. The only thing there, apart from the few meager belongings they'd brought in with them, was the stone pedestal that had been the final resting place of the belt until she and Colin had disturbed it. It would have to do.

"This way," Selene urged as she walked back to the center of the room. Ambrose trailed behind more slowly with the light. She stared at the one thing that could possibly help them escape.

The marble pillar was undoubtedly heavy, but it wasn't like she had much to work with. She bent her knees and wrapped her arms around the stone pedestal, and with an almighty heave she managed to lift it just enough that she could carry it a few feet before having to put it down again. She paused for a few minutes, panting with exertion and pain, before doing it all over again. It was a slow process, but eventually she made it all the way to the gate and tipped the post on its side, right next to the bottom of the portcullis.

While she worked, her angry thoughts kept flicking back to the asshole who had abandoned them in the dark and to Nyx, who was doing God knows what with the belt. There was nothing she could do about either of those things at the moment. She needed to focus on getting herself and Ambrose out of there alive. That was her mission.

After a few minutes of rest, she was ready to try again. At least her wound had mostly stopped bleeding. That had to be a good sign. "Ambrose, I'm going to need your help here. Once I lift this damn gate, I'm going to need you to do your best to wedge the pillar underneath it to prop it up."

"I'll try." He set the light down on the ground and crouched next to the marble post. Selene winced as she saw him flinch in pain. They had to push through. As soon as they got out of there, she could get him to a hospital.

Selene braced herself and bent her knees. With a Herculean effort, she slowly stood, lifting the gate inch by agonizing inch. She locked the muscles of her arms and legs and said, "Now!"

Ambrose grunted as he pushed and shoved the pillar the last few inches so that it was partially in the hallway and beneath the lifted gate.

As soon as the stone was in place, Selene lowered the gate slightly so that it was resting on the marble. Her muscles quivered from the strain as she shook out her arms and legs. The gap they'd created wasn't large, but it was more than they had before. She might be able to squeeze underneath it, even if Ambrose couldn't. That would at least put one of them on the outside. From there, she might be able to grab the sword again and use whatever ancient magic was tied to this place to get the gate to open itself. With a plan in place, she sat on the floor, preparing to shimmy through the tiny gap.

With an earsplitting crack, the marble pedestal snapped apart right where the metal had been resting on it. The portcullis dropped back into place, a metal clank reverberating through the room.

They were trapped. Again.

Colin dashed through the dimly lit corridor, hoping that he wasn't too far behind Nyx and Duran. If he couldn't catch up to them, he would have no idea where they were headed and no way to stop them from carrying out whatever the next phase of their plan was.

He made it back into the room with the thirteen hallways. It was pitch black. He distinctly remembered throwing glow sticks down the tunnel they'd entered from to make it easier to find their way out again. Apparently Nyx and her mercenary thug had grabbed them.

No big deal. He knew how the room was laid out and counted the hallways until he came to the one that would lead him back into the sewer system. He dove in, moving as quickly as he could until he reached the main tunnel and headed back toward the river.

Dominatrix Barbie was nowhere to be seen. Colin quickly snapped off the flashlight, not wanting to draw attention to himself. Luckily, the sun was just starting to come up, and it was bright enough for him to see where he was going. He raced to the stairs that would take him back to street level, hoping that Nyx and Duran would be heading topside as soon as possible.

His mind jumped back to Selene trapped in the underground room. He felt awful that he'd just left her there, but she would surely understand why he'd done it. Her injuries had been slowing her down, and Ambrose hadn't been moving all that quickly either. Colin had been the only one who would have made it out of the room before the gate fell back in place. Nyx and Duran needed to be stopped, and he'd been the only one capable of doing that.

Speak of the devil.

Colin ducked behind a bush to avoid being seen by the very people he was chasing. Nyx and Duran were a few hundred feet in front of him, walking like they were on a mission. Which, to be fair, they probably were. Nyx had clearly taken the time to stop and put on the belt since, even from his hiding place, Colin could see the light glinting off the bronze wrapped around her torso.

He suddenly wished he had a better understanding of the magic imbued into the belt. Selene had said it would take whatever Amazon power she had and amplify it. But how did that work? Did it take time to activate or was it working already? And how exactly would it change her? Selene had mentioned that Nyx had a charismatic personality and a gift for weapons. He was having trouble picturing how the belt might enhance that.

It didn't take him long to figure it out.

Nyx and Duran set a brisk pace as they wove through the streets of Rome. There weren't a lot of people out and about, as it was still on the early side, but folks were starting to emerge from their homes as they headed to work or breakfast or wherever they were going for the day. As each person passed near Nyx, she would say a few words to them, and then they would fall in behind her.

Colin watched as a small crowd formed behind her as she marched through the streets of Rome. On the one hand, the crowd made it easier to stalk Nyx and Duran, because he could blend in with the people trailing behind her. On the other hand, it was suddenly obvious what the belt was doing to her. Her influence on these innocent people was enough that after a few short words they were willing to follow her anywhere.

This was not good.

After almost twenty minutes of walking, the crowd had swelled to several hundred people. Colin kept to the back of the group—not wanting to be spotted by Nyx or Duran—which prevented him from seeing where they were going. Eventually, however, the buildings parted, and they arrived at what was unmistakably one of the most recognizable places in all of Rome, the Trevi Fountain.

At any other time, Colin would have been in heaven. The fountain was an amazing work of art. The central figure of the sculpture was Neptune, the ancient Roman god of the sea, sitting in a chariot being pulled by two horses and two younger sea gods. Water poured around the bottom of the statues and into a lower basin, which glinted in the sun from all the coins people threw into the water for good luck.

The fountain was stunning and took up an entire plaza. Colin itched to get closer and explore as much as he was allowed. Nyx had other plans.

Without any thought or hesitation, she marched straight into the fountain and stood right in front of Neptune himself, not caring about the water soaking her shoes. The crowd pushed and shoved toward Nyx, forcing Colin closer and closer to the middle of the square.

"People of Rome," Nyx began as a hush fell over the gathered throng. "My name is Nyx, and I am the rightful queen of the Amazons. That may not mean anything to you, because it has been brought to my attention that most if not all of you do not even know who the Amazons are or what our purpose is. Allow me to correct that."

Dread sank into Colin's stomach as he frantically looked around. The crowd around him was full of slack-jawed people with almost loving expressions. Many of those people had their cell phones out and were recording Nyx's speech. The secret of the Amazons was about to get out, and he had no way to stop it. *Damn it.*

Selene was going to be so pissed.

"The Amazons are fierce warriors with superior strength and power. We have existed for millennia with the sworn duty to protect others and keep them from being harmed. For centuries, we fought your wars for you. We bested the toughest fighters of the era, all in the name of keeping the populace safe."

Every eye in the plaza was fixed on Nyx. Colin felt a tug inside that wanted him to believe everything Nyx was saying. She was clearly a warrior of old. It was obvious from her stature, her intricate leather and bronze armor, and her weapons, which he had somehow failed to notice before.

"I look about me and see a population that has become soft and vulnerable." Nyx gestured to the people dressed in business suits, exercise clothes, and casual shorts and T-shirts. She pointed out people who were shoving baked goods into their mouths, causing them to lower the food and drop it to the ground. No one wanted to disappoint her. "I come before you with an offer. Clearly your current leaders are doing nothing to help protect you. Not from yourselves and not from others. I can change all of that. I can offer you something that no other ruler can. Power. The power to give up control, to allow someone else to carry your burdens and to fight your battles for you. The power to give yourself to me."

A slow murmur went through the crowd as the bodies pressed closer and closer together. Nyx was electric. She was putting the whole crowd under her spell, Colin included. What she said made sense. Why should he worry about Selene or Ian? It was so much easier to just stop stealing, stop helping, stop fighting. Colin's shoulders relaxed. He barely even remembered why he'd been stalking Nyx in the first place. Obviously it had to have been so that he could offer himself to her. She would take care of him.

As one, everyone in the plaza, Colin included, sank to their knees and looked up at their leader with love and devotion. They would follow her to the ends of the earth and fight anyone that tried to stop them. Nyx was the obvious choice to rule them, and anyone who disagreed was wrong and needed to be put down before they could spread their lies.

"There now. Isn't that easier?" Nyx's smile was enormous.

"Easier isn't always better."

The new voice caused Nyx to whip around, staring in shock at its source.

Selene had appeared out of nowhere. "In fact," Selene continued as she picked her way through the kneeling crowd toward the fountain, "I would argue that easy is boring. I think more people need a little spice in their life."

Duran appeared from wherever he'd crawled off to and leveled a gun at Selene. She returned the favor and pointed hers straight at Nyx. "I wouldn't try that if I were you, lover."

The mental fog was starting to clear from Colin's mind. He knew he should be trying to help Selene, but the force of the compulsion from Nyx's influence didn't let him move. He felt trapped in his body, as if it was no longer his own.

He watched helplessly as Selene slowly circled the fountain, getting closer to Nyx as Duran stalked closer to Selene. Something was going to have to break the standoff.

"Selene, darling. You're looking slightly better than the last time I saw you. No longer bleeding like a sacrificial goat, I trust?"

Colin saw Selene flinch, but she didn't react other than to continue approaching her target. "Nyx, I can't say I missed you much during my exile. You still seem to be as much of a bitch now as you were twenty-five hundred years ago."

Nyx's nose wrinkled like she was smelling something awful. "Charming, as always."

"No more or less than you." Selene finally came to a stop when she was within ten feet of her target. She planted herself on a rock just a few feet lower than where Nyx was standing and glanced over her shoulder at Duran, who had stopped at the same time she did.

Colin strained against the invisible force holding him where he was. Selene was good and she could take care of herself, but even she wouldn't last long against both the wannabe queen and her minion.

A slight movement from Duran caught his eye. Colin squinted, trying to figure out what he was doing, but the bigger man was turned away from him, and Colin couldn't get a clear view. By the time he saw the glint of sunlight on the wicked blade Duran was holding, it was too late.

Chapter Twenty-Eight

"**S**ELENE, BEHIND YOU!"

Colin's shout alerted her less than a second before she sensed the movement behind her. She instinctively leaned sideways just as a razor-sharp knife spun past her head and clanged against one of the two horse sculptures in the fountain.

She glanced over her shoulder at Duran and sent him a smirk. "Tsk, tsk. Careful with that. You could have damaged one of the most famous fountains in the world. That's not a very nice thing to do."

Duran glared at her, his fingers twitching near his waist, where Selene could see several other knives he was clearly waiting to aim at her head. Nyx's lackey was armed to the teeth. Not that she would have expected anything else. All the more reason that she had to figure out how to stop this situation before it went any further. She was sure that the only reason he hadn't tried to shoot her was that if he missed Selene, he might hit his boss.

The square around Trevi Fountain was packed with hundreds of people, with more joining by the minute. Morning commuters would soon give way to tourists, and the numbers would only continue to swell. Selene had to find a way to get the belt off Nyx and break whatever influence she was spreading before it was too late.

As mad as she was at Colin, she had to admit she was glad he was still alive. She scanned the crowds, her eyes seeking the hazel ones she'd thought she had gotten to know so well. She finally found them in the middle of the crowd about fifty feet from where she stood. Once she confirmed that he was uninjured, she brought her focus back to what she had to do.

Selene turned to her former sister and sent her a pitying look. "What's your plan here, Nyx? I hate to be the one to point it out, but you're more than a little out of touch with the world these days. You've been living in a bubble for twenty-five hundred years and, unsurprisingly, the world has changed since the last time you went out into it."

Nyx wrinkled her nose in a sneer. "I've noticed."

Selene acknowledged that with a quick nod. "I'm sure you have. And yet the world is even bigger than you can comprehend. There are entire continents that hadn't been discovered the last time you left Themyscira. Not only that, but the world's population has sort of exploded. There are around eight billion people in the world. That's a whole lot of people to try to bend to your will."

Nyx's eyes narrowed, but Selene could tell that nothing she was saying was making a difference with the other woman. There really was no reasoning with tyrannical insanity.

"I don't understand why you aren't at my side. The Amazons are far superior to these sheep." Nyx gestured widely at the hordes of people staring at her adoringly, hanging on her every word and insult. "By our very design we are better than they are. We should be ruling them, not bowing, scraping, and serving them. I am only doing what should have been done thousands of years ago. It is our right to dominate and control those that are lesser than we are."

"See, that right there is why you're wrong. Yes, Amazons may have strengths and abilities beyond a normal human. But that doesn't make us superior." Selene glanced at the throngs of people who would be hurt if she couldn't fix this situation. Each of those people had their own life, their own family, their own hurdles and challenges. She didn't feel better than them. The fact that they soldiered on, getting through life and all it threw at them—without the extra enhanced abilities granted to the Amazons—humbled her.

Selene had been alive for thousands of years and still regularly felt like she was screwing up. She'd spent the majority of her years in exile, believing she wasn't good enough to be called an Amazon because of her mistakes. Yet here she was, staring at the woman who had stolen the throne from the rightful queen and had ruled her sisters with an iron fist for thousands of years. Selene may not be sure exactly who she was anymore—Amazon, CEO, vigilante—but she did know that she was a far better person than Nyx could ever hope to be.

Nyx cocked her head slightly and put her hands on her hips as she stared Selene down. "Really, Selene. Where does this hostility come from? I am sure we can come to an agreement if we can just get past whatever this grudge is you appear to be holding."

Selene rolled her eyes but stood her ground. "Not going to happen. You and I are due for a reckoning."

"A reckoning? Whatever for? Does this have to do with the disagreement with Kalli over the throne?"

Selene's eyes narrowed, and her hand tightened on the grip of her gun. "That wasn't top of mind, but let's throw that on the pile for good measure."

Nyx tapped her finger against her lips like she was thinking. "Wait, I know." She leered cruelly. "Does this have anything to do with that pathetic village? The one you claimed? What was that silly place called again, Alackia? Akrazia?"

Selene could tell from Nyx's smirk that she knew damn well that it was neither of those and that she was just trying to get a rise out of her. Well, it was working. "It was named Akalia, which I'm sure you remember. And those people were innocent. Hundreds of men, women, and children slaughtered, and for what? Your own ego?" Selene was screaming by the end.

Nyx shrugged like nothing was wrong. "They were going to stop paying. That made them no longer of value to me."

No longer of value? That bitch.

Selene saw red before she charged. She launched herself off the rock she'd been perched on, jumping the several-foot-high rise to land on the level above, about six feet from Nyx. Selene lunged for her opponent's waist—trying to get the belt off her—but Nyx was far too fast for that. She sidestepped the move and lashed out at Selene's arm, smacking her wrist and sending Selene's gun careening over the edge of the fountain and into the pool of water below.

Shit.

With no gun, Selene was forced to pull her backup weapon, her wicked-looking tactical knife. Too bad it would have not only looked awkward but been wildly inconvenient to have been toting her sword through the streets of Rome.

Nyx grabbed a knife with one hand and somehow conjured a whip for her other hand. Not good. Selene had seen exactly how deadly accurate Nyx was with her whip, which would have gotten stronger with the help of the power of the belt. Not to mention, a whip had a significantly longer reach than Selene's eight-inch knife.

Selene was so screwed, and by the predatory grin on Nyx's face, she knew it too.

With a deafening crack, Nyx's whip split the air. Selene felt the smack of the leather lash against her ribs, thankfully on the other side of her torso from the earlier sword wound. She stumbled back a few feet on the uneven stone, her boots slippery and soaked through by the rushing water.

Before Selene could fully recover, Nyx sent the whip flying once more. Selene tried to lift her knife into its path, hoping to damage the leather tail, but instead the tip wrapped around the blade. With a harsh tug, Nyx pulled back on the whip's handle and yanked the knife out of Selene's hands. It landed somewhere behind Nyx with a harsh clang of metal on stone.

Selene was now completely unarmed.

Out of the corner of her eye, she caught a rush of movement. Duran had come up behind her, but before she could even react, someone yelled, "Not so fast!"

Colin, somehow free of the trance that was still holding everyone else, raced through the shin-deep water brandishing his machete and catching Duran off guard. With one swing of the blade, Colin managed to knock Duran's gun out of his hands and into the fountain. At least the odds were a lot more even now that no one had a working gun.

Another painful crack across her ribs brought Selene's focus back to her own fight. Nyx blew her a taunting kiss as she flipped her leather switch back and forth, kicking up splashes of water every time the tip connected with it.

There was no way she could do any damage to Nyx without getting in closer. To do that, she had to deal with the damn whip. This was going to hurt.

Selene leaned forward and reached out like she was going to move in. Predictably, Nyx sent her lash flying and wrapped it around Selene's forearm. Before Nyx could follow through, Selene grabbed the braided leather and pulled with all her considerable might.

Nyx didn't let go of the handle like Selene had been hoping, but the movement did pull Nyx toward her, finally bringing her within arm's reach. Selene wasted no time following up with a knife-hand strike across Nyx's wrist, which finally forced the other woman to drop the handle she was clinging to.

Unfortunately, Nyx still had a knife. The blade glinted in the sun as Nyx swung for Selene's neck, aiming for a killing slash to the artery. Selene lurched sideways, avoiding the blade and taking the whip with her. She wasn't nearly as good with the weapon as Nyx, so instead of trying to use it properly, she swung the rigid handle at her opponent's head, catching her in the temple.

Nyx stumbled back into one of the male statues in the fountain, catching herself before she tripped and fell. Chasing after her, Selene almost rolled her ankle on the uneven surface. Nyx recovered and charged her, forcing Selene to dive behind a statue of a horse to avoid the incoming blade.

Selene ducked under the front legs of the rearing animal and tackled Nyx into something that looked like a giant seashell. Nyx went down hard, her head bouncing off the marble with an audible crack. Nyx let out a pained moan but still managed to roll away and onto her feet before Selene could follow up with a punch.

Selene rolled to her back, brought her knees to her chest, and then flung them outward, using the momentum to flip to her feet. She circled Nyx, driving her away from the crowds of people and toward the building at the rear of the fountain.

From the grunts and clangs behind her, Selene guessed that Colin was somehow holding his own against the mercenary, but she didn't dare take her eyes off her own target. She would not allow Nyx to get the jump on her again.

Nyx lashed out with a punch aimed at the side of Selene's head, but Selene sidestepped the blow and landed a roundhouse kick across Nyx's stomach. She got a kidney punch for her trouble, making her stagger slightly and spreading an evil grin on Nyx's face.

Nyx had always been a good hand-to-hand fighter, but Selene had used the last twenty-five hundred years to study dozens of fighting styles from all over the world. She had the advantage.

Selene faked a punch to Nyx's face and swiftly followed up with a kick to the groin. As Nyx bent over in pain, Selene shoved both of Nyx's shoulders as hard as she could, pushing her closer to the building. But the move didn't knock Nyx off her feet as Selene had intended.

Why wouldn't this bitch go down?

Nyx straightened, gasping for breath, a murderous look on her face. "That was a low blow."

Selene shrugged. "Whatever works, right?" With a primal scream, she dashed forward and practically flew through the air as she tackled her former sister, curling in on herself as she did so. The momentum of her attack sent them both careening into one of the lower windows of the building.

The iron bars on the window groaned as they bent and then snapped, sending both women crashing through the window and onto the hard marble floor of the room inside.

⇥⇥⇥⇥ ⇤⇤⇤⇤

The sound of screeching metal and shattering glass distracted Colin at exactly the wrong moment. A beefy fist cracked across his jaw and sent him stumbling through the shin-deep water of the lower part of the fountain.

Duran easily had thirty more pounds of muscle than he did. He was also a mercenary and trained fighter, neither of which Colin could claim to be. Quite honestly, Colin was astonished he was still alive.

He couldn't even explain how he was mobile when everyone else around him had that trancelike state still going for them. All he knew was that he'd been watching Selene as she approached Nyx and had seen Duran coming up behind her with the knife. He'd yelled a warning, but that hadn't helped with the panic and terror that had gripped him. He knew for a fact that Selene could take care of herself, but two on one were not great odds, especially when those two were Nyx the unhinged warlord and Quinton Duran the murder-happy henchman. He'd felt a sudden surge go through him, and then it was as if a pressure valve had released, and he could suddenly move again.

He'd wasted no time and had booked it across the square, thankfully catching up to Duran just before he'd leveled his gun on Selene. That had, however, turned Colin into target number one. One lone machete wasn't a whole lot to rely on when you were facing off against a trained killer. Too bad he hadn't packed his gun for their nighttime of breaking and entering.

Speaking of a trained killer, Duran had pulled yet another knife from the seemingly endless supply he had sheathed in his belt. The glint in his eyes made it obvious he was some form of sociopath who enjoyed killing and had no remorse for doing so. Colin put his hands up in front of him and started backing away slowly as Duran stalked him through the low water.

A low murmur began from behind Colin, but there was no way he was taking his eyes off Duran long enough to figure out what was going on. The murmur grew into a buzz and then a series of groans and moans.

"What's going on?" a voice behind him asked.

"How did I get here?" another chimed in.

"That guy's got a knife!" The final shout provoked screams from the crowds of people packed around the square.

Chaos erupted as people got off their knees and pushed and shoved to get away. Whatever trance Nyx had put on the people was obviously wearing off now that she wasn't around.

Other than a quick glance around, Duran didn't seem to care that the hordes of followers that Nyx had gathered were escaping. He seemed to have a singular focus.

Colin.

Colin clenched the hilt of his machete as he willed his palms not to sweat. His calves hit the edge of the fountain, alerting him that he'd run out of room to flee. He said a quick mental apology to Selene that he'd never gotten to tell her that he loved her and then braced himself, hoping that whatever fate Duran had in store for him, it would at least be over quickly.

"Stop! You there! What are you doing in the fountain? It is not allowed!" The shout came in both Italian and English. Colin took the risk of glancing in the direction of the voice and almost collapsed in relief.

Two uniformed state police officers were approaching them, guns drawn. Colin immediately dropped his machete and raised his hands. Duran wasn't so compliant. He charged the officers, attempting to slash them with his wickedly sharp blade. Unluckily for Duran, bullets were faster than he was, and both police officers opened fire. Blood blossomed on his chest as he crashed to his knees in the shallow pool. One of the cops quickly approached him and stopped him from falling face-first into the water while the other held him at gunpoint.

Colin didn't wait to see if Duran was still alive. He climbed out of the fountain and ran around to the other side, needing to help Selene. The police shouted after him, but he just gestured toward the smashed window and kept running. He had no idea what had happened to Selene. His heart was pounding out a rhythm of *be alive, be alive, be alive.*

He'd just found Selene, his match and his equal in every way. He wouldn't know what to do with himself if she didn't survive this. Being around her for the short time they'd spent together had already been enough to change him. He was a totally different man than he'd been when he'd shown up on the shores of Themyscira. She'd changed him, and he liked the man he'd become around her. She'd given him the strength to try to find a new path in his life. No one else in his life, with the exception of Mr. Peterson, had ever believed in him.

He had no idea what his new life with Selene would look like, but he needed to find out. And to do that, Selene needed to be alive. Heart in his throat, he arrived at the broken window.

The first thing he noticed was the streak of blood smeared across the white marble floor.

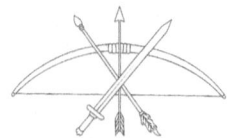

Chapter Twenty-Nine

F OR A FEW SECONDS, there was silence. Then a pained groan came from somewhere on the other side of the large room. Opening her eyes, which she'd instinctively closed when crashing through the window, Selene glanced around to see where they'd landed.

They were in a large open room that had only one thing inside. Oddly, it was another fountain, significantly smaller and simpler than the one outside. This one was made of simple stone and didn't have any carvings or statues. There was a rim around it with some sort of text, but she wasn't close enough to read it.

Ten feet away, Nyx was slowly getting to her feet. She looked rough, but unfortunately for Selene, she was still moving and still wearing the damn belt.

The fight wasn't over yet.

"You should surrender," Nyx said, but the slight pants and gasps Selene could just barely make out gave away that Nyx wasn't as unaffected as she was pretending to be.

"Sorry, no can do. I wasn't on board with you leading the Amazons, and there are only a few hundred of us. There's no way I would let you rule the entire world. Ain't going to happen, sweetheart."

Nyx simply shrugged. "Suit yourself." She reached behind her and pulled out yet another knife.

Where on earth was she hiding them all?

Selene let out a resigned sigh and then took a deep breath, willing each of her muscles to slowly relax. She could do this. She had to do this. She was an Amazon warrior, and it was her duty to protect the world from situations exactly like this. No matter how much it cost her personally.

Her mind briefly flitted to Colin. She had no idea if he was alive or dead, though she was hoping that he somehow managed to make it through all of this. He might have been a selfish asshole, but he didn't deserve to die just because he'd stumbled into Amazon business.

She had no idea how she was going to win this fight—she just knew she had to. She was completely out of weapons. Her opponent had a seemingly endless supply of them. They were both Amazons, so she had no tactical advantage in the strength or speed departments either.

She would win because not winning wasn't an option.

Nyx lunged, her arm slicing through the air. Selene sidestepped but didn't get far enough out of the way. Fire raced across her arm as the tip of the blade skated across her skin. Blood gushed down her arm all the way to her fingertips.

Selene took a few rapid steps back, not letting the bright red of the blood against the stark white floor distract her. She was fine. She could heal anything, right?

The next time Nyx slashed her blade in Selene's direction, she saw it coming early enough to step to the side and chop her hand against Nyx's wrist. Unfortunately, the move didn't work and instead of the knife falling to the floor, Nyx's hand spasmed slightly, gripping the hilt more tightly than before.

Selene danced out of Nyx's reach, her foot slipping in a pool of blood and smearing it on the floor. Luckily, she didn't lose her balance. She backed away from Nyx until her calves hit the fountain in the middle of the room.

She was trapped. There was nowhere else to go.

Nyx lunged once more, sunlight from the window glinting off her viciously sharp blade as it sliced through the air.

Selene tried to dodge the blow but the excruciating pain in her chest told her she hadn't succeeded.

Time slowed as if one of the gods had pushed pause on a giant stopwatch somewhere on Mount Olympus.

Selene glanced down to see the hilt of a knife protruding from the center of her shirt. Blood seeped from the wound, but it almost seemed like an inconsequential amount given the mortal nature of getting stabbed directly in the heart.

Selene was irritated that the last thing she would see in this life was Nyx's triumphant grin. The other Amazon was standing in front of her, the belt safely around her waist, the smile on her face one of a person who knew they had defeated their enemy.

She could already feel her healing ability trying to kick in. She'd always been able to heal almost anything. But that had been before her powers had gone on the fritz. Besides, a knife directly to the heart wasn't *almost anything*. She'd never tested her abilities this much, but as the life force slowly seeped out of her, she guessed it was a bridge too far. Her powers couldn't heal a fatal wound.

She was going to fail. She'd let Nyx win.

"Selene!" The shout from the window almost drove another knife through her heart. Colin had arrived and she was dying. He was no match for Nyx. Nyx would kill him, and then everything Selene and Colin had fought for would be for nothing.

No. She couldn't let that be her last act in this world. If she was going to die, then Nyx was coming with her.

Her hands lifted, almost as if they weren't her own. She watched them grasp the hilt of the knife and tug. It was surprisingly difficult to extract a knife embedded into a rib cage.

Part of her mind heard Colin's shoes hit the marble floor. Another part saw the predatory glint in Nyx's eyes as she turned to meet the newcomer, yet another impossible knife coming from nowhere.

With a strength she didn't realize she still had, Selene yanked the knife from her chest and slashed it across Nyx's throat.

At least Colin would survive.

Selene felt herself falling backward in slow motion, but it was okay. She'd done her duty. Nyx was dead. The world was safe. And most importantly, Colin would live to see another day.

With that information to give her comfort, she allowed herself to float backward into the dark, knowing she'd done everything she could to protect the ones she loved.

⇛ ⇚

"No!" Colin yelled as he sprinted across the cold white floor.

He heard Nyx take her final breath but couldn't even take the time to process that they'd finally won. Duran was in custody and Nyx was dead.

It didn't matter. He'd watched in horror as Selene had pulled the knife from her chest to kill Nyx. He continued to hold his breath as she fell into the fountain, sinking beneath the cool blue water slowly tinging red with her blood.

"Selene," he practically sobbed her name as he skidded to a halt next to the stone basin where she was submerged. Without a thought, he climbed in with her and pulled her head above the surface so that, if nothing else, she wouldn't inhale water.

His heart in his throat, Colin pulled and yanked until Selene was out of the fountain. He laid her flat on the floor and put pressure on her wound, trying desperately to stop the blood that was welling up against his hands. If he could just keep her alive, her healing ability would kick in, and she could save herself.

Nothing.

She was dying, and nothing he could do was going to save her.

Why wasn't her healing ability working? It had never been more important that her gods-given ability protected her, and yet not only had it been working slower than usual for most of the last week, but it suddenly seemed like it was failing her entirely.

Wait.

Something sparked in the back of his mind, fighting to surface from underneath his panic. She had a natural ability to heal. Unfortunately, it wasn't working fast enough to help her heal the fatal wound she'd sustained.

But there was something that might help.

Colin glanced sideways at Nyx, the crazed Amazon whose gifts of influence and warmongering had only increased once she'd donned the belt. The girdle of Hippolyta. A piece of armor rumored to protect the Amazon who wore it and increase their innate powers.

It was worth a shot. Colin sprinted to where Nyx had fallen, doing his best to ignore the blood pooled underneath her lifeless body. Bracing himself, he reached behind her and undid the clasp that secured the belt to her body.

He didn't hesitate before returning to Selene's side. He hastily wrapped the belt around her waist and fastened it. He may not be able to save the love of his life, but maybe magic could.

Sitting back and doing nothing while Selene's life faded in front of his eyes was the worst pain he could possibly imagine. Her breathing was barely visible, the rising and falling of her chest almost undetectable.

Tears pooled in the corners of his eyes. He'd arrived too late. Selene was going to die, and it was all his fault. Well, Nyx obviously had something to do with it, but maybe he could have saved her if he'd been just a fraction of a second faster. If he'd defeated Duran sooner.

Colin sat on the floor then tugged her into his lap. He wrapped his arms around her and clung, his forehead resting on hers.

Tears flowed freely. Selene had gone utterly still. Even his last-ditch effort with the damn belt had failed him. Clearly he hadn't been worthy of her. If he had been, he would have figured everything out sooner. He would have saved her rather than lost her.

How was he going to tell her friends? How was he going to get word to the Amazons? It wasn't like he had their queen's number in his back pocket.

There was one number he did have, however. No matter how much bad blood was between him and Sam Treadwell, he owed this to him and his partner, Kalli.

With a reluctant sigh, Colin pulled his miraculously undamaged phone out of his back pocket. He hit the number saved in his contact list as "Douchey Prof" and waited while it rang.

"Hello?" Sam answered.

"Sam," he said, choking back a sob.

"Colin?" Sam's confused voice came through the line.

"It's Selene. She's . . . hurt. She probably won't make it. You should muster the forces or whatever it is that Amazons do. Rome. Trevi Fountain. Well, I guess the building next to it."

"Colin, what happened?" He could hear the panic in Sam's voice but couldn't find it in himself to care. Colin's heart was dying right alongside Selene, and he had no room for anything else.

"Nyx is dead. Just come." With that he hung up. He slowly sank onto the cold marble floor next to the one person who could never be replaced. His arm went around Selene's waist as he waited for the cavalry to arrive.

Chapter Thirty

H OURS LATER, A RUCKUS of shouted voices and angry
threats pulled Colin from his daze. He hadn't slept—that
would have been impossible—but he'd faded in and out as he kept
vigil over Selene and Nyx.

Neither had moved.

Colin wanted to cry, but all his tears had been spent. Selene was
gone, and nothing he had done had brought her back. He had found
the love of his life only to lose her almost instantly.

Maybe he wasn't destined for happiness. Not everyone was. Some
people just got dealt a crappy hand in life, and there was nothing they
could do about it. It wasn't like they deserved it more than anyone
else. It was just their lot in life that they had won the shit lottery.
Kind of like Colin had.

The chaos of the incoming cacophony drew Colin's gaze to the
only door to the room. Honestly, he'd never paid any attention to

it. He'd come in through the window, and he'd been a bit distracted ever since.

The volume of the incoming noise almost made him miss it. The small hitch under his hand where it rested on Selene's stomach. The slight gasp of breath.

Eyes wide, Colin ignored the insanity descending on them and focused on Selene.

"Selene? Baby?" He leaned over her, his lips inches from hers. "Is this really possible?"

"Why are you hovering over me? If I've told you once, I've told you a thousand times. I can heal from anything." Her voice was weak, but that didn't matter.

Selene was alive.

The door to the room banged open, and a group of people poured in. Colin recognized Kalli, Sam, and Zoe, but he didn't bother trying to remember the rest of their names. "Sorry to bust in on you like this, but the Italian police have been trying to figure out how to get in this room for a few hours." Zoe said.

Colin ignored the newcomers and focused all his attention on Selene who was blinking her beautiful green eyes at him.

"Oh my God," Colin whispered before planting his lips gently on Selene's and stopping the newcomers in their tracks. His eyes closed as he pressed his forehead gently against hers. "I can't believe you survived. There is no way you should have come back from that."

Colin's fingers frantically grasped at her clothes as he ripped open her shirt. The gaping wound that had been seeping blood for hours was gone. Not even a trace of it existed.

"Colin?" Her confused voice was like a soothing balm to his soul. She wasn't dead, and he hadn't had to watch her leave him.

"Selene. Red." He placed another gentle kiss on her lips. "I love you. I can't believe I didn't tell you before now, but you have to know. I need you to know. You're not allowed to leave me ever again."

She started to sit up and he tugged her gently against him in a hug he'd never thought he'd be able to give her again.

"You love me?" she asked, the confusion obvious in her voice.

Colin pulled back, staring her in the eyes, his love radiating from him. "Of course I love you. How could I not?" he asked, a smile spreading across his face.

She sat up fully and shook him off her. If she realized there were other people in the room, she did a damn good job of ignoring them as she pushed herself back into a seated position against the rim of the fountain. "Um, what about the part where you left me to die trapped underground?"

Colin flinched, pulling back but not fully letting her go. "I didn't leave you to die. I went after Nyx and Duran because I knew we needed to stop them."

Selene's eyes narrowed. "Yes, you did. Ambrose and I were trapped underground. Sealed inside a vault that hadn't been opened in more than two thousand years. What made you assume that we weren't going to die down there?"

Colin was baffled. "*You* did." He glanced around at the room and saw the heart eyes coming from a few of their visitors, but he did his best to ignore them. "Selene, you are the most powerful woman, the most powerful person I've ever met. You've never met a challenge you weren't up for. You've never encountered a threat you couldn't conquer. I knew that trapping you in that room would slow you down, but I never thought it would stop you. Your strength amazes me daily. I didn't have a single doubt in my head that you would not only survive, but you would rescue both yourself and Ambrose. Where is he, anyway?" He glanced around as if Ambrose was suddenly going to appear out of thin air.

"The hospital, but that's not the point. There's no way you could have known we would get out," Selene tried to protest, but Colin stopped her with a gentle kiss.

"Of course there is. I know you. Inside and out. You not only saved yourself and your son, but—dare I say it—the world?" He glanced sideways, drawing her eyes to Nyx, who lay dead beside them.

Selene sucked in a sharp breath. "Nyx is dead?"

Colin nodded. "Yes. She is. You did that."

He could see the bewilderment in her eyes as she tried to remember what had happened. He saw the confusion clear as everything came back to her.

"You were coming through the window," she said as she glanced across the room to where he'd entered.

"Yes." He reached his hands out and gently cupped her jaw.

"Nyx was going to kill you," she continued.

"That's probably true," Colin said as he planted gentle kisses on her jaw. "You stopped her."

She shook her head slightly, as if it would help make her memories any clearer. "How am I alive? She stabbed me through the heart. It was a fatal wound. I felt myself falling into the water." She glanced behind her at the red-tinged water of the fountain but quickly found his eyes again.

"Well, you can thank your archenemy for that." He glanced down, drawing her eyes to the leather and bronze belt securely wrapped around her waist.

One of Selene's hands lifted and gently petted the leather band that was securely fastened around her stomach. "I'm wearing it? It worked on my powers?"

Her incredulous question dumbfounded him. "Of course it worked, baby. You're an Amazon. You've always been an Amazon. You may have just forgotten for a while." He winked at her, and she smiled slightly.

"What does this mean?" she asked.

"I'd say it means you saved the world," Kalli said as she joined them next to the fountain. A giant grin crossed her face as she lifted her hand to Selene's shoulder. "I'd also say it looks like you've found yourself a good one here." She winked at Colin before she stood and gestured to Nyx's body. Several Amazons clad in black tactical gear crossed the room and began loading Nyx's body into a body bag and onto a stretcher.

"Oh, there's one more thing," Kalli said as she ushered the crowd of people out of the room. "You may want to take a closer look at that fountain . . ." With that, she pushed the last stragglers out of the room and closed the door behind them.

"What do you suppose that means?" Colin asked as he helped Selene gingerly rise to her feet.

His redheaded seductress turned around and took one look at the fountain before choking on a laugh. "Um, Colin?"

He stepped up next to her, wrapping his arm around her waist. "Yeah?"

She glanced from his feet to his head, closely examining his clothes. "Did you, I don't know, touch the water in this fountain somehow?"

"Um, yes?" Colin said, baffled as to where she was going with this. "You'd been stabbed, and you were drowning in the fountain. Of course I pulled you out of there."

She stifled a laugh. "You may want to check the fine print." She pointed at the inscription that he'd never bothered to read.

Fons iuventutis.

"The Fountain of Youth? Seriously?" Colin wanted to scoff at the ridiculousness of it. There was no possible way that the Fountain of Youth was real. "It's got to be a mistake."

Selene only laughed harder. "You literally just brought me back from the dead by wrapping a four-thousand-year-old piece of leather and metal around my waist, and you're going to call bullshit on the Fountain of Youth?"

"No, really," Colin said. "What are the odds that we wind up in a huge battle and in the middle of it just happen upon the Fountain of Youth in the basement of some random Roman building? It stretches the definition of coincidence too far."

Selene smiled indulgently at him. "Who said it was a coincidence? What do you really know about the Fountain of Youth? Maybe you have some research to do."

Well, when she put it that way.

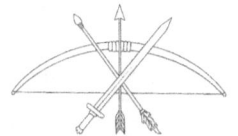

Chapter Thirty-One

*I*MMORTAL.

The word just kept circling around in his head over and over again. He was immortal. One short dip in some magic fountain and his life had changed forever. He still wasn't sure he believed it. He'd been trying to research the fountain on his phone one-handed while trying not to disturb Selene. It wasn't going very quickly, but he wouldn't have it any other way.

Selene shifted in her sleep, pressed against his side. Colin wrapped his arm more tightly around her and kissed the top of her riot of curls. It wasn't just enchanted water that had changed him forever.

The woman in his arms had everything to do with it. She made him want to be a better man. It was long past time that he gave up his vendetta against Sam and his life in the darkness. With Selene by his side, he could be exceptional. He even had some ideas about how they could do that together, though it might take a bit of convincing on her part. Either way, he was up for the challenge.

Most importantly, they had time. Time to rest, recuperate, and just be together in a way that they hadn't quite managed in the whirlwind of their time so far.

Kalli had come in and taken charge of the situation at the fountain like she was born to do it, which, given the fact that she was a queen, perhaps she was. It also helped that they had Zoe the Interpol agent at their disposal to help with the stickier legal aspects of everything that had gone down.

But Colin didn't want to think about any of that right now. His only concern was the woman in his arms.

After leaving the fountain, they'd made their way back to their hotel room and promptly passed out in bed together, Selene tucked up against his side with her arm around his waist and one of her incredibly long legs pinning his to the mattress. He didn't mind. He was more than happy to have her use him and take comfort in him.

He idly traced his fingers up her arm as he waited for her to wake up. He knew they had things to talk about, and he was looking forward to clearing the air. No more secrets going forward.

When Selene finally stirred, it was hours later, and Colin's stomach was protesting loudly. The sound must have disturbed her, because she chuckled quietly and patted his stomach before lifting her head and smiling at him. "I guess we need to feed you." She planted a quick peck on his lips, which he deepened into something more sensual. With a low moan she sank into the kiss for a few heartbeats before pulling away again. "Food first," she said with a laugh.

"Room service?" he asked hopefully.

"Sounds perfect."

They placed their food order with the hotel, but once Colin hung up the phone, the silence stretched between them. They both knew they had things to work through, but neither of them wanted to go first.

"Selene, I . . ."

"Colin." They spoke at the same time.

"You go first. Please." He gestured to her.

She took a deep breath, then sat up taller on the bed, where they were camping out. "Tell me about Ian."

Colin shook his head in surprise. Ian wasn't the very last thing he would have expected her to bring up, but he was definitely near the bottom. "What do you mean? I told you who he was. That we were friends growing up and that he was the one that got me into thieving in the first place."

She nodded in acknowledgment. "Tell me about two days ago."

Two days ago? His forehead pinched as he racked his brain. God, had it really been that recently that Ian had called him? So much had happened since then that the conversation felt like a lifetime ago rather than a mere thirty-six hours. But how would she even have known about their conversation?

"Ian called me to ask for help with a job that he was trying to pull. He's in deep with a bad dude in Chicago and owes him way more money than he could possibly pay back." That about summed it up. Ian was obviously an idiot, but he wasn't sure why that bothered Selene so much.

Her lips pressed into a thin line as her shoulders slumped. "So when do you head out?"

Realization dawned as Colin figured out what she was getting at. He tucked his finger under her chin and brought her gaze up to meet his. "I'm not leaving."

Her eyes widened. "But you said . . ." She glanced down at the rumpled duvet like she was trying to remember something. She squared her shoulders and looked at him dead on. "You told him you were going to help him."

"How do you know what I said? Did you tap my phone?" he asked, mostly jokingly, since he didn't think she would go quite that far.

A blush bloomed on her face. "Oh, um. No. Though, if we're getting it all out in the open, I did plant a tracker on you. That's how I found you and Nyx at the fountain." She had the decency to look ashamed of that. "As to the phone call, you weren't exactly quiet." She pointed at the open window across the room. The window that would have been directly above where he'd been standing outside the hotel on his phone.

Colin was slightly miffed that she'd felt the need to track him, but given how handy that little device had been once they'd gotten separated, he couldn't complain too hard. "Yes, I did agree to help him, but not in the way you think," he rushed on before she had time to pull away from him. "I'm giving him the money he owes on one condition. That we're done. I told him we were even and that he was never to contact me again."

Her mouth dropped open. "You're doing what? How much does he owe?"

He chewed on the bottom of his lip for a second before answering. He wanted to be honest with her, but he had no idea how she was going to react. "Um, $1.2 million."

"Are you kidding me?" she asked, her hand going to her chest. "You're telling me you have a spare million dollars that you can just give away?"

Colin ran his fingers through his hair. "I mean, don't we all?" He tried to make a joke about the situation, but her narrowed eyes told him she wasn't buying it.

"I've been alive for thousands of years and run a multibillion-dollar company. I know why I have that kind of capital." She sighed and her shoulders slumped. "I guess I just selectively forget parts of your life."

Colin cocked his head sideways as he studied her face. "Would you feel better if I gave it all away?" He would do it if she wanted him to. Being with her was far more important to him than whatever fortune he'd amassed.

She choked slightly. "You must be joking."

He shrugged. "It's only money. I can make more. Especially now that I have a very long life ahead of me. I have an idea on that front if you're interested."

"You're serious." It wasn't a question.

He reached across the bed and grasped her hands between his own. "Selene, you're not getting this. Who I was before doesn't matter. I'm no longer that man, and I don't want to be that man ever again. You're more important to me and my future than whatever ill-gotten gains I have stashed away. You're more important than the toxic relationship I have with a childhood best friend. I have amends I need to make, most importantly to Sam. He and I have some shit we need to sort through, but I'm one hundred percent on board with doing that. I want to make you happy and be everything you need. Apparently I now have a thousand lifetimes to live, and I want to spend each and every one of them with you. I love you."

In a flash, Selene crash-tackled him to the bed and fused her mouth to his. He was startled but relaxed into the kiss. Eventually she pulled away, her kisses getting softer and gentler. "I can't believe I'm finally saying this after more than four thousand years, but I love you, too, Colin. I love you so much."

"Now that we've established that," Colin said with a quick peck on the lips, "We need to talk about your healing ability. I know you have the belt now, which can give you a boost, but we need to figure out why your powers have been on the fritz."

Selene sighed. "As much as I hate to admit it, you were right. I've been getting more reckless and getting injured more frequently than usual. I've been relying on my gift to save me. It's supposed to act more like a failsafe, and I've been treating it like another tool in my toolbelt. Luckily I now have a very good reason to remain whole and healthy." She winked at him.

A knock on the door announced the arrival of their food. "Seriously? They have terrible timing." With a reluctant huff, Selene pulled away from him and rolled off the bed to grab the plates from the server. She handed him his before digging into her own meal. "So what's the great idea you have?"

Nerves flooded his stomach. Why was this more difficult to discuss than his feelings for her? "So, yeah." He started talking, then stopped and cleared his throat. He started over again. "Blackburn Industries is a security company."

She smirked. "I believe we've established that."

Colin put his breakfast sandwich back on his plate and wiped his hands on a napkin. "Right. Of course. But I still beat you."

Selene bit into her hashbrowns and rolled her eyes. "Thanks for reminding me. I still don't know how you pulled some of the jobs you did."

He shifted in his seat. "That's exactly my point. Maybe, you know, if you're interested . . ." He knew he was babbling and forced the rest of it out. "I could help you with that." He rushed on before she could respond. "No big deal if you're not interested. I just thought I would toss it out there." He grabbed his sandwich and took way too big a bite, almost choking on his food.

Waiting for her to respond was agonizing. Blackburn Industries was her baby. She'd founded the company and turned it into a global powerhouse in the security and tech industries. Who was he to think he could help her or that she couldn't do it herself? She was an Amazon, for Christ's sake. She could do anything.

"You mean like as a consultant?" She blinked a few times. Her nose got an adorable wrinkle in it, and her dimples popped out.

"Well, yeah. But only if you want." He finally managed to answer her after swallowing his enormous mouthful of food.

A smile bloomed on her face, one that reached all the way to her eyes. "You mean you're finally going to give me all your secrets?" she teased.

"Well, I don't know about all of them . . ."

She grabbed a pillow and lightly hit him upside his head. "Tease."

He brought her in for a searing kiss. "Just one of the many things you love about me."

"Well, you're not wrong."

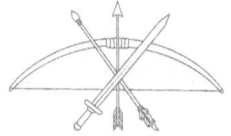

Epilogue

"**Y**OU MEAN THIS WAS here all along?" Kalli asked, her voice rising in disbelief.

"Yep." Zoe responded as she stared at the oddly humble marble ring that made up the Fountain of Youth. "Unsurprisingly, Sam and Colin are all over this like butter on hot toast. They filled me in." The mention of Kalli's fiancé had a sweet smile spreading on her queen's lips, but Zoe plowed on. "While this building is currently a museum, it wasn't always. Apparently, in true narcissistic fashion, some rich nobleman built this place as a shrine to himself. He had it built to encompass the Fountain of Youth so that only he and his high-society cronies could access it. Eventually, they commissioned the Trevi Fountain right outside the window because they thought it was amusing that they could look out upon the crowds gathered around its grandeur, all the while knowing that they had the real treasure to themselves."

Kalli sighed and rolled her eyes. "Men."

"Right? Well, maybe not all men," Zoe said as she winked and nodded toward Sam, who was crouched across the room, inspecting the fountain up close.

"True," Kalli said with a smile.

"Anyway. Apparently, over the centuries of their newly immortal lives, the friends eventually came to blows, each one wanting sole access to the fountain. They wound up killing each other off. The head butler of the house when the last nobleman passed sealed the room from the outside so that no one could be tempted to use it again."

"That explains the difficulty we had getting in here but not how we're going to secure and protect the fountain going forward." Kalli sighed.

Zoe's gaze traced every square inch of the room once more, as if the details had suddenly changed in the last few minutes. There was nothing else inside the room except the fountain. Nothing to help them hide or contain the treasure within. The door they'd broken down to get to Selene and Colin was now damaged beyond repair and would have to be replaced. But how on earth were they going to keep people out of here permanently to prevent them from using and abusing the fountain's power?

Zoe could already feel a headache coming on.

Her phone buzzed in her pocket, and she tugged it out. There was a text message waiting from Gabriel, her coworker at Interpol. It was a short message that just said, "Holy crap! Have you seen this?" A link popped up, and her phone helpfully showed her a preview of the video it linked to. An image of the Trevi Fountain filled the screen.

Dread pooled in her stomach as she clicked the link.

The video was handheld and wobbly, and the sound wasn't great, since the person filming hadn't been particularly close to the action, but Zoe still managed to catch every word. "People of Rome," Nyx began as a hush fell over the gathering. "My name is Nyx, and I am the rightful queen of the Amazons . . ."

"Oh shit," Zoe said.

The secret of the Amazons was out.

Acknowledgements

This book would not have been possible without a host of people who believed in me and made it happen. Among those I should thank are my beta readers Jessi and Chris, my copy editor James Gallagher of Castle Walls Editing, and my cover designer Graphic-SoulArt. And, as always, my brainstorming partner/marketing director/social media coordinator/all-around go-to person Chris.

About the Author

Elizabeth Salo is a Michigan native who loves magic, myths, and mayhem. She writes paranormal romance, romantic suspense, and urban fantasy books and is a sucker for a strong female lead. She firmly believes she should have been born with superpowers, but since she wasn't, she'll have to make do with writing about people who do.

She currently lives in Michigan with her family and more fur babies (and feathered babies, and scaly babies...) than is probably wise.

http://www.elizabethsalo.com/

Also By Elizabeth

Did you miss Kalli and Sam's story? Get it at Amazon:

Amazon in Exile
Amazons of Themyscira Book One

Wondering what's going to happen now that the secret is out? Stay tuned for:

Amazon in Hiding
Amazons of Themyscira Book Three
coming soon!